"I'm glad n   Vidicon said.

Tony stared. "Your what?"

"My message," said the saint. "That's why I fed that virus into the mainframe of one of your company's clients—because I needed a troubleshooter. Specifically, you."

"Why me?" Tony asked.

"Because you have the right turn of mind."

"What kind of troubles would you want me to shoot?"

"Anything people call me for, when I'm already trying to fix another problem," Father Vidicon said. "When I finish this trip through Hellmouth, maybe God will grant me the power to be in many different locations at once; but even then, I think I'll need some help." He stiffened suddenly. "A call's coming in. Here, see it with me and analyze the problem."

He caught Tony's hand, and whether the technician wanted to or not, he saw what the saint was seeing and heard what he was hearing—a despairing, many-voiced cry for help, and the background of the predicament . . .

SAINT VIDICON
TO THE RESCUE

CHRISTOPHER STASHEFF

ACE BOOKS, NEW YORK

THE BERKLEY PUBLISHING GROUP
Published by the Penguin Group
Penguin Group (USA) Inc.
375 Hudson Street, New York, New York 10014, USA

Penguin Group (Canada), 10 Alcorn Avenue, Toronto, Ontario M4V 3B2, Canada
(a division of Pearson Penguin Canada Inc.)
Penguin Books Ltd., 80 Strand, London WC2R 0RL, England
Penguin Group Ireland, 25 St. Stephen's Green, Dublin 2, Ireland (a division of Penguin Books Ltd.)
Penguin Group (Australia), 250 Camberwell Road, Camberwell, Victoria 3124, Australia
(a division of Pearson Australia Group Pty. Ltd.)
Penguin Books India Pvt. Ltd., 11 Community Centre, Panchsheel Park, New Delhi—110 017, India
Penguin Group (NZ), Cnr. Airborne and Rosedale Roads, Albany, Auckland 1310, New Zealand
(a division of Pearson New Zealand Ltd.)
Penguin Books (South Africa) (Pty.) Ltd., 24 Sturdee Avenue, Rosebank, Johannesburg 2196, South
Africa

Penguin Books Ltd., Registered Offices: 80 Strand, London WC2R 0RL, England

This is a work of fiction. Names, characters, places, and incidents either are the product of the author's imagination or are used fictitiously, and any resemblance to actual persons, living or dead, business establishments, events, or locales is entirely coincidental.

SAINT VIDICON TO THE RESCUE

An Ace Book / published by arrangement with the author

PRINTING HISTORY
Ace mass market edition / April 2005

Copyright © 2005 by Christopher Stasheff.
Cover art by Christian McGrath.
Cover design by Judith Murello.
Interior text design by Kristin del Rosario.

ISBN: 0-441-01271-X

ACE
Ace Books are published by The Berkley Publishing Group,
a division of Penguin Group (USA) Inc.,
375 Hudson Street, New York, New York 10014.
ACE and the "A" design are trademarks belonging to Penguin Group (USA) Inc.

PRINTED IN THE UNITED STATES OF AMERICA

10 9 8 7 6 5 4 3 2 1

This book is dedicated to
Eleanore Stasheff
in recognition of her truly major contribution

The author would like to thank
Chris Clayton
and all the other good people,
such as Katharine Moore,
who have told me
of their own encounters with Finagle

TO THE READER

The point has been raised that a fictitious saint shouldn't be able to hear people cry out to him. However, those people are fictitious, too—well, most of them, anyway.

Prologue

THE MARTYRDOM OF ST. VIDICON OF CATHODE

"Praise God, from Whom electrons flow!
Praise Him, the Source of all we know!
Whose order's in the stellar host!
For in machines, He is the Ghost!"

"Father Vidicon," Monsignor reproved, "that air has a blasphemous ring."

"Merely irreverent, Monsignor." Father Vidicon peered at the oscilloscope and adjusted the pedestal on Camera Two. "But then, you're a Dominican."

"And what is *that* supposed to mean?"

"Simply that what you hear may not be what I said." Father Vidicon leaned over to the switcher and punched up color bars.

"He has a point." Brother Anson looked up from the TBC circuit board he was diagnosing. "I thought it quite reverent."

"You would; it was sung." The Monsignor knew that Brother Anson was a Franciscan. "How much longer must I delay my rehearsal, Father Vidicon? I've an archbishop and two cardinals waiting!"

"You can begin when the camera tube decides to work, Monsignor." Father Vidicon punched up Camera Two again, satisfied that the oscilloscope *was* reading correctly. "If you insist on bringing in cardinals, you must be prepared for a breakdown."

"I really don't see why a red cassock would cause so much trouble," the Monsignor grumbled.

"You wouldn't; you're a director. But these old camera tubes just don't like red." Father Vidicon adjusted the chrominance. "Of course, if you could talk His Holiness into affording a few digital cameras . . ."

"Father Vidicon, you know what they cost! And we've been the Church of the Poor for a century!"

"Four centuries, more likely, Monsignor—ever since Calvin lured the bourgeoisie away from us."

"We've as many Catholics as we had in 1355," Brother Anson maintained stoutly.

"Yes, that was right after the Black Death, wasn't it? And the population of the world's grown a bit since then. I hate to be a naysayer, Brother Anson, but we've only a tenth as many of the faithful as we had in 1960. And from the attraction Reverend Sun is showing, we'll be lucky if we have a tenth of that by the end of the year."

"We've a crisis in cameras at the moment," the Monsignor reminded. "Could you refrain from discussing the Crisis of Faith until they're fixed?"

"Oh, they're working—now." Father Vidicon threw the capping switch and shoved himself away from the camera control unit "They'll work excellently for you now, Monsignor, until you start recording."

The Monsignor reddened. "And why should they break down then?"

"Because that's when you'll need them most." Father Vidicon grinned. "Television equipment is subject to Murphy's Law, Monsignor."

"I wish you were a bit less concerned with Murphy's Law and a bit more with Christ's!"

Father Vidicon shrugged. "If it suits the Lord's purpose to give authority over entropy into the hands of the Imp of the Perverse, who am I to question Him?"

"For the sake of Heaven, Father Vidicon, what has the Imp of the Perverse to do with Murphy's Law?" the Monsignor cried.

Father Vidicon shrugged again. "Entropy is the loss of energy within a system, which is self-defeating; that's perversity. And Murphy's Law is perverse. Therefore, both of them, and the Imp, are corollary to Finagle's General Statement: 'The perversity of the universe tends toward maximum.' "

"Father Vidicon," Monsignor said severely, "you'll burn as a heretic some day."

"Oh, not in this day and age. If the Church condemns me, I can simply join Reverend Sun's church, like so many of our erstwhile flock." Seeing the Monsignor turn purple, he turned to the door, adding quickly, "Nonetheless, Monsignor, if I were you, I'd not forget the Litany of the Cameras before I called 'roll and record.' "

"That piece of blasphemy!" the Monsignor exploded. "Father Vidicon, could St. Clare care enough about television to be its patron?"

"She did see St. Francis die, though she was twenty miles away at the time—the first Catholic instance of 'tele-vision,' 'seeing-at-a-distance.' " Father Vidicon wagged a forefinger. "And St. Genesius *is* officially the patron of showfolk."

"Of actors, I'll remind you—and we've none of those here!"

"Yes, I know—I've seen your programs. But do remember St. Jude, Monsignor."

"The patron of the desperate? Why?"

"No, the patron of lost causes—and with those antique cameras, you'll need him."

The door opened, and a monk stepped in. "Father Vidicon, you're summoned to His Holiness."

Father Vidicon blanched.

"You'd best remember St. Jude yourself, Father," the Monsignor gloated. Then his face softened into a gentle frown. "And, Lord help us—so had we all."

Father Vidicon knelt and kissed the Pope's ring, with a surge of relief—if the ring was offered, things couldn't be all that bad.

"On your feet," Pope Clement said grimly.

Father Vidicon scrambled up. "Come now, Your Holiness! You know it's all just in fun! A bit irreverent, perhaps, but nonetheless only levity! I don't *really* believe in Maxwell's Demon—not quite. And I know Finagle's General Statement is really fallacious—the perversity's in us, not in the universe. And St. Clare . . ."

"Peace, Father Vidicon," His Holiness said wearily. "I'm sure your jokes aren't a threat to the Church—and I'm not particularly worried by irreverence. I don't really think the Lord minds a joke now and then. But I've called you here for something a bit more serious than your contention that Christ acted as a civil engineer when He said that Peter was a rock, and upon that rock He'd build His Church."

"Oh." Father Vidicon tried to look appropriately grave. "If it's that feedback squeal in the public address system in St. Peter's, I'll do what I can, but . . ."

"No, I'm afraid it's a bit more critical." The hint of a smile tugged at the Pope's lips. "You're aware that the faithful have been leaving us in increasing droves these past twenty years, of course."

Father Vidicon shrugged "What can you expect, Your Holiness? With television turning everyone toward a Gestalt mode of thought, they've become more and more inclined toward mysticism, needing doctrines embracing the Cosmos and making them feel vitally integrated with it, but the Church still offers only petrified dogma and logical reasoning. Of *course* they'll turn to ecstatics, to a video demagogue like Reverend Sun, with his hodgepodge of T'ai-Ping Christianity, Taoism, and Zen Buddhism . . ."

"Yes, yes, I know the theories." His Holiness waved Father Vidicon's words away, covering his eyes with the other palm. "Spare me your McLuhanist cant, Father. But you'll be glad to know the Council has just finished deciding which parts of Teilhard's theories *are* compatible with Catholic doctrine."

"Which means Your Holiness has finally talked them into it!" Father Vidicon gusted out a huge sigh of relief. "At last!"

"Yes, I can't help thinking how nice it must have been to be Pope in, say, 1890," His Holiness agreed, "when the Holy See had a bit more authority and a bit less need of persuasion." He heaved a sigh of his own and clasped his hands on the desktop. "And it's come just in time. Reverend Sun is speaking to the General Assembly Monday morning—and you'll never guess what his topic will be."

"How the Church is a millstone around the neck of every nation in the world." Father Vidicon nodded grimly. "Priests who don't pass on their genes, Catholics not attempting birth control and thereby contributing to

overpopulation, Church income withheld from taxa-
tion—it's become a rather familiar bit of rhetoric."

"Indeed it has; most of his followers can recite it
chapter and verse. But this time, my sources assure me
he intends to go quite a bit further—to ask the Assembly for a recommendation for all U.N. member nations
to adopt legislation making all these 'abuses' illegal."

Father Vidicon's breath hissed in. "And with so large
a percentage of the electorate in every country being
Sunnite . . ."

"It amounts to virtual outlawing of the Roman
Catholic Church. Yes." His Holiness nodded. "And I
need hardly remind you, Father, that the current majority in the Italian government are Sunnite Communists."

Father Vidicon stared. "They'll begin by annexing
the Vatican!" He had a sudden nightmarish vision of a
Sunnite prayer meeting in the Sistine Chapel.

"We'll all be looking for new lodgings," the Pope
said drily. "So you'll understand, Father, that it's rather
important that I tell the faithful of the whole world, before then, about the Council's recent action."

"Your Holiness will speak on television!" Father
Vidicon cried. "But that's wonderful! You'll be . . ."

"My blushes, Father Vidicon. I'm well aware that
you consider me to have an inborn affinity for the video
medium."

"The charisma of John Paul II with the appeal of
John the XXIII!" Father Vidicon asserted. "But what a
waste, that you'll not appear in the studio!"

"I'm not fond of viewing myself as the chief drawing card for a sideshow," His Holiness said sardon-
ically. "Still, I'm afraid it has become necessary. The
Curia has spoken with Eurovision, Afrovision, PanAsia-
vision, PanAmerivision, and even Intervision. They're

all, even the Communists, willing to carry us for fifteen minutes . . ."

"Cardinal Beluga is a genius of diplomacy!" Father Vidicon murmured.

"Yes, and all the nations are worried about the growth of Sun's church within their borders, with all that it implies of large portions of their citizenry taking orders from Singapore. Under the circumstances, we've definitely become the lesser of two evils, in their eyes."

"I suppose that's a compliment," Father Vidicon said doubtfully.

"Let's think of it that way, shall we? The bottleneck, of course, was the American commercial networks; they're only willing to carry me early Sunday morning."

"Yes, they only worry about religion when it begins to affect sales," Father Vidicon said thoughtfully. "So I take it Your Holiness will appear about 2:00 P.M.?"

"Which is early morning in Chicago, yes. Other countries have agreed to record the speech and replay it at a more suitable hour. It'll go by satellite, of course . . ."

"As long as we pay for it."

"Naturally. And if there's a failure of transmission at our end, the networks are *not* liable to give us postponed time."

"Your Holiness!" Father Vidicon threw his arms wide. "You wound me! Of *course* I'll see to it there's no transmission error!"

"No offense intended, Father Vidicon—but I'm rather aware that the transmitter I've given you isn't exactly the most recent model."

"What can you expect, from donations? Besides, Your Holiness, British Marconi made excellent transmitters in 1990! No, Italy and southern France will receive us perfectly. But it would help if you could invest in a few spare parts for the converter that feeds the satellite earth station . . ."

"Whatever that may be. Buy whatever you need, Father Vidicon. Just be certain our signal is transmitted. You may go now."

"Don't worry, Your Holiness! Your voice shall be heard and your face seen, even though the Powers of Darkness rise up against me!"

"Including Maxwell's Demon?" His Holiness said dourly. "And the Imp of the Perverse?"

"Don't worry, Your Holiness." Father Vidicon made a circle of his thumb and middle finger. "I've dealt with *them* before."

" 'The good souls flocked liked homing doves,' " Father Vidicon sang, "or they will after they've heard our Pope's little talk." He closed the access panel of the transmitter. "There! Every part certified in the green! I've even dusted every circuit board . . . How's that backup transmitter, Brother Anson?"

"I've replaced two chips so far," Brother Anson answered from the bowels of the ancient device. "Not that they were bad, you understand—but I had my doubts."

"I'll never question a Franciscan's hunches." Father Vidicon laced his fingers across his midriff and sat back. "Did you check the converter to the earth station?"

" 'Converter'?" Brother Anson's head and shoulders emerged, covered with dust. "You mean that huge resistor in the gray box?"

Father Vidicon nodded. "The very one."

"A bit primitive, isn't it?"

Father Vidicon shrugged. "There isn't time to get a proper one, now—and it's all they've given me money for, ever since I was 'promoted' to Chief Engineer. Besides, all we really need to do is to drop our fifty-thousand-watt transmitter signal down to something the earth station can handle."

Brother Anson shrugged. "If you say so, Father. I should think that would kick up a little interference, though."

"Well, we can't be perfect—not on the kind of budget we're given, anyhow. Just keep reminding yourself, Brother, that most of our flock still live in poverty; they need a bowl of millet more than a clear picture."

"I can't argue with that. Anyway, I did check the resistor. How many ohms does it provide?"

"About as many as you do, Brother. How'd it test out?"

"Fine, Father, it's sound."

"Or will be, till we go on the air." Father Vidicon nodded. "Well, I've got two spares handy. Let the worst that can happen, happen! I'm more perverse than Finagle!"

The door slammed open, and the Monsignor was leaning against the jamb. "Father . . . Vidicon!" he panted. "It's . . . catastrophe!"

"Finagle," Brother Anson muttered, but Father Vidicon was on his feet. "What is it, Monsignor? What's happened?"

"Reverend Sun! He discovered the Pope's plans and has talked the U.N. into scheduling his speech for Friday morning!"

Father Vidicon stood, galvanized for a second. Then he snapped, "The networks! Can they air His Holiness early?"

"Cardinal Beluga's on three phones now, trying to patch it together! If he brings it off, can you be ready?"

"Oh, we can be ready!" Father Vidicon glanced at the clock. "Thursday, 4:00 P.M. We need an hour. Anytime after that, Monsignor."

"Bless you!" the Monsignor turned away. "I'll tell His Holiness."

"Come on, Brother Anson." Father Vidicon advanced on the backup transmitter, catching up his tool kit "Let's get this beast back on line!"

"Five minutes till air!" the Monsignor's voice rasped over the intercom. "Make it good, reverend gentlemen! Morning shows all over the world are giving us fifteen minutes—but not a second longer! And Reverend Sun's coming right behind us, live from the U.N."

Father Vidicon and Brother Anson were on their knees, hands clasped. Father Vidicon intoned, "Saint Clare, patron of television . . ."

". . . pray for us," finished Brother Anson.

"Saint Genesius, patron of showfolk . . ."

"One minute!" snapped the Monsignor. "Roll and record!"

". . . pray for us," murmured Brother Anson.

"Rolling and recording," responded the recording engineer.

"Saint Jude, patron of lost causes . . ."

". . . pray for us," murmured Brother Anson.

"Slate it!" Then, "Bars and tone!"

They could hear the thousand-cycle test tone in the background, whining. Then it began beeping at one-second intervals.

"Ready mike and cue, ready up on one!"

"Five!" called the assistant director. "Four! Three!"

"Black! Clip tone!" the Monsignor cried. "Mike him! Cue him! Up on One!"

Television screens all over the world lit up with the grave but faintly-smiling image of the Pope. "Dearly beloved in Christ . . ."

The picture flickered.

Father Vidicon darted a glance at the converter. Its tally light was dead. Beside it, the light glowed atop the back-up converter.

"Quick! The big one died!" Father Vidicon yanked open the top of the long gray box and wrenched out the burned-out resistor.

"There are a few points of theology on which we can't agree with Reverend Sun," His Holiness was saying. "Foremost among these is his concept of the Trinity. We just can't agree that Reverend Sun is himself the third Person, the 'younger son' of God . . ."

Brother Anson slapped the spare resistor into Father Vidicon's palm.

". . . nor is the sharing of a marijuana cigarette a valid form of worship, in the Church's eyes," the Pope went on. "But the Council does agree that . . ."

The screen went dark.

Father Vidicon shoved the spare into its clips and threw the routing switch.

The screen glowed again. ". . . have always been implicit in Catholic doctrine," His Holiness was saying, "but the time has come to state their implications. First among these is the notion of 'levels of reality.' Everything that exists is real; but God is the Source of reality, as He is the Source of everything. And the metaphor of 'the breath of God' for the human soul means that . . ."

"Yes, it's gone." Father Vidicon yanked the burned-out resistor out of the backup "The manufacturers must think they can foist off all their defectives on the Church."

Brother Anson took the lump of char and gave him a new resistor. "That's our last spare, Father Vidicon."

Father Vidicon shoved it into its clips. "What're the odds against three of these blowing in a space of ten minutes?"

"Gunderson's Corollary," Brother Anson agreed.

Father Vidicon slapped down the cover. "We're up against perversity, Brother Anson."

The tally blinked out on the main converter as the little red light on the backup glowed into life.

"We're out of spares," Brother Anson groaned.

"Maybe it's just a connection!" Father Vidicon yanked open the cover. "Only four minutes left."

"Is it the resistor, Father?"

"You mean this piece of slag?"

". . . the oneness, the unity of the cosmos, has always been recognized by Holy Mother Church," the Pope was saying. "Christ's parable about the 'lilies of the field' serves as an outstanding example. All that exists is within God. In fact, the architecture of the medieval churches . . ."

A picture of the Cathedral of Notre Dame appeared on the screen. The camera zoomed in for a close-up of the decorative carving . . .

. . . and the screen went blank.

"It died, Father Vidicon," Brother Anson moaned.

"Well, you fight fire with fire." Father Vidicon yanked out the dead resistor. "And this is perversity!" He seized the lead from the transmitter in his left and the lead to the earth station in his right.

Around the world, screens glowed back into life.

". . . and as there is unity in all of Creation," the Pope went on, "so is there unity in all the major religions. The same cosmic truths can be found in all, and the points on which we agree are more important than the ones on which we disagree—saving, of course, the Godhood of Christ, and of the Holy Spirit. But as long as a Catholic remembers that he is a Catholic, there can certainly be no fault in his learning from other faiths, if he uses this as a path toward greater understanding of his own." He clasped his hands and smiled gently. "May God bless you all."

And his picture faded from the screen,

"We're off!" shouted the Monsignor. "That was masterful!"

In the transmitter room, Brother Anson chanted the *Dies Irae*, tears in his eyes.

The Pope moved out of the television studio, carefully composed over the exhaustion that always resulted from a television appearance. The Monsignor dashed out of the control room to drop to his knees and wring the Pope's hand. "Congratulations, Your Holiness! It was magnificent!"

"Thank you, Monsignor," the Pope murmured, "but let's judge it by the results, shall we?"

"Your Holiness!" Another Monsignor came running up. "Madrid just called! The people are piling into the confessionals—even the men!"

"Your Holiness!" cried a cardinal. "It's Prague! The faithful are flocking to the cathedral!"

"Your Holiness—New York City! The people are streaming into the churches!"

"Your Holiness—Reverend Sun just cancelled his U.N. speech!"

"Your Holiness! People are kneeling in front of churches all over Italy, calling for the priests!"

"It's the Italian government, Your Holiness! They send their highest regards and assurances of continued friendship!"

"Your Holiness," Brother Anson choked out, "Father Vidicon is dead."

They canonized him eventually, of course—there was no question that he'd died for the Faith. But the miracles started right away.

In Paris, a computer programmer with a very tricky program knew it was almost guaranteed to hang. But he prayed to Father Vidicon to put in a good word for him with the Lord, and the program ran without a hitch.

Art Rolineux, directing coverage of the Super Bowl, had eleven of his twelve cameras die on him, and the twelfth started blooming. He sent up a quick prayer to Father Vidicon, and five cameras came back on-line.

Ground Control was tracking a newly-launched satellite when it suddenly disappeared from their screens. "Father Vidicon, protect us from Finagle!" a controller cried out, and the blip reappeared.

Miracles? Hard to prove—it could've been coincidence. It always can, with electronic equipment. But as the years flowed by, engineers and computer programmers and technicians all over the world began counting the prayers, and the numbers of projects and programs saved—and word got around, as it always does. So the day after the Pope declared him to be a saint, the signs went up on the back wall of every computer room and control booth in the world:

"St. Vidicon of Cathode, pray for us!"

Chapter 1

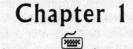

The door was all glass with the company's name and logo etched in:

RODRIGO AND ASSOCIATES
Market Analysis

Inside all was chrome, glass, and plush. Everyone was dressed to the nines, so Tony was glad he had elected to wear a suit that day, even if it was somewhat rumpled. Computer troubleshooters didn't have to dress up, but Tony tried to fit in with the employees at whatever company he was visiting. From the Wall Street address, he'd guessed these people believed in formality.

He pushed on through the door. The receptionist looked up with a smile. "Good morning. What can I do for you?"

Tony stepped up to the desk and handed the young man his card. "Business Systems Solutions."

"Ah." The receptionist nodded and gestured toward a chair. "Would you like to sit down? Ms. Clavier will be with you in a moment.

"Thanks." Tony stepped over and sank down into plush so thick it seemed to embrace him—not an entirely pleasant experience. He took advantage of the opportunity to give the reception area a more thorough examination. Everything screamed "Now!" and "Rich!" The receptionist's desktop was thick glass, its legs chrome; the floor was thick burgundy carpet with such a deep pile that it had to be synthetic. The only organic note was the walnut panelling, and it seemed out of place. Rich, but out of place. The room was obviously designed to impress visitors with the firm's wealth and stability, both rather necessary on Wall Street.

A young woman came in, and Tony forgot to breathe for a minute or two. She was beautiful, that was all there was to it, from the auburn hair cut in a sleek bob to the tailored jacket and skirt that let eighteen inches of shapely calf show above the slender shoes. But it was her face that really caught Tony's attention, the look of a pixie grown up—and she was coming toward him!

"Mr. Ricci?" She held out a hand. "I'm Sandra Clavier, the company's network administrator."

Tony stood and took her hand as his stomach sank; network administrators didn't like calling for help. If you had to bring in an outside specialist, it meant you didn't know everything about your job. Normally it didn't bother him, but the other people he dealt with weren't quietly gorgeous. Nonetheless, he managed to screw up his courage, and say, "Puh-pleased to meet you, Ms. Clavier."

"Call me Sandy," she invited, "and if you can make our computers work smoothly again, I'll be very pleased to have met *you*." She turned toward the door.

"I'll show you to a cubicle where you can work, if you'll follow me."

Tony would have followed her anywhere for the sheer joy of it. The graceful sway was hypnotizing and made him feel like a lumbering elephant as he followed.

Well, no, a lumbering log was more like it—Tony was lean, at least; all his working out did that much for him. Other than that, following a fascinating creature like this, he felt awkward and weird, like a gargoyle in a jacket and tie. His hair was the color of straw and not much more manageable; he knew his nose was too long, his eyes too narrow, and his chin too much of a lump. He might not be all that bad to look at most of the time, but compared to Sandra Clavier, he must be downright ugly.

She led him through a door and into a huge room filled with standard-issue cubicles. She navigated the maze with ease and stopped by a gray-walled enclosure like all the rest, except that it held only a chair, desk, and filing cabinet; the desktop was bare, and so were the walls. "We cleared one for you to work with," Ms. Clavier said. "If there's anything else you need, just give me a call; I'm extension two-eight-four-one."

"Two-eight-four-one," Tony repeated, that being all he could think of to say, and sat down so that he would look a little less awkward. He should have booted the desktop, but that would have required looking away from her. "You've been having interruptions in service?"

"Yes, the strangest kind." Sandy frowned, and Tony stopped breathing again. "I've never seen a virus like this one. Every now and then, for no reason I can pinpoint, all the screens go blank. Then text starts to scroll up, bits and tags of some story in a weird archaic style, like something out of the King James Bible—but the

Bible doesn't describe a modern man going down the road to Hell."

Not having read the Book, Tony frowned and tried to look wise. "That's a new one on me, too. Any idea what triggers it?"

"None." Sandy was beginning to sound exasperated. "I've asked everyone to keep logging their work, and whenever one of the interruptions occurred, I had them print out the few minutes before and went through them—but I can't find any word or phrase that's entered every time. No number, either, for that matter."

"A real puzzle." Tony grinned in spite of himself, then tried to squelch it.

But Sandy smiled. "You like puzzles too, huh? Well, I guess it goes with the territory. Do you want the print-outs?"

"If you don't mind." Tony nodded, then took refuge in more talk about the problem—what else could he say to a creature like this? "How long do the interruptions last?"

"Six minutes," Sandy said. "Always six minutes to the second; I've timed them. Then the screens revert to the current work without any changes at all, almost as though it had been saved." She sighed. "No damage, really—just a very frustrating inconvenience. Add up all the interruptions, and it's really hurting productivity. Six minutes is enough to break a worker's concentration so badly that it takes a while to get it back, so it's costing the company a great deal of time—especially since the staff has figured out that the interruptions always last just long enough to work in an extra coffee break. Then it takes another five minutes to get them back to their desks and working again." She shook her head, clearly frazzled.

"Sounds like you're being hacked, sure enough,"

Tony said. "Well, let me talk to your mainframe and see what I can find."

"A cure, I hope." Sandy flashed him a dazzling smile. "Get that priest out of our system, Mr. Ricci, and I'll owe you a big one."

Priest?

She turned and glided away. Tony watched the folds of her suit amplify her movements as long as he could, then turned away with a distinct sense of disappointment and reached down to power up the desktop.

As it booted, he let himself envision Sandy's face. Contemplating the memory, he wondered why she had cast such a spell over him. He forced himself to be as analytical as possible—it was the only defense against the emotions she raised—and had to admit that she was only moderately pretty; the suit only hinted at a figure, and neither the tilt of her nose nor the curve of her lip was exceptional—until she smiled, of course—and her complexion wasn't quite flawless. The slight touches of makeup were applied perfectly, but Tony was old enough to know the difference between art and nature, though he had to admire skill. He decided it was her eyes that had cast the spell over him. They were dark, a wonderful shade of green (like old jade, he thought) with long, thick lashes; very, very large—and, Tony decided, horribly distracting.

He'd never been very good at talking with women, though, so as the terminal screen unfolded from the top of the desk, revealing a glass window through which he saw a keyboard, he banished the vision of jade eyes and turned his attention to the glowing rectangle. He plugged in his laptop and ran the diagnostic program. The screen lit up with the trademark for a few seconds; then the results box came up. Tony glanced and nodded; as he'd expected, the hardware was sound. He hit a few keys, and the diagnostics program began checking the software. It had almost finished, showing no viruses or unauthorized programs, when the screen went blank.

Tony stared; this wasn't the usual procedure.

Then white type started scrolling up the screen and merry calls echoed from cubicle to cubicle. Chairs rolled and footsteps hissed across carpet as the workers, chatting gaily, headed toward the coffeemaker.

Tony stayed in place, of course, running program after program with staccato bursts of keystrokes, trying to track the streaming letters to their source and ignoring the happy conversation in the coffee alcove. With his gaze mostly on his laptop's screen, he caught only quick glimpses of the text on the terminal, but those piqued his curiosity savagely. Still, while the program was actually running was golden time, and he didn't dare pay attention to anything but his own trace programs.

Then the last line of type scrolled off the top of the screen. Tony watched the blank rectangle, fingers poised, and in the alcove, somebody called, "Okay, six minutes. Back to work."

As though it had heard him, the screen came to life with its virtual desktop.

Tony relaxed, sitting back and studying the test readouts on his laptop screen.

A soft footstep made him look up, then freeze, because Sandy was leaning on the cubicle screen and smiling down at him. "That tell you anything?"

Tony threw off the strange paralysis she induced and gestured at his laptop. "Yeah, a little bit. As far as I can tell, the problem's in the system."

"Inside?" Sandy frowned. "You mean it's not coming from outside?"

Tony managed to start breathing again—even her

frowns were affecting him—and said, "The signal originated inside the mainframe."

"Then it's infected." Sandy's frown darkened with concern. "Can you kill the virus?"

"Can't say for sure." Tony turned his gaze resolutely to the laptop screen. "I'll give it everything I've got."

"I hope you can," Sandy said. "It's going to be very, very expensive if we have to junk the mainframe."

"We can put in a new one in twenty-four hours," Tony said, "but let's not play the funeral hymn until we're sure it's dead. After all, I've got a lot of results to analyze."

"Oh." Sandy's face cleared. "Of course—while the text was scrolling, you were running test programs and saving the results. You haven't had a chance to check them yet."

Tony nodded. "It's going to take some time. If my bugcatcher doesn't find the problem, I'll have to print out the code and analyze it line by line."

Sandra shuddered. "I wish you luck."

"Thanks." Tony started hitting keys and studying results; he was about to turn and tell Sandra the latest (negative) report when he realized she'd gone. He sighed and let the bugcatcher run. While it did, he called up the code and scanned it quickly. With just a light once-over, it looked to be the standard operating system, nothing different, nothing alien.

Then he realized that the virus might be buried in the text of the story itself.

He cleared the code and opened the log of the text. He started to scan it, too, but within two lines, he was caught and found himself reading the story.

When that the blessed Father Vidicon did seize upon a high-voltage line and did cleave unto it, aye, even unto death, so that the words of our blessed Holy Father the Pope might reach out through the satellites to all the television transmitters of the world, for the saving of our most Holy and Catholic Church—aye, when that Father Vidicon did thus die for the Faith and did pass into one enduring instant of blinding pain, he was upheld and sustained by the knowledge that, dying a martyr, he would pass straightway to Heaven and be numbered among the Blest.

How great was his dismay, then, to find himself, as pain dimmed and awareness returned, to be falling through darkness amidst a cold that did sear his very soul—for in truth, he was naught but soul. Distantly did he espy certain suns, knew thereby that he did pass through the Void, and that his eternal fall was not truly so, but was only the absence of gravity. Indeed, he knew the place for an absence of all, and fear bit him sharply—for thus, he knew, must Hell be: a place of lacking, an absence of being.

Then, in his terror, did he cry out in anger, "My God! For Thee did I give my life! Wherefore hast Thou doomed me?" Yet no sooner were the words said than he did repent, and cursed himself for a faithless fool, thus to doubt even now in death, that the Christ would uphold him.

And straightway on the heels of that thought came the shock of insight—for he saw that, if he did die to cheat the Imp of the Perverse, defeating Finagle himself by his very perversity, he must needs expect reversal of expectation—which is to say that, if he died expecting the vistas of Heaven, he would most certainly discover the enclosures of Hell.

Then courage returned, and resolution; for he did come to see that the struggle was not ended, but only begun anew—that if he did desire Heaven, he would have to win to it. Then did he wonder if even the saints, they who dwelt in God, could count their toils ended—or if they chose eternally to struggle 'gainst greater forces.

Then did his Mission become clear to him, and the Blessed One knew wherefore he had come to this Void. The enemy 'gainst whom he had striven throughout his life endured still—and now would Father Vidicon confront him and look upon his face.

With the thought, his fall slowed, and he saw the mouth of a tunnel ope in the darkness before him, and it did glow within, a sullen red. Closer it did come, and wider, stretching and yawning to swallow him; yet Father Vidicon quailed not, nor attempted to draw back. Nay, bravely he stood, stalwart in nothingness; yea, even eagerly did he strain forward, to set foot upon infirm fungoid flesh and stride into Hellmouth.

As he strode, the sullen glow did brighten, gaining heat until he feared it would sear his flesh, then remembered that he had none. Brighter and hotter it flowed, until he turned thorough a bend in its tube and found himself staring upon the Imp of the Perverse.

Gross it was, and palpable, swollen with falsehood and twisted with paradoxes. Syllogisms sprouted from its sides, reaching toward Father Vidicon with complexes of bitterness, and it stood, but did not stand, on existential extensions.

"Turn back!" roared the Imp in awesome

sardonicism. "Regress, retrograde! For none can progress that do come within!"

"Avaunt thee!" cried Father Vidicon. "For I know thee of old, bloody Imp! 'Tis thou who doth drive every suicide, thou who doth strengthen the one arm of the Bandit who doth rob the gambler compulsive, thou who doth bring down freezing snow upon the recumbent form of the will-leached narcotic! Nay, I know thee of old and know that he who retreats from thee, must needs pursue thee! Get THEE behind ME—for I shall surpass thee!"

"Wilt thou?" cried the Imp. "Then look to thy defense—for I shall undo thee!"

So saying, it reached toward Father Vidicon, twisting its hand—and of a sudden, thirst unbearable did seize the priest, a craving that could be slaked only by cheap rum. The Imp did hold out to him a bottle of brown glass with a garish label, and Father Vidicon's hand stretched out seemingly of its own accord. Appalled, the priest did pull back his hand, and the Imp did laugh at the shock that filled his face. "Surrender, cleric," it cried, "for soon or late, thou shalt take of this bottle and drink till that thirst is slaked!"

With dismay, Father Vidicon felt his hand rise and fought muscle against muscle to keep it from stretching toward that bottle.

A shout of anger escaped; shocked, Tony realized it had come from his own lips. He stared, astounded—could he really care that much whether or not the fictitious character took a drink? Surely not! He shook off the spell and punched in the commands necessary to reveal the code that underlay the letters. It would be subtle and devious, but the unknown hacker might have buried a virus in the shapes of the letters themselves.

The code appeared; he started scanning with a frown. No need to slow down and study—it was all familiar. He could have scanned the whole six minutes' worth, of course, but a sudden hunch had him checking the interval before the message, and sure enough, a few keystrokes brought another burst of code to the screen.

Now Tony did slow down and study character by character. This code was new, nothing he had ever seen before. He took a pencil and pad out of his briefcase and started trying to unsnarl it. As he worked, his frown deepened to a scowl. Faster and faster his pencil worked until it was fairly flying across the paper as he tried combination after combination.

"Mr. Ricci?"

Tony started as though he'd been bitten, head snapping up.

"Gee, sorry," Sandy said. "No harm intended."

"Me neither." Tony closed his eyes, wiping a hand across them. "Sorry—I was just concentrating so hard . . ."

"I could see that." Sandy smiled. "Think you could use a lunch break?"

"Definitely. My brain was beginning to go around in circles." Tony closed his laptop and stood up—and was amazed how his joints hurt. "Ouch!"

"Yes, too intense by far." Sandy smiled. "The restaurant next door is pretty good, nothing special. There's an excellent Chinese place down in the next block, though."

"I probably couldn't tell the difference between 'pretty good' and 'excellent' anyway," Tony confessed. "The restaurant next door will be fine."

They joined the line filing into the elevator, and an

uncomfortable silence fell—uncomfortable for Tony, at least. He scanned his memory for possible conversational topics, and tried, "How long have you been here?"

"Three years," Sandy said. "It's a good place to work, and I'm learning a lot about telling a good stock from a bad one."

"Must come in handy," Tony said. "Just knowing how to analyze a stock isn't insider trading, is it?"

"Far from it," Sandy said, amused. "In fact, it's very much from the outside."

The elevator stopped, and they moved slowly with the tide of other lunch-bound workers. "It does take a lot of research, though," Sandy said.

"I'll bet." Tony pursed his lips. "How do you start— with a company's earnings report?"

"That's one place," Sandy said, "but there are others . . ."

Tony managed to keep her talking for most of the next hour, but he didn't really register much about market research, though he did become an offhand expert on Sandy's hair, on her eyes, her nose, the expressiveness of her lips and gestures. By the time they were back in the office, she was calling him Tony, and he was very much afraid he had fallen in love—afraid because it couldn't be mutual. After all, she was beautiful, and he was a nerd—maybe pretty stylish, as nerds go, but still a nerd.

With a sigh, he stepped back into the cubicle and settled into the chair, hoping the streams of numbers would banish the vision of huge eyes and mobile lips. He lit the laptop, picked up his pencil, and began analyzing.

It worked; in a few minutes he was so deeply immersed in code that the outside world ceased to exist. He glanced at the desktop from time to time, of course, but most of his attention was on the yellow pad.

Then something changed. He glanced at the desktop and saw the screen was blank. His heart leaped; with three keystrokes, he opened a new file and started copying just in time for the first line of type to rise from the bottom of the screen. Dimly, he heard the workers' whoop of delight and their chatter as they moved toward the coffee alcove, but he stayed in his chair, dying to know whether Father Vidicon took the bottle or not.

Chapter 2

Appalled, the priest did pull back his hand, and the Imp did laugh at the shock that filled his face. "Surrender, cleric," it cried, "for soon or late, you shall take of this bottle and drink till that thirst is slaked!"

With dismay, Father Vidicon felt his hand rise and fought muscle against muscle to keep it from stretching toward that bottle. The Imp's laughter grew till it seemed to fill the whole darkened tunnel, and that cacophony did make the priest feel alone, isolated, with no person or spirit on whom he might draw for strength.

But the extremity of that emotion itself was like cold water dashing in his face, waking him from the stupor of despair the Imp of the Perverse had raised in him, making him mindful that no matter where he stood or how isolated he seemed, there was always One from whom all human folk can draw comfort and rely upon for strength.

Then a great calm came upon the Blessed One, and he slowly stood straight, smiling gently, and saying, "Nay, I shall not—for I know now that to become defensive is to bend thy sword so that it strikes against thyself. I shall not defend, but offend!" And so saying, he leaped upon the Imp, striking out with his fist.

But the Imp raised up a shield, a plane of white metal, flat as a fact and bare as statistics, and polished to so high a gloss that it might not have existed. "See!" cried the Imp, full of glee. "See the monster thine offense hath wrought!"

And staring within, Father Vidicon did behold a face twisted with hatred, tortured with self-doubt, barefaced as a lie and bound by the Roman collar of law.

Yet the Blessed One did not recoil. Nay, he did not so much as hesitate to question himself or his cause; only, with a voice filled with agony, did he cry, "Oh my Lord! Now preserve me! Give me, I beg of Thee, some weapon against the wiles and malice of this Imp's Shield of Distortion!"

He held up his hands in supplication—and Lo! In his left, a blade did appear, gleaming with purity, its edge glittering with exquisite monofilament sharpness—and in the Blessed One's palm, its handle nestled, hollow to the blade folded.

The Imp sneered in laughter, and cried, "See how thy master doth requite thee! In exchange for thy life, he doth grant thee naught but a slip of a blade which could not pierce so much as a misapprehension!"

But, "Not so," cried Father Vidicon, "for this Razor is Occam's!"

So saying , he slashed out at the shield. The Imp screamed and cowered away—but the Blessed One pursued, slicing at the Shield of Distortion, and crying, "Nay, thou canst not prevail! For I could have wasted eternity wondering where the fault lay in me, that could so twist my face and form into Evil! Yet the truth of it is shown by this Razor as it doth cleave this Shield!"

So saying, he swung the blade, and it cleaved the Shield in twain, revealing hidden contours, convexities and concavities of temporizing and equivocating. The Imp screamed in terror, and the Blessed One cried, " 'Tis not my image that is hideous, but thy shield that is warped!"

Dropping its shield, the Imp spun away, whirling beyond Father Vidicon to flee toward the Outer Dark.

Filled with righteous rage, the Blessed One turned to follow it—but he brought himself up short at a thought, for 'twas almost as though a voice spoke within him, saying, *Nay! Thou must not seek to destroy, for thus thou wouldst become thyself an enemy of Being. Contain only, and control; for the supporting of Life will lead Good to triumph; but the pursuit of Destruction in itself doth defeat good!*

The Blessed One bowed his head in chagrin— and there, even there in the throat of Hell, did he kneel and join his hands in penitence. "Pardon, my Master, that in my weakness, I would have forgotten the commandment of Thine example." And he held up the Razor on his open palm, praying, "Take again the instrument wrought for Thee by Thy faithful servant William. I need it not, now, for thou, oh

God, art my strength and my shield; with Thee, I need naught."

Light winked along the length of the blade, and it was gone.

Father Vidicon stood up then, naked of weapons and devoid of defense, yet his heart was light and his resolution was strengthened. "Whither Thou wilt lead me, my Lord," he murmured, "I shall go, and with what adversaries Thou wilt confront me, I shall contend."

So saying, he strode forth down the throat of Hell, but the song that rose to his lips was a psalm.

The last line scrolled off the top of the screen just as someone called, "Six minutes!" and sure enough, the lines of code flashed across the screen again. Tony was surprised to find he was as disappointed to have no more story to read, as he was happy for Father Vidicon.

Regretfully, he looked up from his laptop—to see Sandy standing at the doorway to his cubicle, leaning on one of the screens with a smile.

"I don't know what you did, troubleshooter," Sandy said, "but you fixed our system."

Tony stared at her—not hard to do—while he let the statement soak in. Of course, he hadn't done anything.

Then he realized that St. Vidicon's victory had probably also chased the Imp out of the mainframe. Of course, it could also be that, having contacted Tony, the priest had pulled his story out—but Tony instantly discounted the idea; he wasn't that important.

"Glad to help." Tony didn't like claiming credit for other people's work, but under the circumstances, there wasn't much choice. He closed the laptop and stood up. "I can't be sure the fix will last, though. If you have any more trouble, give me a call." He slipped a business card out of his pocket and held it out, then with a sudden inspiration turned it over and wrote on the back. He handed it to Sandy. "That's my home number. Computer problems don't always happen during business hours." It was a good excuse, anyway.

"Thanks, soldier." The merry glint in Sandy's eye told him he hadn't fooled her for a second. "How about a drink to celebrate? On the company's tab, of course."

"I'd love to. Just a sec . . ." Tony disconnected the cable that joined his laptop to the terminal and packed them both. "Okay, let's go."

Off they went, down the central aisle between cubicles, and Tony sailed blithely through a gamut of dagger glares from people who had just lost their extra coffee breaks. Tony was impervious to their resentment—he was going for a drink with a beautiful girl.

As the door closed behind them, Sandy shuddered. "I hate being stared at!"

"Really?" Tony asked. "I should think you'd be used to it. Not that kind of stare, of course."

Sandy frowned up at him. "Why would I be used to it?"

"Because you're a beautiful woman," Tony said. "Men must stare at you all the time."

Sandy blushed and looked away, and Tony suddenly realized he might have been a little too frank.

"I'm not beautiful," Sandy said. "Well, maybe kind of pretty, but not much."

Tony was flabbergasted. How could the woman not know how lovely she was? "You must have noticed men watching you."

"Sure, but that's because they don't know how to run their computers, and I do. They want to ask but they can't take the blow to their pride."

Tony was surprised at her bitterness. "It never occurred to you that it might be because you're"—opening the door of the cocktail lounge gave him a chance to catch himself, and to pause long enough to keep from saying "beautiful" again—"attractive?"

"No, but it's nice of you to say so." Sandy gave him a smile that lit up the gloom of the lounge. She paused by a table just long enough for Tony to pull out a chair. She flashed him another smile as she sat.

Tony sat next to her. "I'm surprised to hear that you think men would resent a female computer guru. The guys I know are delighted when they find a woman who knows code."

"Sure, but you're engineers," Sandy said.

The conversation was shelved as the server came up to take their order. As he went, Tony turned back to Sandy. "Sorry, but I need to correct a mistaken impression. Being an engineer doesn't mean we don't know how to talk about anything but our work."

"I know that from the inside now," Sandy said, "but I didn't learn to write code in college. If you'll pardon me for saying it, women must have been in short supply in your major."

"Yeah, but we all found ways to make social contacts," Tony said. "Me, I volunteered for tech work in the college theater. One of my buddies got a job at a fast-food place, and another joined the student radio station. We didn't get many dates, but at least we got to talk to girls."

Sandy laughed, a sound that struck Tony as distinctly musical. "Still, finding a girl you could talk computers with must have been a treat."

"It didn't happen much in college," Tony said. "Of course, now that I'm in the working world, I'm running into more and more of you—though I'll have to admit some of them wear glasses they don't need, tie their hair in buns, and don't wear makeup."

"Yeah." The bitterness was back. "A girl shouldn't have to be plain for guys to believe she knows what she's talking about."

"Or to resent her for knowing it?" Tony risked looking into her eyes and smiled. "I'm glad you practice what you preach."

"I'm glad you can appreciate it." Almost reluctantly, Sandy smiled again.

"Oh, believe me, I can."

"Which?" The smiled hardened. "My not dressing down, or my knowledge?"

"Yes," Tony said.

Sandy stared at him, then laughed. The waiter must have taken it as a signal, because he brought their drinks.

All in all, it turned into a very pleasant evening, and even though Tony did get to take the taxi to Sandy's apartment building and got away with walking her up the steps to the door, there wasn't any sign that he had been promoted from business associate to friend. Sighing as he went back to the cab, he told himself that these things take time.

He wondered if he would have any more of her time to take.

Ridiculous! He shook off the mood as he came in the door, took off his coat, sat down at his own computer and banished the screen saver with a flick of the mouse. Time to work on the program he'd been frittering around with. He wondered why the prospect didn't fill him with the excitement it usually did, then decided he must be more tired than usual. He'd fiddle with it for fifteen minutes or so, though, and see if the pleasure of writing code didn't banish the weariness.

He puttered around, trying one approach after another, then on a whim decided to try a four-dimensional structure.

It made sense.

Unfortunately, it made sense because the lines of code had turned into lines of words. Tony barely had time to start capturing before the end of the second sentence.

Long did St. Vidicon stride onward down that darkly ruddy throat, till he began to tire—then heard a roar behind him, rising in pitch and loudness as though it approached. Looking back, he saw . . .

Saw what? Did it have to break off right there? Blood pounding—though whether at his eagerness to solve the puzzle or his hunger to follow Father Vidicon's adventures, was hard to say. Tony entered a dozen lines of code into the desktop, then ran the four-dimensional structure—and the code turned into lines of biblical English, scrolling slowly up the screen. Enthralled, Tony read, the maroon hallway becoming clearer and clearer to him—until he realized, with a shock, that it was real, or virtually so. If he looked up or down, he saw not acoustical tile nor gray carpet but moist and pulsating blood-red curves—and if he looked ahead, he saw Father Vidicon striding down that sinister throat.

On the other hand, Tony couldn't see his own body.

He was an objective viewer, then. As a disembodied presence, he drifted after Father Vidicon.

Looking back, Father Vidicon saw an airplane approaching, the propeller at its nose a blur. He stared, amazed that so large an object could navigate so small a space, then realized that it was a model. Further, he realized that it swooped directly at him, as shrewdly as though it had been aimed. "Duck and cover!" he cried, and threw himself to the floor, arms clasped over his head. The aircraft snored on past him, whereupon he did look up to remark upon it, but heard the pitch of its propeller drop and slow as the craft did lower, then touch its wheels to the palpitating deck and taxi to a halt, its propeller slowing until it stopped.

Father Vidicon stared in wonder, then frowned; it seemed too much a coincidence, too opportune, that a conveyance should present itself when he was wearied. Still, a machine was a challenge he could not ignore; the thrill of operating a strange device persisted even after life; so he did quicken his steps until he stood beside a fuselage not much longer than himself, with an open cockpit into which he might squeeze himself—and so he did.

Instantly the propeller kicked into motion, in seconds blurring to a scintillating disk, and the aircraft lurched ahead, bouncing and jogging till it roared aloft and shot onward down that darkling throat. St. Vidicon, no stranger to ill chance, searched for a seat belt, but there was none, and shivered with the omission. The plane's arrival might be mere chance, the lack of a seat belt might be only coincidence, but he braced himself for a third, and surely planned, unpleasant occurrence.

Sure enough, the engine coughed, then sputtered, then died; he stared in horror at a propeller that slowed to a halt. Galvanized by ill fortune, he seized the wheel, set his feet to the rudder pedals, and glanced at his gauges. There was fuel, so he dealt with malfunction.

Enough! The plane did tilt downward, rushing toward that obscene and gelid floor. Father Vidicon did haul back upon the wheel and the nose did tilt upward again. Relying on what little he'd read, he held his wing flaps down, keeping the airplane's nose upward as the craft settled. It struck that fleshly floor with as much impact as though it had hit upon grass; it bounced, then struck again, bounced again, and so, by a series of bounces, slowed until at last it came to rest.

Father Vidicon clambered down from that falsely-welcoming cockpit, telling himself sternly that never again would he operate a machine that he had not inspected—for once may have been accident and twice coincidence, but this third time was definitely enemy action.

But which enemy?

There was as yet insufficient data for a meaningful conclusion. Staggering for his first few steps, then stabilizing to stride, he made his way onward down that darkling throat, lit only by the luminescence of certain globular growths upon the walls.

An object loomed before him, at first dim and indistinct in the limited light, then becoming clear—and Father Vidicon stared upon a scaled-down Sherman tank, a treaded fortress scarcely higher than his shoulder, that sat in the middle of the tunnel as though waiting for him, though in friendly fashion, for its cannon pointed ahead.

The Blessed One reminded himself that he had but minutes before promised himself never to drive a mechanism unverified, so he examined the treads most carefully, then opened the engine compartment and scrutinized the diesel. Satisfied that nothing was defective—ready but wary—he set foot upon a tread, climbed up, and descended through the hatch.

The slit above the controls showed him that dim-lit tunnel. He sat before it, grasped the levers to either side, and pushed them forward quite carefully. The tank cranked, then coughed, then clanked into motion. Warily, though, Father Vidicon held its speed to crawling, not much faster than he could walk. His gain was that he could travel sitting down, but in truth 'twas the thrill of adventure in operating a device hitherto unknown.

So he went grinding down that tunnel, allowing a little more speed, then a little more, until he was traveling at a pace quite decent—till a sudden crash did sound upon his right, and the tank did slew about.

The telephone rang.

Tony gave the clock a quick glance, saw it was only twenty after nine, and picked up the receiver. "Hello?"

"Tony?" said a somewhat shaken voice on the other end. "Sorry, I know we've just met, but I had to talk to somebody."

It was Sandy! "Well, I'm honored! What's the matter?"

"Nothing I can say," Sandy answered. "I just get to feeling like this at night sometimes."

Tony waited and heard only shaky breathing, so he asked, "Like how?"

"Oh . . . like I'm not good enough for anything, and everything's just going down the drain." Then, more quickly, "I know I do my job well, and that there's no shame in having to call in a specialist, and it doesn't mean a woman's a failure today if she isn't married by the time she's thirty—but it's hard to remember that when you're all alone and it's dark outside."

"Yeah, I know," Tony said, with feeling. "Best cure is not to be alone when it's dark. Is there a coffee shop near you that's still open? Or a neighborhood tavern?"

The line was silent for a few seconds; Tony could almost feel Sandy's surprize and hoped it wasn't his imagination. Had he blown it, scared her away?

Then her voice came, definitely pleased. "There's Espresso Service just down the block. Think I ought to go there?"

"Yeah, but I think I should escort you," Tony said. "What's your address?"

"I'm on West Adams," she said, "fourteen twenty-two. Are you sure? I mean, it's so late . . ."

"Yeah, we should have met about seven-thirty," Tony agreed, "but nine-thirty's better than not meeting at all."

Sandy laughed, not as silvery as earlier in the day, but ready to be polished. "I'll get dressed and wait in the foyer, then."

"See you in . . ." Tony considered the distance and the chance of getting a cab. "Twenty minutes, maybe. Certainly half an hour."

"Twenty minutes," Sandy said, her tone half-wondering. "'Bye."

She hung up, and so did Tony, exulting. "Thank you, St. Vidicon," he said, and half expected to hear a reply, but the room stayed as quiet as a city apartment can, and besides, if the saint said anything, Tony was in too much of a rush to hear.

He was in such a hurry to get out the door that he didn't even notice the lines of text that had begun to scroll upward on his screen again.

He only lived eight blocks away and a cab came along just as he burst out the door, so neatly that Tony suspected saintly intervention. He flagged it down and stepped in, saying, "Fourteen twenty-two West Adams, please." At least he had remembered her address. He'd written it down, of course, but that's not the same thing.

The cab pulled up at 1422, and sure enough, there was Sandy, waiting behind her glass door, looking as fresh as she had when he'd met her that morning. Tony wondered how she did it.

"Eight thirty-two, Mac," the cab driver said.

"We're going on another block or so," Tony said. "Wait just a minute, will you?"

"Don't think about stiffing me," the driver warned.

"I won't," Tony said, and got out to run up the steps. Sandy saw him coming and came out. Tony said, "Sorry to be late."

"But you're right on time," Sandy looked confused. "You said half an hour."

"But you've been waiting ten minutes." Tony offered his arm.

"Ten minutes! Oh! How will I ever last?" Sandy asked in her most melodramatic tones and pressed the back of a limp-wristed hand to her fevered brow.

Tony laughed as they came down the steps. He opened the door. "Bet you were the best actress in your high school."

"In high school," Sandy agreed. "Not in college." She slipped into the taxi.

Tony closed the door, went around, and climbed in. "Espresso Service in the next block, okay?"

"You got it, folks." The driver put the car in gear.

Tony turned to Sandy. "So you started finding computers more interesting than audiences?"

"Not *more* interesting," Sandy said, "but I heard hopeful actors can make a living taking temp work, so I figured I'd better learn some office applications—and I started wondering how they could make all those exotic functions happen just by manipulating ones and zeros."

"How about manipulating ten twenty-three?" the driver asked.

Tony looked up and realized they had stopped. "Yeah, thanks." He handed the driver twelve dollars, then got out and came around to open Sandy's door. She managed to make it look graceful as she slipped out and took his arm again. They went in, found a table, and Tony draped his overcoat over a seat. "What would you like?"

"Raspberry mocha." Sandy sat.

As he brought the drinks, Tony couldn't help thinking that she looked much more cheerful than she had sounded on the phone and dared hope he might be doing something right. He sat down, and asked, "Did you take classes or just read books?"

Sandy looked at him blankly, then laughed and reached out to press his hand. "I thought you meant acting. No, I actually took some courses. I was amazed how fascinating it was."

"Bet you took calculus in high school."

Sandy looked surprized, then smiled. "Yeah, math skills deteriorate fast, don't they? But when I was a sophomore, I had a date with a sexist senior who told me women couldn't learn math."

Tony grinned. "Proved him wrong, huh?"

Sandy grinned back. "Luckiest insult I ever had. Sophomore year of college, I found out that the brain is still growing during high school."

"Didn't know the logical centers kept growing too. Doesn't seem as though they've stopped."

"Use it or lose it." Sandy raised her cup in a toast, then blushed for some reason and covered it with a quick sip.

Tony swallowed a teaspoonful of cappuccino. "So you graduated with a B.S. and three certificates?"

"Four." Sandy held up fingers. "One in networking and three in operating systems."

Tony nodded. "I still haven't found one in hacking."

"Bet you could teach it, though."

"Who, me?" Tony was all astounded innocence. "I, who am dedicating my life to the betterment of humanity through computing?"

"And computer security," Sandy said, "which I'm sure you're constantly testing—unofficially, of course."

"Only when the site advertises a hacking contest."

"You win, of course," Sandy said.

"I'm flattered," Tony said, "but there are lots of hackers out there who are better than I am."

"Spending too much time doing legal stuff these days, huh?"

Her spirits certainly seemed to have improved. Tony let himself feel a little elation. "Started thinking about people's rights, too. Kind of dulled my edge."

"People are important." Sandy's eyes were soft and deep.

"Yes," Tony said with a sigh, "but computers are so much easier to understand."

Sandy laughed and squeezed his hand, and the rest of the evening passed quickly and pleasantly. They were both surprised to realize midnight was approaching— so Tony whisked her back to her apartment in a yellow cab, no golden coach being available, and told her good night on her doorstep. She seemed a little surprised but thanked him for a wonderful evening, then went in, and Tony turned back to the cab with his heart singing. Only after he had given the driver his address did he wonder if she had been expecting him to try for a kiss.

Feeling normal again—which is to say, gauche and clumsy—he paid the driver and went back to his apartment. He went into the bathroom and studied his image critically, then shook his head. Good thing he hadn't tried for that kiss. Even with his hair neatened with gel, he was no match for a lovely creature like Sandy. Sport coat was probably way out of fashion, too.

He sighed; he might do as Sandy's friend, but he would be hopeless as anything more. He changed into pyjamas, then went to the kitchen to heat up a drink—hopeless or not, he was going to have to calm down a bit before he'd be able to sleep.

As he came back into the room, he noticed the lines of text on the screen. Frowning, he went over to the computer, sat down, saved, scrolled back to the top, and began to read.

Father Vidicon did throttle down, and the tank slowed dutifully—but slewed as it slowed, and the good priest realized that he was swinging about and about in a circle.

He pulled back on the levers, killed the engine, then clambered out of the hatch, setting foot down onto the right tread—and found nothing there beneath his step. He froze, then levered himself up and turned about to climb down the left-hand tread instead, then walked around the machine and saw that the right-hand tread was gone indeed. Looking back down the tunnel, he saw it lying like a length of limber lumber on the ground. Frowning then, he came close and sat upon his heels to study the end, and saw where the connection had broken, crystallized metal fractured, as indeed it might have if this Sherman tank had really sat in wait through six decades. " 'Nature always sides with the hidden flaw,' " he mused, then stiffened, remembering that he quoted a corollary of Murphy's Law, which was itself a corollary of Finagle's General Statement.

Yet he had defeated the Imp of the Perverse—so which other of Finagle's henchmen had engineered this mishap?

Or was it a henchman? It might well have been a monstrosity quite equal, for many were the minions of Finagle.

Suspending judgment, the Blessed One rose to stand and turned his face ahead. Onward he strode down the tunnel.

Tony pushed his mouse and followed, feeling as though he were an invisible camera rolling forward in a tracking shot. In fact, the screen seemed to expand until the dark red tunnel surrounded him, almost as though he really were inside it—virtual reality without goggles. Father Vidicon was a quick walker, but Tony could match him, since he had no feet. However, he didn't even try to harmonize with the priest's whistling. Besides, he'd never liked that hymn, anyway.

Then a voice called, "St. Vidicon, save me from Finagle!"

The priest stopped, gazing off into space, and Tony asked, "Who was that?"

"A mother of three," St. Vidicon answered, "who is trying to get them out the door to school while one has taken her lunch box before it was packed, another has cleared the table but dropped a glass which shattered, and the third cannot find her jacket, all the while the telephone is ringing." His smile turned nostalgic. "How my sainted mother managed, I have no idea." He was silent a moment, then said, "There. I have given her what strength of spirit I may, and it has sufficed for her to shepherd all three of them out the door . . . no, she has forgotten her own attaché case . . . There, now she has it, and is into the car just in time to keep her daughter from punching her son."

"Where is her husband during all this?" Tony asked.

"He works the early shift in the factory's personnel office, so he was gone before seven . . . Ah! The poor woman! The car has refused to start." The priest's eyes lost focus again. "Perhaps a little more energy in the battery . . . No, that helped not at all; it must be a loose connection. No help for it but to send a part of my consciousness probing the circuits to find and restore it."

An evil laugh echoed down the hallway, and Father Vidicon spun to face it, crying, "Finagle! There would come another enemy upon me while I must deal with a call for help."

"Let me take care of the engine," Tony offered. "I may not be much on mechanical things, but I know circuits."

"Would you, then?" The saint turned to him and touched his shoulder. "I shall speed you on your way."

Tony just had time to realize he had a shoulder again, which really must have meant that he was actually in that fetid hallway, before a rushing sensation seized him, the world seemed to blur, and he found himself arrowing through reddish brown fog.

Chapter 3

Tony wondered what the reddish brown mist was, then recognized the color—copper! No. He couldn't be inside a wire. After all, where would the light be coming from?

Electrons, of course. What did he think was propelling him?

So why hadn't he been electrocuted?

Because he was pure energy himself—a spirit, or a fragment of spirit that was conveying information back to his mind. After all, his body would scarcely fit inside a wire, would it?

He decided he must have fallen asleep at his desk and be dreaming—but if this was a dream, he might as well enjoy it. He shot on through the wire, exulting in really getting into a circuit.

He barely had time to reflect that this was certainly a new view of electronics, before the electrons jerked to a halt and he found himself staring at a vast canyon.

A canyon? Inside an engine?

Well, of course—from an electron's point of view, and Tony couldn't be much bigger than an electron right now. No wonder the loose connection seemed like the Grand Canyon! But how to bring it closer? In frustration, he reached out toward the terminal from which the wire had come loose—and was amazed to see his arm, then see it stretching and stretching until his hand closed around the terminal. He pulled and watched his arm shrink while the terminal came closer and closer.

Well, why not? If he was pure energy himself, the arm was only a metaphor for his efforts anyway.

The terminal touched his wire, and the woman must have turned the ignition key again, for there was a burst of sparks that filled Tony's vision, then faded into darkness.

"Wake up, Tony! It wasn't really a shock, you know. Your mind just interpreted it that way from force of habit."

Tony blinked, looking up, and saw Father Vidicon leaning over him—and sure enough, he felt completely awake and not the slightest bit woozy. He sat up. "The mother! What happened to her?"

"Oh, the car started, thanks to you," St. Vidicon said. "She's on her way to drop the kids at school before she goes to work. You don't know how much you've improved her spirits."

"Glad to hear it." Tony rolled to his knees, then stood up with Father Vidicon's help. "That roar down the tunnel . . ."

The roar came again.

"Still making noise," Father Vidicon said. "I think it's hoping to intimidate me before it appears."

"I'll help!"

"Believe me, you've been a great help already," the

priest said, "but you have your own life to live. Back to your body, now, before more than a few nanoseconds of your time have passed."

"Body?" Tony looked down at himself, saw his shoes and the slacks of a business suit with legs inside them, presumably his. He stared at his arms and hands, turning them over and wriggling them. "What's this?"

"A memory of your body that you brought here with your spirit," Father Vidicon said, "as soon as you volunteered to troubleshoot that engine for me." The priest waved a hand. "Back to your real body now, for it needs at least some sleep before you go to work again tomorrow."

Tony started to object, but Father Vidicon faded away before his eyes. So did the dark red tunnel, and he found himself staring at his bedroom ceiling, striped with sunlight through the windows, and heard the early-morning roar of city traffic. He sat up, looked down at his blanket-covered legs, and wondered how he had made it from the computer to the bed. All he could think of was that it was a good thing he'd shifted to pyjamas.

The only problem with helping St. Vidicon was that Tony couldn't brag about it to Sandy—but he could talk to her. More to the point, listen—if he had the chance. Heart hammering, he dialed her number. "Hello?"

"Sandy? This is Tony."

"Tony! How nice of you to call!"

He wondered why she sounded so surprised even as he swallowed and plucked up his faltering nerve. "I was, uh, wondering if"—he reminded himself that he was a capable professional in his own field—"if you'd like to go to, uh, to dinner Friday night."

"Why, I'd love to! Thanks very much. Where shall I meet you?"

Tony hadn't thought that far ahead, but he improvised. "Well, I've always liked the Marinara. Unless you don't like Italian?"

"I love Italian! I'll meet you there at, oh . . . seven-thirty?"

"Sounds great. But, uh, I could pick you up—just a cab, of course . . ."

"That's very sweet of you, but not at all necessary." Her voice had become very firm. "I'll meet you at the Marinara at seven-thirty Friday night, then."

"Seven-thirty," Tony confirmed, heart in his throat. "Uh . . . good day."

"Good-bye," Sandy said sweetly, and hung up.

So did Tony, with a shaky hand and a sigh of relief. "Thank you, St. Vidicon!"

It might have been his imagination, but he thought he felt a glow of reassurance surround him for a minute.

Somehow Friday seemed a very long way away, and the day stretched on interminably, especially since Tony was sent out on a call to troubleshoot a local area network. It took him most of the morning to track down the terminal whose user had decided to try a little programming of his own, then all of the afternoon to remove the traces of the amateurish attempt at writing code from the server and the other terminals. The only bright spot of the day happened during afternoon coffee break when Tony, obsessed with the problem as usual, brought his cup back to his cubicle-away-from-home and found text beginning to scroll up. He punched a few keys to start capture and sat down to read.

Instead, a banner appeared across the top of the screen:

To arms, Tony! Help the poor fellow whose computer has crashed!

Yrs. Trly,
Fr. Vidicon

Tony stared. Surely the saint didn't think he could
help during working hours!

The phone rang. Tony picked it up and heard his
boss, Harve, saying, "Grab your tool kit and go, Tony!
Fifty-first and Seventh, Suite Twenty-thirteen! Just a
computer crash, but you never know."

"On my way." Tony hung up, reflecting that one of
the nice things about this business was that you never
knew what would be coming next.

Then he realized that he had known. Apparently St.
Vidicon had given the clerk whose computer had
crashed the good sense to call for help.

He started for the door, but hesitated. Better see if his
saintly benefactor had any background information. He
went back to his keyboard and typed in, "Someone else
needing help?"

A text box appeared with print scrolling. "A software
engineer who's trying to run a new application he has
designed, but it keeps freezing his system."

Tony typed back, "Blue Screen of Death?"

"Indeed," the screen answered.

"Be glad to, Father!" Tony was delighted to dive into
something he could understand. Code made sense, unlike relationships.

At the office of SubWare Development, Inc., Tony
was taken to the cubicle of a very shamefaced engineer
who, unless Tony was completely mistaken, had lingering traces of acne on his face. "Hi. Something wrong
here?"

"Yeah, a lot!" The young man held out a hand. "Richard Arkin."

"Tony. What were you doing when it crashed?"

"Running a new program I'd just finished—well, tried to run it, anyway. It's none of the standard bugs, I can tell you that."

"Sounds like fun." Tony grinned and sat down at the keyboard. "You take lunch yet?"

"Well, no. I wanted to finish the program."

"This might be a good time, then. See you in an hour." Tony rebooted the computer, ignoring Richard's yelp of dismay, then called up the code for the new program. As he studied it line by line, the numbers seemed to reach out to surround him, and he knew it was one of his better days.

It was just an illusion, of course, but he seemed to be inside the program and was shocked to see deformed and twisted digits drifting aimlessly, not flowing as they should. On closer look, he saw the "digits" were really clumps of ones and zeros, so deformed they almost seemed to resemble . . .

Insects.

To be more exact, bugs.

Tony began to get a very nasty feeling. He rose up as high as he could, trying to get a new perspective on the situation, and looked down on the drifting digital bugs. Instantly, he saw that they formed a gyre, an expanding, rising spiral. He cross-referenced, found its center, and dived back.

There it lay, a pair of vertical spirals, a double helix— but cramped and distorted, with uneven amounts of distance between turns. Tony's hair stood on end as he recognized a virus.

The debate still continued as to whether or not organic viruses were living things. They were molecules, but they exhibited some of the symptoms of life, such as the ability to reproduce—and this one was generating offspring, and those offspring were bugs. Definitely it was as alive as any information could be, and was mumbling to itself:

"One, ten, eleven, one hundred twelve!"

Twelve?

"Data drives the driven drivel, info forms formations forgone!"

On and on it mumbled, pure gibberish—because, Tony realized, it might have been pure information, but it had no intelligence—so it constantly spewed code which made no sense of any kind and was therefore guaranteed to stop any program in its tracks, maybe even to scramble all the data on a hard drive. Tony had to find a way to stop it, and stop it fast, before it escaped into this engineer's address book and e-mailed itself to thousands of other computers.

How do you kill something that isn't quite alive but that generates chaos?

By opposing it to obsessive order, of course. Tony remembered a college friend's computer's address. He dived into the data stream, surged upward and upward, traced the route to the DSL port, and shot out into the Internet.

He found it still on the hard drive of the mathematician's computer—apparently he moved his All-Purpose Bug Killer with him whenever he upgraded. It was certainly a new perspective on the tool—instead of lines of code, from the inside, it looked like a giant comb. "Come on, Bug Killer! I've got a job for you!" Tony grabbed the comb—and was surprised when it turned on him. It pounced, and for the first time, Tony realized that those teeth were very sharp.

He dodged at the last instant, and the teeth bit deeply

into the electron stream. Sparks cascaded from it as it leaped up and struck again.

Tony decided to find another bug killer and shot back through the circuit toward the DSL port. Just before he left the computer, he glanced back over his shoulder—but the giant comb was still coming, leaping after him in coruscating bounds. Tony shouted in panic and shot out into the Internet.

He dodged through the connections and portals back to Richard's computer, but he could tell from the sound of sparks fizzing behind him that the comb was still coming. He began to wonder how getting back into Richard's computer was going to help anything, but what else could he do?

He flashed through the port and down into the program—maybe the bugs would hide him. He swerved around behind the virus, putting the dense cloud of bugs it was emitting between himself and the comb—but through the snowy cascade, he saw the giant comb slow, then stop, then begin raking the tide of twisted digits, breaking the bugs back into their components. In its wake, it left straightened, orderly ones and zeros that snapped back into their original places in Richard's program. Relentlessly, the comb advanced on the virus.

Tony left the two of them to battle it out and swam out of the infected computer. He found the pure stream of an antivirus program, lingered long in its cleansing jet, then finally, limp and exhausted, limped home to his body.

Tony recovered from the limpness and weakness in the cab back across town and was almost himself by the time he walked back in the door and made it to his cubicle. There he collapsed in his chair, staring at his screen saver. After a few minutes, he flicked the mouse and saw some text that hadn't been there when he'd left. He glanced at his watch—half an hour till quitting time: not enough time to accomplish anything useful, but plenty to find out what St. Vidicon had been doing while he'd been gone. Feeling a bit more settled, he smiled and began to read.

Down that hallway darkly red did the good priest wander, but had not paced long ere he came to a bank of recorders whose reels spun two-inch-wide tape. He frowned, remembering such things from his youth, but finding no television cameras or control chains nearby—though his eye did light upon an antique electric typewriter without a platen. "A computer terminal!" he cried in delight, and went to sit by the console and log on.

Behind him reels did hum, and he froze, reminding himself that he dealt with a device unknown. Casually, then, he typed in a program he knew well—but when he directed the computer to run, the reels spun only for a minute before the printer chattered. Looking over to it, he saw the words, "Error on Line 764"—but the type-ball flew on until it had drawn a picture in marks of punctuation. Peering closer, Father Vidicon beheld the image of a beetle. "It doth generate bugs!" quoth he, then realized that he was in a realm in which any device would have a hidden flaw.

Rising from that place, he resolved most sternly that he would ignore any other device he found, and onward marched.

Well! Now Tony knew why he'd succeeded with Richard's computer. His patron had been shutting down the archetypal Bug Generator for him! He read on.

Full ten minutes did Father Vidicon stride before a doorway blocked his path, and a lighted panel lit above it in the yellow-lettered word "RE-HEARSAL." The Blessed One's pulse did quicken, resolution forgotten, for in life he had been a video engineer, and he quite clearly did approach a television studio much like the one in which he first had learned to operate a camera, in the days of his youth.

He wondered if he should enter, but saw no reason not to, if the souls within were only in rehearsal. He hauled open the sand-filled door, discovering a small chamber four feet square with a similar door set opposite him and another in its side, as a proper sound lock should have. He closed the door behind him carefully, so that sound might not be admitted, then opened the door to the side and stepped into the control room.

It lay in gloom, with three tiers of seats rising, all facing bank upon bank of monitors—the first tier of seats for the engineers, the second for the switcher, director, and assistant director, and the third for observers. Each position sat in its own pool of light from tiny spotlights hung above.

None were peopled. He stood alone.

Looking out through the control room window, he saw the studio likewise unpeopled, but with huge old monochrome cameras aimed at easels, each with a stack of pictures. Even as he watched, the tally light on Camera One went out as its mate atop Camera Two came on, and on Camera One's easel, one picture fell to the floor, revealing another behind it.

Father Vidicon frowned; it was clearly an automatic studio, and even more clearly a temptation.

Still, he saw no harm in it, and since the studio blocked the tunnel, it had to be navigated—so he sat down before the switcher, smiling fondly as he saw only a preview bank and two mixing banks with not even a downstream key cluster; the memories that it evoked were dear.

But he could not wallow long in nostalgia, for a voice called from the intercom, "Air in five . . . four . . . three . . ."

Quickly, the saint split the faders and went to black.

". . . two . . . one . . . You're on!" the voice cried.

Father Vidicon faded in Camera One, seeing a vision of St. Mark's Plaza appear on the program monitor as a mellow voice began to narrate a travelogue. Father Vidicon glanced at Camera Two's monitor, saw a close-up of the gilded lion, and readied a finger over the button Two on the air bank. As the voice began to speak of the lion, he punched the button and the close-up of the lion appeared on the line monitor. Grinning then, he began to fall into the old rhythm of a program, taking from one detail to another, then seeing a photograph of a gondola on a canal and dissolving to it.

Just as the image became clear, though, the picture fluxed, shrinking, then expanding, then shrinking to die. Instantly did Father Vidicon dissolve back to Camera One—and it too bloomed and died.

"Telecine!" he roared, that his voice might be heard through the director's headset (since he wore none). "Trouble slide!"

And Lo! The telecine screen lit with a picture of an engineer enwrapped in layers of videotape as he spooled frantically through an antique videotape recorder, attempting to clear a jam. It was a still picture only, so Father Vidicon leaned back with a sigh, then rose on rather wobbly legs. "I should have known," he muttered, "should have remembered." Then he walked, though rather unsteadily, back into the sound lock, then on into the studio. Around the cameras he went and drew aside the heavy velvet drape that hid the back wall—and sure enough, it had hidden also the double door to the scenery storage room. He hauled open the portal, stepped in among the ranked flats, threaded his way through piled sofas and stacked chairs, and found the entry door beyond. He opened it, stepped through, and found himself back in the dim light of the maroon tunnel.

The priest set off again, mouth in a grim line, for, said he unto himself, "Now, then, we know which minion of Finagle's we shall face," for surely there could be no doubt who sided with the hidden flaw, who made machinery fail in crucial moments, who was attracted to devices more strongly as they became more complicated, and it was not Nature.

And Lo! The monster did approach—or, more precisely, the saint did approach the monster, who smiled as he saw the Blessed One come nigh, glanced down to make a check mark on his clipboard, then looked up again to grin—or his lips did; Father Vidicon could not see his eyes, since they were shadowed by a visor of green, and his face that of a gnome, not a man. He wore a shirt that was striped and held by sleeve-garters, its collar tightened by a necktie, though over it he was clothed in coveralls (but they were pin-striped), and his left hand bore socket wrenches in place of fingers. Clean-shaven he was, and round-faced, smiling with delight full cynical, the whiles his right hand did play upon a keyboard.

Then Father Vidicon did halt some paces distant, filled with wariness, and declared, "I know thee, Spirit—for thou art the Gremlin!"

"I do not make policy," the creature replied, "I only execute it."

"Seek not to deceive!" Father Vidicon rebuked. "Thou art the one who doth seek to find the hidden flaw and doom all human projects."

"'Tis in the nature of humans to bring it out," the Gremlin retorted. "I only execute what they themselves have overlooked."

"Wouldst thou have me believe 'tis Nature who doth side with the hidden flaw, though well we know that Nature makes not machines?"

"Nature sides with me," the Gremlin returned. "Canst thou blame me for the nurture of the natural?"

"'Tis not Nature thou dost serve, but Entropy!"

"What else?" the spirit gibed. "Humans seek to build, when 'tis the way of Nature to fall apart."

"Only in its season," Father Vidicon admonished, "when the time of growth is behind."

"Not so," the Gremlin answered, "if the flaw's inherent in the new-born creature. Thus only when it doth come to maturity doth its undoing become manifest."

"And what of those whose flaws emerge before they're grown?"

The Gremlin shrugged. "Then they never come to the age at which they can build, and only looking backward can they see a life worth living."

"Thou dost lie, thou rogue," Father Vidicon said sternly, "for that cannot be behind which is before!"

"Oh, so? Hast thou, then, heard never of the Mule?" The Gremlin's hand did beat upon the keyboard, and letters of a glowing green did glimmer in the gloaming 'fore his face: "BOOT MULE." Father Vidicon did step back with a presentiment of foreboding; then the words did vanish, and beside the Gremlin stood a stocky quadruped, with longish ears laid back, teeth parting in a bray.

"I should have thought," the priest did breathe. "This is the beast most susceptible to thee, for 'tis also the most contrary; when we most wish it to work, it will not."

"All who will not work are with me," the Gremlin answered, "as are those who, in the name of standing firm, give way to stubbornness." He reached out to stroke the beast, and chanted,

> " 'The mule, we find,
> Hath two legs behind,
> And two we find before.
> We stand behind before we find
> What the two behind be for.' "

And the saint did find the mule's tail confronting him, and the hooves kicked up and lashed out at his head.

But St. Vidicon did bow, and the feet flashed by above. "Affront me not," quoth he, "for I do know this beast hath fallibility."

"Then make use of it," the Gremlin counselled, "for he doth set himself again."

'Twas true, the mule did once again draw up his hooves to kick. Father Vidicon did therefore run around the beast up toward its head.

But, "What's before, and what's behind?" the

Gremlin cried. "Behold, I give the beast his head, and he doth lose it! For if we know what that behind be for, then assuredly, what's behind's before!"

Father Vidicon did straighten up before the mule's face—and found it was a tail, with hooves beneath that did lash out.

"Surely in his stubbornness," the Gremlin said, "the mule has lost his head!"

The good priest did shout as he did leap aside, quickly, but not quite quickly enough, and a hoof did crack upon his shoulder, and pain shot through his whole side. He cried out, but his cry was lost in the Gremlin's laughter, which did echo all about.

"Thou canst not escape," the spirit cried with gloating glee, "for if thou dost run around the beast, thou wilt but find what thou hast lost!"

Hooves slashed out again, and the priest did throw himself upon the ground. The mule's feet whistled through the air above him, then drew back to stand, and began to hobble toward him.

"Come, come!" the Gremlin cried. "Thine heart was ever in thy work! Wouldst thou now lie about and trouble others? Wouldst thou be underfoot?"

But the priest had scrambled to his feet, a-running, and heard the thunderous echo of galloping hooves behind. At a thought, however, he turned back. "Two backward sets both running must go against each other; they thereby must stand in place!"

Assuredly, the poor beast did; for each pair of legs, in leaping forward, did naught but counter the other's thrust.

"Let it not trouble thee," the Gremlin counselled, "for I've held him close thus far—yet now I'll give the beast his head!"

Father Vidicon knew then that he had but a moment to draw upon the strength of Him to Whom he was in all ways dedicated; and holding up his hands to Heaven, he did pray, "Good Father, now forgive! That in my pride I did think myself equipped to defeat the Finder of Flaws. Lend me, I pray Thee, some tool that will find and hinder all contrariness that this creature doth embody!"

Of a sudden, his hands weighed heavy. Looking there, he found a halter.

A bray recalled him to his conflict, and he saw the mule's tail grow dim, then harden again to show forequarters topped by a head that did reach out, teeth sharp to bite, as the Mule leaped forward.

Chapter 4

Father Vidicon shouted and spun aside, flailing at the Mule with the halter—and sure enough, it caught. The Mule swerved and reared, braying protest, but Father Vidicon did hold fast to reins and turn the Mule toward its master, then leaped upon its back. Still under the Gremlin's mandate to attack, it galloped ahead, teeth reaching for its master.

"How now!" the creature screeched, drumming at its keyboard. "How canst thou turn my own artifact against me?"

The mule disappeared, leaving the saint to plummet toward the floor, the halter still in his hand—but he landed lightly.

"Thou didst expect that fall!" the Gremlin accused. "How couldst thou have known?"

"Why, by preparing 'gainst every eventuality,"

the saint replied, "then expecting some other malfunction that I could not name because I had not
thought of it."

"Thou dost not mean thou didst expect the un-
expected!"

"Surely, for I have always expected thee, since
first I learned to program Cobol." The saint approached, holding out the halter. "Know that with
my Master's power, these straps can harness any
who their energy expend." Still he advanced, the
halter outheld.

"Thou dost speak of those who embody Entropy," the Gremlin protested, and did back away.

"'Tis even so," the saint replied, "for to live is to
expend energy, but to grow is to gain structure."

"You are not fool enough to think to reverse entropy!" the Gremlin cried, still backing.

"Only for some little while," the saint replied,
"but each little while added to another can constitute a lifetime entire."

"Yet in the end your race shall die! In mere bil-
lions of years, your sun will explode, and all will
end in fire! Thus all is futile, all is done in vain, all's
absurd!"

"Yet while life endures, it contradicts absurdity—
if it has structure." Father Vidicon relaxed the halter, then swung it at the Gremlin to ensnare.

The Gremlin wailed and winked out as though
he'd never been.

Father Vidicon stared at the place where he had
stood and bethought him somberly, "He is not truly
gone, but will recur wheresoever people try to
build—for 'gainst such as him we struggle to find
meaning." Then he looked down at the halter, contemplating it a moment before he held it high in of-

fering. "O Father, I thank Thee for giving Thine overweening servant the means to banish this Foe of Humankind, no matter how briefly. I return unto Thee the Halter of one of the beasts who witnessed the birth of Thy Son, and of another who bore Him to His triumph in Jerusalem."

For half a minute the halter began to glow, then scintillated as it vanished.

The Blessed One stood alone, reflecting that once again he was unarmed; but he recalled the words of the psalm and murmured them aloud: "'For Thou, O God, art my wisdom and my strength.' Nay, I shall never lack for defense within this realm, so long as Thou art with me."

So saying, he strode forth once more, further downward in that tunnel, wondering what other foe the Lord might send him to confront.

The text rolled off the screen, and Tony sighed, wishing for more. He glanced up at the clock, saw it was almost quitting time, called the front desk to make sure there were no calls for him and felt irrationally disappointed when there weren't—after all, Friday was still two days and one night away.

He had dinner at his favorite restaurant, but it seemed more lonely than it ever had, and his paperback didn't hold his attention. All in all, it seemed a good idea to go to bed early and try to sleep.

Not just "try to"—sleep came surprisingly easily. Of course, the surprise evaporated when Tony found his dream self pacing down the maroon, soft-floored corridor beside Father Vidicon.

The priest looked up, startled. "Tony! A pleasure to see you." Then he frowned. "But you shouldn't be here."

"Are you kidding?" Tony said. "This is where the action is."

"You should be resting, though, not working." Father Vidicon held up a hand. "Oh, don't get me wrong, I'm delighted to have company—but this isn't your fight."

"Are you kidding? The number of times you've helped me out when a program wouldn't run?" Tony grinned. "Besides, how often does a guy get to play sidekick to a saint?"

Father Vidicon still held up the cautioning hand. "I haven't been declared a saint yet, Tony. Indeed, my journey through this tunnel may be the ordeal that shows whether or not I'm worthy of a place in Heaven."

"You're kidding, of course," Tony said. "You're a martyr."

"Well, yes, but I try not to take things for granted." St. Vidicon turned and started down the squelching hallway again. "I really should see where this pathway leads me, though."

Tony fell in beside him. "You don't really think it's the road to Hell, then?"

"I'm beginning to suspect otherwise, yes."

It seemed the most natural thing in the world to be talking with a saint—until St. Vidicon said, "I'm glad my message finally reached you."

Tony stared. "Your what?"

"My message," said the saint. "That's why I fed that virus into the mainframe of one of your company's clients—because I needed a troubleshooter. Specifically, you."

"Why me?" Tony asked.

"Because you have the right turn of mind," St. Vidicon told him. "You inherited it from your ancestor Mateo."

"My ancestor? None of my great-grandfathers was named Mateo!"

"No, but your forefather in the sixteenth century had a cousin named Mateo—a Jesuit who founded the China Mission and wrote the first treatise in comparative religion, comparing Confucianism to Christianity to try to discover if people could develop a sound moral code without Divine intervention." Father Vidicon smiled. "He decided they could. It was troubleshooting in advance, laying the groundwork for religious tolerance. The trait has bred true all the way down to you."

Tony's father had worked for a satellite communications company, troubleshooting earth stations; his great-grandfather had done the same thing with the phone company's landlines. He saw St. Vidicon's point. "But what kind of troubles would you want me to shoot?"

"Anything people call me for, when I'm already trying to fix another problem," Father Vidicon said. "When I finish this trip through Hellmouth, maybe God will grant me the power to be in many different locations at once; but even then, I think I'll need some help."

"That's interesting but not informative."

St. Vidicon stiffened suddenly. "A call's coming in. Here, see it with me and analyze the problem."

He caught Tony's hand, and whether the technician wanted to or not, he saw what the saint was seeing and heard what he was hearing—a despairing, many-voiced cry for help, and the background of the predicament.

Up on the wall, right where you see it when you come in the door of the lab, is a sign that says,

"We have everything we need to build an electric car. We have the motor, the transmission, the steer-

ing, and the headlights. All we need now is a battery
that will last long enough."

—T. A. Edison

That's our job—developing an electric car for one of
the Really Big Auto Makers—and our "lab" looks like
a cross between a machine shop and a clinic. The Eagle,
our prototype electric car, sits on a hoist that hasn't
lifted in months, sits there with its hood up to show an
engine so clean you could cook on it—and a great big
gaping hole where the battery ought to be.

The battery, at the moment, was sitting on an insu-
lated bench with two technicians hovering over it in
protective gear and masks that would have done credit
to an astronaut. Behind them, Sally Barley was beaming with motherly pride. She was fiftyish, neat, tidy, be-
spectacled, and Director of Development. She was also
an attractive woman who wasn't aware of the fact. She
wore a lab coat, bifocals, and coiled braids. Just looking
at her made me feel like a slob.

Not that I was, of course. The waistline isn't showing too much bulge for a man in his early forties, and
the creases in the slacks are still sharp. Sure, I wore
gym shoes, but they were very trendy and cost more
than I'd want to admit, if everyone else I knew didn't
know the figure to the penny (including tax). And I
wore polo shirts because my generation was more ca-
sual than hers, not to show off my biceps and pecs (not
that they weren't worth showing). The hairline hadn't
receded too much and there weren't too many wrinkles.
Too bad I'd never had time for that nose job.

"This is Eagle Fifteen," I reminded her, "and the
fourteenth one only ran for thirty hours at in-town
speed. You really think you've managed to double that,
for highway speeds, in just one generation?"

"Oh, yes." Sally nodded. "Of course, I wouldn't let the stockholders know about that yet. We still have a month of trials and fine-tuning."

Which raised the question of why she had called me in—but there are advantages to keeping the public relations director on your side. Besides, I had a triple-A clearance from company security, so I'd been following the project ever since Eagle 1 came off the drawing board.

"How come you're so sure it's going to last so much longer?"

"Because the new motor and power train use much less current—and that next-generation electrolyte is a wonder. Too bad NASA didn't think of it sooner."

It made sense, after all. A battery that could keep a robot explorer going for two months on an ice moon around Saturn shouldn't have had much trouble lasting sixty hours on an American highway—and like everything else NASA developed, it was free. We didn't have to pay royalties or a licensing fee or anything. Sometimes I wondered just how much more money NASA put back into the economy than it cost us in taxes.

The two technicians finished sealing the battery and, very carefully, lifted it and started toward the car.

"Gently, boys, gently," Sally cautioned. "That's the crown jewels, there—or at least the diamond."

I was glad she'd qualified that. The battery couldn't have been worth any more than the Koh-i-Noor. It was the whole car whose development cost probably dwarfed St. Edward's Crown.

The two techs were good at their jobs. In fact, they were top experts. Sally knew that. Even so, she breathed a huge sigh of relief as the battery settled into place and they started screwing the clamp down.

"You knew they weren't going to drop it," I reproved her.

"Yes, I knew," she admitted, "but accidents happen."

"It's a disaster!"

We both spun to stare at Joe Sanders, fresh off his college track team and breaking his own record for the sixty-yard dash. He skidded to a halt beside Sally, and the way he was gasping couldn't have been due to the distance between the door and the Eagle.

"Calm down, Joe," Sally said in her most soothing tone. "Nothing's that bad—unless the whole car blows up, of course. Now take a deep breath and tell me what happened."

Joe gulped, made a visible (but unsuccessful) effort to relax, then blurted, "It's the boss! He wants to drive the Eagle."

Since our boss was Sally, Joe could only have meant the Big Boss—the CEO of the whole blamed company. Sally turned visibly pale but said with monumental restraint, "When?"

"Two-thirty." Panic edged Joe's voice.

It was contagious. I went into panic mode too, and Sally froze. It was one-forty-five.

Then she turned to the boys and started rapping out orders. "Bill, check all the connections! Jodie, take it once around the track! Then turn it over to Anna and Tom for a quick wash!" She would have had them checking the onboard computer too, but microprocessors had only been invented ten years before.

They were just polishing the last drop off the Eagle when the Boss walked in.

He went straight up to Sally with a politician's smile and an outstretched hand. "Dr. Barley, your lab has to be the cleanest room in the building! And your whole staff does you credit."

She took his hand and gave him back smile for smile. "Thanks, Mr. Bridge. I'm proud of them all. I understand you'd like a progress report on the Eagle."

"No, I want to drive it."

Well, it had been a nice try, anyway. I pulled out my camera and got a quick shot of them before Sally's smile faded.

I didn't need speed; she kept the mouth curved. They tell me some corpses do that. "It's an honor, Mr. Bridge. I do have to advise you, though, that we haven't really tested the new battery on the track yet—only once around to make sure the connections were sound."

"Oh, that's all right." Mr. Bridge waved it away. "I don't mind being your test driver." He opened the door and slid in behind the wheel before any of us could argue. "Now, where's the ignition? . . . I see. And here's the gearshift . . . accelerator and brake in the usual places, hm? Well, wish me luck!"

We did. We wished us luck too, as the Eagle rolled out the door and onto the track.

"Just once around." Sally's voice had the tone of a prayer. "Once around is all he needs. He's just making sure it runs and seeing how it steers and stops."

Beside her, Bill nodded. "Once is plenty."

The Boss turned the far curve and came back toward us, gaining speed.

"Pull up," Julie pleaded. "Pull up like a nice little executive and let us finish fine-tuning it!"

For a minute there, we thought he'd heard her. The Eagle came up opposite us, slowing—then went right on into the turn. A massed groan came from the dozen engineers.

"He was only slowing for the curve," Shirley lamented.

"He wasn't really meaning to tease us," Jodie said beside her.

"Okay, twice around," Tom wheedled. "Twice around is plenty. Just bring it back to us like a good little manager."

Again, the Boss seemed to hear, because instead of speeding up on the straightaway, he slowed.

There was a massed gasp behind me as the engineers held their breaths.

The Eagle turned ninety degrees, out through the gate toward the city streets.

The engineers let out another massed groan.

The journalist in me took over. I sprinted down to the gate, whipped out my camera as I turned, and managed to get a clear shot of the security guard waving the Eagle through the main gate. So much for secrecy.

The Eagle vanished into the city traffic.

My heart down in my boots, I headed back toward the lab, wondering why I cared. It wasn't my job that was on the line, after all.

Then I looked up and saw the track was bare. I frowned. I'd expected the engineers to be lined up along it, ready to cheer the Boss as he came back—after they were done cursing him under their breaths. I went through the huge open door into the lab.

There they were, clustered together in the middle of the huge space with heads bowed, Sally in front of them, intoning, "St. Vidicon, patron of all who toil with screwdriver and soldering gun . . ."

"Pray for us," the engineers chorused.

"St. Vidicon, upholder of order and foe of chaos . . ."

"Pray for us."

"St. Vidicon, straightener of electron paths and adjuster of energy states . . ."

"Pray for us!"

I edged up to the back row and muttered to Tom, "I thought you guys were all agnostics."

"Pretty much," he said, "but at a time like this, you gotta pray to somebody!"

Beside him, Julie nodded. "St. Vidicon's only a character in a story, so he's okay."

I tried to figure out the sense in that while Sally went on with her impromptu litany.

"What a fascinating toy!" the Gremlin said to itself as it swam through the Eagle's circuits. "A triumph of ingenuity! Now, how best to make it stop working? Just loosen the battery cable—but no, that would be too obvious; no chance it would scuttle the project. Weaken the electrolyte? Again, too easy to discover. A thinning of the windings in the motor and a burn-out that would follow? Yes! It will be days before they think to look at brand-new coils!" It stretched out a long and knobby finger.

"Wait!" said a voice.

Frowning, the Gremlin turned and saw Gunderson, swimming beside him in the current.

"Not now, when the car is on a lightly-travelled street," said Gunderson. "Remember, the least desirable possibility must always exert itself when the results will be most frustrating. Wait until he is in the heaviest traffic and the breakdown will cause a mass collision."

The Gremlin pulled its finger back with a grin. "I like your style, Scandinavian."

"St. Vidicon, foe of Gunderson and the Gremlin," Sally called.

"Protect us from breakdowns!" the engineers answered.

•   •   •

Tony groaned. He too knew better than to trust management with an engineering problem. "The CEO of a corporation driving a prototype car into city streets!"

Head cocked to listen, St. Vidicon asked, "Hear that, Tony?"

Tony listened but heard a slow beat so low-pitched it was scarcely audible. Frowning, he shook his head.

"Touch my sleeve," Father Vidicon said.

Tony took hold of his arm and heard a voice. Dimly, he heard a woman call, "St. Vidicon, engineer of philosophies"—and a dozen people finished her thought—"make the world logical!"

St. Vidicon smiled. "Not even a saint can do that, Tony."

Tony stared, wounded. "You mean it isn't?"

"Not the human world, at least," the priest answered. "Still, I can straighten a few crooked ways."

Tony became absolutely still, listening to the minds and hearts of the engineers a generation before his own, until he understood the scope of the problem, and his eyes widened in horror. "Where is he?"

"I'll search." Father Vidicon looked down, and Tony wondered how he could see anything but the undulating floor. Still, he had no doubt the priest was scanning the city streets outside the research plant. "Not that car," Father Vidicon muttered, "nor that one, nor that—they all stink of exhaust . . . That one! The one that runs with no fire inside!" He probed, thoughts delving into the circuitry—and somehow Tony was there with him in the copper-colored fog, staring at . . .

"Begone, impertinent priest!" the Gremlin hissed.

"We meet again, fell spirit," St. Vidicon answered.

"This car is mine!"

"Yes, wait for the next one," Gunderson agreed.

"If you two have your way, there will never be a next

one," St. Vidicon retorted, then closed his eyes in prayer. "Dear Lord, I pray thee, send some tool to correct whatever foul-ups these two may make in the situation normal."

His palm tingled. Looking down, he saw a roll of copper in it. Grinning, he closed his eyes, picturing the inside of the motor until it began to seem real, then became real, and knew that some part of him was inside it.

The Eagle turned onto a boulevard that should have been lightly travelled at that time of afternoon, but Gunderson began to mutter under his breath, suggestions that sent sudden insights into every nearby motorist who was frustrated by traffic, and they all turned onto the boulevard to find easier going. In minutes, the little Eagle was surrounded by trucks and taxis and vans.

"Now!" Gunderson said.

The Gremlin touched a wire; it shrivelled. He reached out for another—but phantom hands with nimble fingers appeared, stretching ghostly wire that sank into the coil and strengthened it. The Gremlin cried out in frustration and touched the new wire, but it refused to shrivel. Cursing, the creature touched winding after winding—but the ghostly fingers kept pace with him, replacing wire after wire.

"A pox upon you, priest!" the Gremlin cried.

"Too late," Father Vidicon's voice said. "I've left my body behind." Then he reached out to the Boss with a suggestion.

It had been fun, the Boss decided, but it had turned into just another drive. The Eagle hummed along as smoothly as his town car and considerably more quietly. Besides, the traffic was getting thick and beginning to get on his nerves. Who made all these cars, anyway? He turned at the next light and started back to the track.

Inside his motor, the Gremlin went on touching wire after wire frantically, even stooping to loosen the battery cables, but as quickly as he wrecked, Father Vidicon fixed.

I decided somebody had to stand sentry, so I left the engineers trying to buck up their spirits and headed back to the gate, camera at the ready. I paced and waited, waited and paced, then heard the chime as the outer gate rose. "The Eagle is landing!" I shouted and whirled, whipping the camera up to my eye, and caught the Eagle as it glided through the inner gate and back onto the track, the Boss smiling behind the wheel. It would make a great photo for the article about the Eagle on the future day he decided to unmask it—officially, that is. I got another shot of the engineers swarming back onto the track to line up and cheer as the Eagle rolled between them and back into the lab. Then I sprinted for the door.

I got there in time to see the Boss climb out of the car and shake Sally's hand. "Congratulations, Dr. Barley! First-rate work, the kind that has made this company great!"

The engineers all glowed with pleasure, and Sally beamed. "Thanks, Boss—but it's still a prototype, and we have quite a few improvements to try out."

"I'm sure they'll make the car thoroughly marketable by the time we need to put it in production!" The Boss turned toward her office. "But we need to talk about the conversion problem. People won't buy an electric car, after all, if they can't recharge it while they're on the road . . ."

Sally fell in step beside him, and they headed for her

office, talking about setting up a network of service stations with half a dozen high-speed charging stations apiece. "With restaurants, of course," Sally was saying, "so the family can have lunch while they're having the battery topped up . . ."

"Well, Tom, you made it," I said.

"Yes, thank Heaven!" Tom joined his hands and looked up at the roof piously. "And thank you, St. Vidicon!"

"Amen!" the engineers chorused.

Then they shut up and whirled, looking shamefaced at the CEO who stood in the lab doorway, waving and calling, "Congratulations on a job well done! Good to know we have hard-working, loyal employees. I'll look forward to a production model this time next year!" And waving a cheery farewell, he turned and went out.

The team stood stunned, Sally most of all. Then, with one massive groan, they all staggered away in different directions.

Tom sidled up to Shirley. "Do you suppose it's too early to start praying yet?"

"A lucky accident, priest!" the Gremlin snarled. "I'll lock horns with you again, be certain!"

"Oh, I'll never doubt it," Father Vidicon returned, and withdrew his ghostly touch within his own spirit again.

Tony staggered at the suddenly-infirm footing. Looking around, he saw they were back in the maroon tunnel.

"I shall have to fight him till time's end"—Father Vidicon sighed—"again and again, I'm sure."

Tony frowned. "That doesn't seem fair."

"Oh, fair enough," Father Vidicon said, "for once having defeated him here on his home ground, I'm bound to win whenever I confront him on earth." He turned to Tony with a grin. "But that's enough fantastic adventure for you for the time being. Back to your own reality, now, and the young woman who is a far more worthy goal than helping a foolish monk combat invisible villains."

Tony started to object, but St. Vidicon raised his hand in blessing and farewell, and Tony found himself staring at his bedroom ceiling again, pale with the light of false dawn that filtered through his curtains. He just had time to wonder how much rest he'd had when the alarm clock went off.

Thursday seemed to drag worse than Tuesday or Wednesday, but it did eventually expire. Suddenly Friday had come, and Tony didn't feel ready. Nonetheless, he phoned the Marinara to make sure he still had a reservation for two, dressed in his best suit, and called the cab.

He walked into the Marinara and went to the lectern to wait. The maître d' came back a minute later and raised his eyebrows in polite inquiry.

"Ricci," Tony said. "Anthony."

The maître d' checked his list and nodded. "It will be a few minutes. Would you like a seat in the bar, sir?"

"No, I'm waiting for someone."

"I'll direct your guest to you, sir."

Tony started to object, but just then the door opened and Sandy walked in. She was radiant in a white satin dress decorated with an arc of seed pearls, her chestnut hair gleaming in a wave, her makeup minimal and flawless, and Tony found himself breathing, "Thank you."

Sandy smiled, pleased, but asked, "For what?"

"Uh—for being on time!" Tony offered his arm. "The maître d' offered us a seat in the bar."

"Wonderful way to begin." Sandy took his arm, and they went into the opulent gloom of damask and polished mahogany.

As he held her chair, Tony was amazed that so far, he seemed to have said the right things—and he thought he knew why. *St. Vidicon, don't desert me now!*

Chapter 5

Tony didn't actually hear any answer, but he felt massively reassured.

Over dinner, he found himself asking sensible questions—about Sandy's week and her work—then listened, fascinated as much by the sound of her voice and the animation in her face as by what she was saying.

". . . so then I routed the fibrillator into the framistan and ran a recursive routine," she finished.

Tony stared. "You did what? With what data?" Then the earlier words reregistered and he asked, "What's a framistan?"

Sandy laughed, lightly, gently, and reached out to squeeze his arm. "Just wondering if you were listening."

"Every syllable." Tony relaxed a little. "Thank heavens! For a moment there, I thought you were tying up your system with a recursive fractal!"

"I wouldn't be quite that silly." Sandy pursed her

lips, gazing off into space for a minute. "Framistan . . . fractal . . . I suppose it makes sense."

"Maybe," said Tony, "if I knew what a framistan was."

"A nonsense word from my childhood," Sandy said merrily, then turned as the dessert cart rolled up with the server behind it. "No, thanks. Couldn't eat another bite."

"Maybe a liqueur?" Tony offered.

Sandy cocked her head to the side, considering. "Cointreau would be nice."

"And I'll have cappuccino," Tony told the server, who nodded and disappeared, dessert cart and all.

They came out, Tony still asking questions and Sandy still answering merrily. "Cab?" the doorman asked.

Sandy sighed, looked directly into Tony's eyes, and said, "I'm not ready for the evening to be over yet."

Tony's pulse leaped, but he managed to keep his reaction down to a smile. "How about the Aftermath?"

"Sounds great!"

The Aftermath might not have been the most luxurious cocktail lounge in the city, but it was certainly the most welcoming for computer people, probably because it was the retirement project of a former systems analyst and three former software engineers. Tony and Sandy sat down at a small table that had clearly started life as a printer stand, feeling right at home. Track lighting displayed portraits of computer pioneers, framed sets of punch cards, sorting needles, and antique keyboards—their natural environment. Sandy ordered an old-fashioned; Tony had Irish coffee. He'd been here often enough that the bartender knew to go light on the Irish. Sandy was talking about the latest experiment in artificial intelligence, and Tony agreed that it was a nice try but that no one would ever mistake the talking head on the screen for a real human being. "It's too clearly animated."

"But a very good attempt," Sandy said, "and if you're only listening to it over the phone, you'd swear it's real."

"Oh, sure, by words alone it passes the Turing test," Tony agreed, "but somehow, when I'm listening, I never lose track of the fact that I'm hearing a machine that's executing a program."

"Pretty soon, you'll be aware of that when you see a face on your viewphone," Sandy predicted.

Tony smiled. "Good thing I try to be polite even when I know I'm talking to a machine."

Sandy stared. "You do? Why?"

"Habit," Tony said. "If I let myself start being rude to a robot, I might slip and start being rude to a human being. Besides, you never know, the voice might be real."

"But is it any the less real because it comes from a computer than if it comes from a person?" Sandy gave herself a shake. "Now, that is definitely too serious for an evening's fun. Let's dance!"

Tony's heart dropped three inches; he knew his own limitations. But he forced a smile, tried to sound cheery as he said "Sure!" and got up to take Sandy's hand and step out onto the dance floor.

It was a disaster. Well, maybe only a qualified disaster—but that was certainly how it felt to Tony. He'd had some lessons in the lindy long years before but not much practice since. At least, with fast dancing, he couldn't step on Sandy's feet. He thought he faked it fairly well, standing in the same spot and moving his feet a little while he clasped her hand and pulled and pushed when he thought she wanted, and Sandy managed to keep her smile, but by the time the music ended, it was definitely strained.

The band shifted to a slow tune, and Tony tried to be game, holding up his hands, but Sandy shook her head. "That was fun, but I think I'd better finish my drink."

Tony followed her back to the table with a feeling of doom.

Sandy managed some bright conversation while she was finishing her drink, but shifted to asking him what he did in his spare time. Tony couldn't think of an interesting lie, so he had to tell the truth. "Well, lately, I've been helping St. Vidicon with some miracles."

"St. Vidicon of Cathode?" Sandy stared. "When have you been doing that?"

"When I'm asleep, mostly."

"Oh, dreams!" Sandy folded her hands under her chin, eyes bright. "Tell me!"

So Tony told her about countering a virus with a bug-catcher/comb, and Sandy laughed with delight. "You certainly have wonderful dreams! Tell me another one on the way home."

So while they waited for the cab, Tony told her about helping with the electric car, and as they rode back to her place, he told her about the mother whose car wouldn't start—so he was able to keep the evening from ending on a note of defeat. As he came back to the cab from seeing her to her door, though, he felt gloom settle over him. The evening had definitely lost its magic when he'd stepped onto the dance floor. As the cab bore him homeward, he vowed to learn to dance.

Sleep was slow in coming, but gradually images of Sandy faded into darkness. Then the darkness turned reddish, a redness that took on form and substance, and Tony found himself walking down the moist maroon hallway with St. Vidicon. "Thanks, Father," he said fervently. "I don't seem to have put a foot wrong until I actually had to move my feet, but I couldn't have done it without you!"

"Oh, I think I may have had less to do with it than you think," the priest said, amused. "You do have some instincts, you know."

"Yes, and they're all usually wrong."

"Not really, if you'd trust them more often." Father Vidicon smiled. "But enough of pleasant realities. Let's see what else awaits us in this dream-realm. Do you know 'Amazing Grace'?"

"Of course." Tony said.

"Then let us walk." Father Vidicon linked arms with him, and together they strode down the darkling hallway through deepening mauve, singing the words of the hymn, knowing that sooner or later, they would wind up in the same key.

Then, suddenly, St. Vidicon stopped, and because Tony's arm was in his, he too could hear the young man and young woman who called out to the martyr.

"A complicated situation." Father Vidicon frowned. "We'd better find out how they got into this mess."

And, so help me, he scanned their section of the time line, back to when the whole predicament started.

Happy hour was just starting when the Gadget came in. Her name was Gidget Farnum, really, but for her classmates in engineering, the temptation had been too great, so she'd been Gadget since her first day on campus. That had been twelve years and two towns ago.

"So how's things in the motor pool?" I asked as I set her scotch and soda in front of her.

"Very funny, Nick," she said, with a look that could

electrocute. "You know the union threatened a walkout if they ever saw me with a wrench in my hand."

"You and all the other drawing board jockeys." Actually, I doubted the union even knew she existed—just one more indentured servant toiling in the bowels of Research and Development. "How's the lawsuit?"

Legal action had nothing to do with the Company, who knew they couldn't claim the next-generation carburetor she had invented in grad school. It was the petroleum lobby who had persuaded Congressmen Annihile to introduce the bill banning manufacture of ethanol-burning cars; his speech to the House had painted a lurid picture of alcohol stations sprouting up all across the country, with legions of alcoholics lining up to sip from the nozzles.

"The suit went down faster than an Empire State Building elevator," Gadget said, looking more like a bloodhound with each word. "The bill passed. Ethanol-burning cars are now illegal in the United States, before they ever had a chance to go into production—or invention, for that matter."

I shrugged. "What was to invent? All they had to do was plug your carburetor into the engine instead of the old-fashioned kind, and voilà! You could fuel up from a cornstalk!"

"You left out a few steps, such as harvesting and distilling." But Gadget looked at me with new awareness. "How much do you know about automobiles?"

"Enough to know that with the oil reserves down to the dregs and everybody buying electric cars, your patent is the only real hope Detroit has to avoid scrapping their old lines completely," I said, "and as much as three years studying chemical engineering could teach me."

Gadget stared.

"Because I forgot to graduate." I answered the question she was too polite to ask. "I interned with Amalgamated Chemicals the summer before my senior year, and in July, they made me an offer I didn't refuse."

Gadget winced; like everybody else in the country, she knew what had happened to Amalgamated.

"Hey," I said, "it was a great job for a year and a half."

"How come you didn't go back to school?"

"With what money?" I said. "I lived really well for that eighteen months. Who knew it was going to end?"

"Only Amalgamated's accountants," Gadget said darkly.

She didn't even bother asking about a computer job. America's youth had finally listened to reason and made sure they could all troubleshoot a program on their way out of high school. Result? A huge oversupply in skills.

Gadget's eyes widened. "Thanks."

I frowned. "What for?"

"Making me feel a little less sorry for myself."

I actually laughed. "Yeah, sounds like we've both run afoul of Finagle."

Gadget's turn to frown. "As in 'Finagle's Variable Constant'?"

Any engineer knew that the Constant (also known as the Fudge Factor) was the number you added to or subtracted from the answer you worked out, to make it equal the answer in the back of the book.

I nodded. "Also the mythical author of human doom and source of Finagle's General Statement."

Gadget frowned. "Which is?"

" 'The perversity of the universe tends toward maximum,' " I quoted. "Its corollaries are endless, including Catch-22, Parkinson's Laws, the Corollary of Stasheff the Elder, Stasheff's Law of Reversal, and, of course, Murphy's Law."

"Impressive." Gadget didn't realize she was smiling. "But Finagle is master of them all?"

"The spirit behind the human urge to self-defeat," I proclaimed. "He has minions, such as the Gremlin and Poe's Imp of the Perverse, but he does pretty well even without them."

The smile widened as she asked, "Is there no hype?"

"Plenty of it," I said, "unless you mean 'hope,' in which case I should quit serving you."

"All right, 'hope.'" She shoved out her glass. "And about serving . . ."

I poured. "Of course there's hope. Finagle has an antagonist—St. Vidicon of Cathode."

Gadget gazed off into space, tracking a memory. "Isn't he in a book somewhere?"

"Yes, but not *Lives of the Saints*—he's fictitious."

Gadget frowned. "I've heard engineers pray to him when they're really frustrated."

"Done it myself," I said, "and whatever I am, I'm not Catholic—but anybody who's fighting to make things come out right has my vote. Presumably St. Vidicon founded an order of monks, but to qualify for membership, you had to be an engineer."

Gadget actually grinned. "Sounds like we could both stand to send him a quick prayer."

"Let us pray," I said solemnly, and we both bowed our heads with tongues firmly placed in cheeks. "St. Vidicon, patron of all who labor with calculator and soldering gun, send aid, we pray, for two suffering souls who have fallen afoul of human bureaucracy. Enlighten the politicians, St. Vidicon, that they may see that the benefits of ethanol for the many must be accounted greater than the fruits of human greed for the few—and while you're at it, O Worthy One, if you could inspire some entrepreneur to start a new chemical company that needs engineers who didn't graduate, I'd appreciate it vastly."

"Amen," Gadget said solemnly.

We both burst out laughing, and I knew I had done my good deed for the day. Then the laughing slackened and our eyes met, and I suddenly felt totally aware of Gadget, of her warmth, her humor, and her femininity— and from the way her eyes widened, I knew she had suddenly developed a corresponding awareness of me.

Then she looked down, blushing a little and muttering something about needing to be home.

"Yeah, me too," I said, but she went out the door and I didn't.

Father Vidicon paused in midstride, hearing the laughter, but also hearing the heartfelt cry, fighting despair, unworded beneath. The good priest shuddered.

"What is it, Father?" Tony asked, concerned.

"Two young people who have invented a car that runs on ethanol," the priest answered, "but have seen pure alcohol outlawed as fuel by an Act of Congress. They want me to persuade the politicians to unmake that law—but what do I know of politicians?"

"I thought you were the expert on perversity!"

"In machinery, yes," Father Vidicon said. "Certainly in electronics, even atoms—but I know little or nothing of those who govern! I might be able to bring these two young folk out of their denial of their attraction for one another—any priest has had to counsel those who run afoul of pride and prejudice in affairs of the heart—but the use and misuse of political power? I'm afraid not."

Tony frowned, pondering. "What excuse did the politicians use for outlawing the ethanol car?"

"Some of their number managed to whip up fear of the threat of a plague of alcoholism."

"Something most politicians can relate to, yeah." Then inspiration struck, and Tony grinned. "What if people can't drink the ethanol that's being manufactured for fuel?"

"An ingenious thought!" Father Vidicon clapped him on the shoulder—and Tony felt the saint's power flowing through him. "Suggest that to the young chemist, would you?" Father Vidicon asked.

Tony opened his mouth to ask how he was supposed to do that, then felt the answer bloom in his brain along with an awareness of the mind of the young chemist. "Yes, sir!" Grinning, he focused his attention on the young man who had offered the prayer, searching the time line for the moment when he would be most receptive—and hoping that, unlike so many, he would not prove so busy talking to the saints that he would forget to listen.

I sat up in bed, instantly awake, awed at my own genius. Visions of carbon rings danced in my head and faded, but I held on to them long enough to turn and scribble a diagram on the pad I kept on the bedside table. Then I turned on the light and started translating the diagram into formulas. When I finished, I straightened up, gazing at my handiwork and beaming. I allowed myself five minutes to congratulate myself on being a genius.

Then I reached for the phone and called Gadget.

"H'lo," said a very sleepy and somewhat grumpy voice.

"Gadget?"

Silence. Then, with gathering anger, "Do you know what time it is, Nick?"

"Time to make a fortune," I said. "I just invented an additive that will give ethanol such a disgusting flavor that nobody will be able to get past the first sip. Worse—if they do force themselves to choke it down, it'll come right back up."

Silence again. Then, fully awake and holding down excitement: "Don't tell me you mixed up a batch already!"

"No, but I won't be able to get back to sleep until I do."

Silence yet again, but I could almost hear her thoughts racing. They settled on the least important: "I can't pay you."

"That's okay," I said. "I'll settle for a half interest in your company. You can have an option on a half interest in mine if the ethanol car takes off the way we think it will."

"Uh—don't those halves kind of cancel out?"

"Don't worry—I'll charge your company through the nose."

"I suppose that's fair," she said dubiously. "My lawyer's Charlotte Russe. Meet you at her office tomorrow."

"Make it day after," I said. "I've got some serious sleeping to do tomorrow, 'cause tonight I've got a cocktail to mix. Want to stop over for the taste test?"

"Taste test?" she said. "I'll be there to watch you brew—and I'll bring a rat!"

The rat was of the rodent variety, white with a pink nose, and he had far too much sense actually to sip my concoction. One sniff and he was cowering against the other side of the cage, even though it was only one percent additive.

"I don't blame him." Gadget wrinkled her nose. "One sniff almost had me gagging."

"Better him than us." I took the additive out of the cage and swapped it for a mayonnaise jar lid of water with a touch of sleeping powder.

We waited.

The rat took a step or two away from the bars, his nose twitching.

We held our breaths.

He came, light-footed and hesitant, to sip from the lid—anything to wash away the smell of that last sample. We both restrained a shout of triumph as he lapped up the water. He hadn't even finished before he fell asleep.

"Didn't kill him, did it?" Gadget said with doubt.

"I didn't put in *that* much." I had to admit, though, that I was no expert on dosing rodents. Carefully, I pried his jaws open, poked in an eyedropper, and squeezed in a cc of additived ethanol. Then we stood back, watching and feeling guilty.

The little guy's belly twitched. It buckled. It heaved, and the water gushed back out the way it had come in.

"Quick!" Gadget didn't wait—she picked the wee tim'rous beastie up by the tail and let him hang so the last drops came trickling out. "Don't want him to choke," she explained.

Her compassion warmed my heart. "Good enough for me," I said, "and I'll be very surprized if it isn't good enough for the FDA, too."

"But Congress?" she asked, still doubtful.

"The law only affects pure ethanol," I said. "Anything we add this to will no longer be pure."

The look on her face was all the corroboration I needed.

Tony gave himself a shake and realized he was back in the deep mauve of the tunnel to Hell. He turned to see Father Vidicon beaming fondly on him—but the priest's hair was mussed and his cassock was disarrayed. Alarmed, Tony cried, "What happened to you?" Then he realized what the answer had to be. "You had to fight another supernatural enemy, didn't you? And you sent me out of the way to make sure I wouldn't get hurt!"

"No, I sent you to answer a prayer," Father Vidicon said. "I didn't know I would encounter an antagonist as soon as you were gone—but if you hadn't been here, I couldn't have helped those two young folk while I was fighting another Spirit of Perversity. Thank you, Tony. Did you manage to break through to Nick?"

"And how! I just hope they'll be willing to introduce their product without too much fanfare."

Saint Vidicon's head snapped up, and his eyes glazed. After a few seconds, though, his eyes focused on Tony again, "Introduce their products without too much fanfare? No, they didn't."

Chapter 6

Maybe we shouldn't have started out with a full-dress press conference, especially since it was such a rousing success. The media showed up with cameras already rolling as I poured a fifth of no-longer-pure ethanol into Gadget's enhanced jalopy (what better way to make the point that the fuel was alcohol, and any conventional car could use it with only a change in carburetor?). She started up, drove off northward, and turned the corner.

"She'll come in from the south," I said helpfully.

The cameras panned to follow my pointing hand and kept recording.

The jalopy rolled around the corner, pulled up to the curb, and stopped.

I breathed a sigh of relief. The first time we had tested the fuel, the engine wouldn't stop; turning off the ignition had absolutely no effect. It dieseled, which would have been great for heavy equipment but not so great if you wanted to use it in a conventional car. We'd had to wait for it to run out of fuel—not hard, since I'd only put in a quart. Of course, we'd advertise the diesel fuel separately, but for the ordinary consumer, I'd had to put in another additive—which was great when it came to getting it past the FDA.

How about the American public?

They lined up at repair shops and the orders from mechanics skyrocketed—for a week. That's how long it took the petroleum lobby to file charges with a federal court. The cease-and-desist order hit us on Thursday and the warrant hit us on Friday. Ms. Russe, Gadget's lawyer, fought a valiant holding action but called us in for a warning.

"The law says no pure ethanol cars," she told us.

"It isn't pure anymore," I said.

She nodded but told me, "The lobby's lawyers will make it look as good as. After all, you're only adding three-quarters of a percent of other chemicals."

"Which make it undrinkable," Gadget said, "and the whole purpose of the law is to prevent alcoholics from tanking up."

"Right—but the law as written doesn't say anything about 'why.' It just says, 'No pure ethanol.' Period."

"Can't we do something with the intent of the law?" I asked.

"I'll try," she said, "but I'm outgunned. They've got ten lawyers to my one, they're all much more experienced than I am, and they can bring in enough expert witnesses to keep the jury in the box for a year."

"So what do we do?" Gadget asked.

"Pray," she said.

Gadget looked at me. I looked at Gadget.

There weren't any fictitious churches for praying to fictitious saints—at least, none we could actually walk

into—so we cobbled up a virtual chapel. We down-
loaded a 3-D image of the inside of Notre Dame de
Paris, put on our goggles, and started down the nave,
then swerved over to a side altar, where I had pasted a
picture of St. Vidicon as I imagined him to be, complete
with little yellow-handled screwdriver in the breast
pocket of his monk's robe—never mind that the story
said all that had been invented after he died.

"St. Vidicon," I intoned, "protect us from the petroleum lobby."

"Amen," Gadget said. "St. Vidicon, protect us from
specious logic and rigid interpretations of the law."

"Amen," I said. "St. Vidicon, protect us from judges
who want everything the way it was in 1928."

"Amen," Gadget agreed.

We took off our goggles, and Gadget said, "I don't
feel good about this. Isn't it sacrilegious or something?"

"Only irreverent," I assured her. "It may seem to be
making fun of religion, but believe me, there's a very
real need underlying it."

"Amen to that," Gadget said fervently, then did a
double-take at her own words.

"Besides, what harm can it do?" I shrugged. "And it
might bring some good. St. Vidicon may be fictitious,
but the saint who's really in charge of lawyers and
courtrooms could hear us."

"We don't believe in saints," Gadget objected.

"Does that matter?"

"Father Vidicon," Tony said hesitantly, "can the road
to Hell really be so soft and squishy?"

"I came in through Hellmouth"—the priest sighed—
"so I suppose this is its throat—and as you know,
throats are notoriously . . ." He broke off, staring into
midair.

"What is it?" Tony asked, then anxiously, "It isn't Nick and Gadget again, is it?"

"The very ones," Father Vidicon answered. "They've been indicted."

Tony stared. "What for?"

"For manufacturing a car that burns pure alcohol."

"Quick! You've got to save them! Inspire their lawyers! Talk to the judge!"

Father Vidicon threw his arms wide in bafflement. "Lawyers! Courts! They're completely beyond my experience. As to the judge, if even God is always talking to us but can't make us listen, how is a poor martyr to manage?"

"But you're the expert on perversity!"

"Only in machines."

"No, in systems, too," Tony pointed out, "and the law is a system."

Father Vidicon frowned, thinking that one over. Then he shook his head. "How am I supposed to know anything about the contrast between the precise language of the law and the twists and turns of people's minds that could bend it out of its original purpose? How could I know anything about constructing a legal argument or talking forcefully in front of a panel of judges?"

Tony stared, at a loss—and stricken to see Father Vidicon confounded.

Then a bell seemed to chime inside his head; he grinned. "Don't martyrs have an inside track when it comes to calling on other saints?"

Father Vidicon stared at Tony, then smiled as a feeling of warmth enfolded him, and he remembered that he wasn't alone in the long struggle for the souls of humanity. "You're right, Tony. It's time to pray to a *real* saint."

"That's talking!" Tony grinned. "Which one?"

"St. Genesius."

Tony frowned. "Isn't he the patron saint of actors?"

"The very one." Father Vidicon nodded. "He performed for the amusement of a Roman emperor in a play mocking Christians and collapsed, felled by an explosion of enlightenment—God talking to him, and he finally listened. He converted to Christianity and died a martyr's death."

Tony frowned. "Why is an actor going to help us?"

"Because," said Father Vidicon, "he is also one of the patrons of lawyers." Folding his hands, he prayed, "Oh Genesius, patron of performers, epileptics, and lawyers, hearken, I pray you, to the cries of these earnest younglings who seek, in their way, to better the lot of all people! Defend them, St. Genesius, from the casuistry and specious claims of those who would defeat their efforts in a court of law! "

"Enough, Father Vidicon! I hear you!"

Father Vidicon looked up in surprize and saw a round clean-shaven face with the close-cropped Roman haircut smiling upon him, as though a round window had opened in midair, showing the saint from the waist up.

Tony stared, awestruck.

"O holy one!" Father Vidicon cried, and would have fallen to his knees had not a hand stretched forth from that window to prevent him. "None of that, Father Vidicon! You lived a more holy life than I for much longer, and died a martyr's death even as I did—and as for my being real and you not, bear in mind that actors are always closer to fiction than most."

St. Vidicon straightened his legs, staring at the window in midair, then realized that a canonized saint could not, of course, step into the throat of Hell. "O Sainted One . . ."

"Yes, well, if I have the title of 'saint,' that goes without saying. Be done with your high-flown language, Father Vidicon, and address me as an ordinary mortal, or we shall take forever in this chat! Tell me in plain language what you want of me."

"Why, that you inspire their lawyer, St. Genesius, with arguments to confound the opponents who want to use law as a shield while they loot the earth of its last treasures!"

"Rather broad, isn't that? Remember, I knew little enough of physics or chemistry while I was alive and haven't had occasion to ask the Almighty to enlighten me since! Exactly how would you suggest I help these two young people?"

"Ah, if I had the slightest notion, I would not have called upon you!" Father Vidicon protested. "How should I know the mind of a lawyer?"

"Because you're a Jesuit and have learned the skills of logic and argumentation, of course! Still, I'll admit I can probably advise more effectively on those points, since they require an impassioned delivery as much as clear thought. Now tell me for whom these lawyers will be arguing, and why."

Father Vidicon gave him a summary of the motives and actions of the petroleum lobby and of the valor of the two young inventors who dared oppose them. As he finished, St. Genesius nodded. "The cause is clear, then, and the younglings' ambition does not diminish the good they may do. But I cannot urge speech without thoughts to put into words, engineer! What facts can you tell me that I can urge upon this earnest lawyer?"

"Well!" St. Vidicon said, and decided to begin from the beginning. "The alcohol molecule is a string of a hydrogen atom, two oxygen atoms, a carbon, and a hydrogen, bonded by . . ."

He spoke on, and St. Genesius listened with rapt attention, fascinated by an aspect of existence he had never contemplated before. When Father Vidicon was done, the saint said, "I'll have to think this over for a bit—but rest assured that I'll inspire their lawyer as soon as I see the precedents they must cite. In the meantime, good priest, you might want to make sure the news of this lawsuit reaches an executive at the National Sugar Board."

He disappeared, leaving Father Vidicon staring at the space where his window had been.

"Sugar?" Tony asked, bewildered.

The priest strove to flatten his forehead with the heel of his hand, crying, "How blind I am! Naturally the Board would encourage these inventors!"

He knew, of course, that the exploding popularity of artificial sweeteners had hurt the sugar industry badly and that it had sponsored a score of research projects to find other uses for sucrose. Gadget, however, had never thought to submit a proposal to them—if she had, she would surely have had strong allies in Congress.

As she would now.

Father Vidicon touched Tony's arm so that the young man would know what he was doing as he turned his attention to the Americas, where they lay slumbering in the dark, scanning the sleeping people to discover executives of the Board. Finding the chairman, he inserted a thought into his sleeping mind ever so gently, then expanded it into a full-fledged dream, confident that when the man woke, he would attribute his insight to his subconscious and his newspapers, never to a saint.

That done, Father Vidicon sighed, and said, "That's

all we can do for tonight, Tony. Back to your body, now, and wake rested."

"Wish you could rest."

"Time enough for that when I reach Heaven. Besides . . ." Father Vidicon gave him a crooked smile. "Not having a body to haul about, my spiritual energy lasts a great deal longer. You, however, are still mortal, so back to sleep with you!" He raised a hand as if in blessing, and Tony sank into the depths of slumber.

Alone again, Father Vidicon turned to pace onward down the throat of Hell, whistling as he went.

Gadget hadn't quit her day job, of course, though she wasn't looking forward to another eight hours of advising mechanics by videophone. She was on her way out the door when her phone rang. Torn between the thought of worsening rush-hour crowds on the trolley and the chance that I might have woken up early with another brilliant idea, she hesitated, knowing how a call would slow her down, then pulled out the phone as she headed for the corner. She punched at the phone as she walked, scolding her pulse rate for picking up its tempo at the thought of me and my delightful ideas.

Hey, I know how conceited that sounds—but stop and figure out how I know. She told me herself, after things had really gotten going. No accounting for taste, as my mother said—but I'm not about to complain.

Her spirits were dashed by the sight of the mature man who looked out of the screen at her—another bill collector! Or maybe not—he sounded far too cultured as he asked, "Miss Farnum?"

"Yes," Gadget said warily.

"I'm Hiram Mather and I chair the National Sugar Board. We'd like to talk to you about your lawsuit."

Gidget stood frozen for a second while her engineer's mind searched for possible correlations and hit on them. Of course! And here all along she'd been thinking of a boost for the grain farmers! "A pleasure to talk with you."

"I hope so," Mather said, with a smile of amusement. "We understand you've developed a carburetor that lets conventional cars run on ethanol."

"Yes, but my colleague Nick Smith had to invent an additive that slows down ethanol's combustion rate," Gadget said. "It really works better as a diesel fuel."

"Oh, we don't mind appealing to the commercial market as well as the consumers." Mather's smile widened into a grin.

Gadget found she was smiling, too; the man's good spirits were infectious. "I assume you know Congress passed a law outlawing ethanol as a sole fuel instead of as an additive."

"Oh, we were quite well aware of that, I assure you." Mather's smile turned sardonic. "We also knew it was the patenting of your carburetor that triggered the petroleum lobby to push for that law. But we hadn't known you had developed a way around . . . I mean, that you had modified your carburetor to comply with that law."

Gadget was sure the slip had been deliberate. "Actually, it was mostly Nick's doing. I just made a few modifications to accommodate his additives."

"I think one of our companies might have a position that would interest him," Mather said thoughtfully. "I'd like to discuss the issue with you in some detail, Ms. Farnum. Shall we say, lunch?"

When Gadget disconnected, it finally occurred to her to wonder where on earth Mather was. She hoped his jet wouldn't run into any delays.

Then she punched another number into her phone as

she started walking again, waited impatiently through the rings until she heard my voice say, "Hi!" She blurted, "Nick, you'll never guess . . ."

"I'm probably sleeping right now," my voice went on, ignoring hers, "so please leave a message at the tone, and I'll call you when I wake up."

Gadget cursed silently while she waited for the beep, then said, "Nick, the National Sugar Board called! I think they're going to give Charlotte a lot of high-powered legal help! I'm talking to their chairman over lunch—call me before you go to work!" She pressed the disconnect button and hurried the rest of the way to the corner, arriving just in time to watch the trolley pull away.

The Coq d'Or was only a few blocks from her office. As she stepped through the door, the maître d' came up to her, eyebrows raised as though to tell her she wasn't rich enough for this place—so she said quickly, "I'm with a Mr. Mather."

"Ah, yes, m'amselle." The maître d' nodded as though he'd expected someone dressed as she was all along, then led her to the best table in the house—no mean feat, since the Coq d'Or claimed all its seats were the best in the house, but this one was next to the fireplace. Mather stood, stretching out a hand as she came up. "Ms. Farnum, a pleasure to meet you."

Gadget took his hand. "The pleasure's all mine, I'm sure." At least she hoped it would be. She realized the maître d' was holding out a chair for her and sat; he settled her, assured them their waiter would be with them when they'd had a chance to consult the menu, and vanished.

Gadget did and gasped with horror because there weren't any prices listed. Apparently if you needed to know how much dinner would cost, you didn't belong at the Coq d'Or.

"I understand the veal piccata is very good today," Mather confided.

An image of a calf locked into a narrow stall flashed through Gadget's mind. "It sounds wonderful, but I never have that much appetite in the middle of the day. I'll just have a salad, if that's all right."

"Certainly," Mather said as though he'd been expecting it. "Caesar?"

Gadget managed to keep herself from looking around for Julius's statue. "Yes, thanks."

When the waiter had brought the appetizers, Mather seemed to relax a little. "Now, Ms. Farnum," he said, "what we would suggest is that your attorney consult with our defense team."

Gadget managed to nod while she was catching her breath. "That would be fine."

"We'll underwrite all your defense costs, of course," Mather said, "and since the news of your, ah, accomplishment seems to have already leaked to the press, I'd recommend you let us assign bodyguards to yourself and Mr. Smith."

Gadget stared. "The news channels?"

"It will be on the Net tomorrow," Mather assured her.

Gadget had a notion who had leaked the information and made sure it would be published.

"The bodyguards will be extremely discreet," Mather assured her. "Neither of you will ever know they're in place."

Gadget relaxed a little. "That would be fine." Then, quickly, "Of course, I can't speak for Mr. Smith."

"I would appreciate it if you'd discuss the situation

with him," Mr. Mather said. "Of course, we would be expecting something in return for our support."

Gadget braced herself and tilted her head with an inquiring look.

"We would like to arrange rights to selling your carburetor, installed," Mather said.

Gadget's heart leaped, but she managed to hide it with a frown. "Isn't that a little outside your ordinary line of work?"

"We have several subsidiaries that participate in other businesses," Mather said, amused. "We were envisioning setting up another, to franchise filling stations all across the country selling Mr. Smith's formula."

Gadget let herself begin to imagine dollar signs. "That sounds wonderful, but I'm afraid you'll have to talk with Mr. Smith about that."

"We will, as soon as he wakes up." Mather managed to say it without even a hint of irony. "Of course, we'll ask our attorneys to discuss the terms with your attorney—if the basic concept is agreeable?"

Gadget's heart leaped. "Oh yes, very agreeable."

"Good." Mather's smile was warm, and if there was amusement in that warmth, it wasn't offensive in the slightest. He raised a glass of water. "To partnership!"

"To partnership," Gadget agreed, clinking her glass against his. She only managed a tiny sip, though.

My alarm went off at two and Gadget's call came at two-fifteen. I hit the ACCEPT button, ready to chew back at the boss because I was nowhere near late yet—but it was Gadget, bright-eyed and breathless. "Nick, you'll never guess! The most wonderful thing happened today!"

It was the glow in the eyes that made me catch my breath—no, the way excitement spread the glow to her whole face. "Tell me, tell me!"

She did.

I stared.

"Nick, isn't that wonderful?"

"Absolutely fantastic," I said, staring back at her, but I wasn't talking about Mather.

The window opened only a few minutes after it had closed, and St. Genesius leaned out with a smile. "These Americans have let their laws develop in most amusing ways, Father Vidicon."

"Have they really?" the priest asked. "I'm afraid I haven't paid much attention to the law, except to make sure I don't break it."

"You're hardly alone," St. Genesius said with some irony. "Still, I'm going to need some explanation about this carburetor the lawyers will be arguing over. I have the facts, but I don't understand why they're a cause for debate. Explain why the ability to burn alcohol troubles them."

"Ah, well—that's more a matter of money than of mechanics," Father Vidicon said, and explained.

When he was done, the saint smiled broadly. "Now I know what to tell the lawyers!"

Chapter 7

"The court reminds counsel that this is only a prelimi-
nary hearing to discover if there is enough evidence to
warrant sending this case to the grand jury," the judge
said. The fact that we were in his chambers instead of a
courtroom should have been enough reminder of that,
but it never hurt to make sure.

"Your Honor," Charlotte said, "we move to dismiss."

The judge raised an eyebrow. "Really, Ms. Russe?
On what grounds?"

"The law as it is written is unconstitutional, Your
Honor. It operates in restraint of trade and restricts the
development of a system that may well prove vital to
national welfare."

"An interesting notion," the judge said drily, "and
one we'll let the appellate court deal with once this case
is resolved. Council for the prosecution?"

"Thank you, Your Honor." The bright young assistant district attorney stood up; surely the half dozen

gray-haired, hard-faced lawyers behind her were only there as observers. I imagined them all wearing name tags that said, PROPERTY OF AMALGAMATED OIL. "May it please the court," the young lawyer said, "it's clear the defendants have willfully broken the law by planning to manufacture automobiles that will burn pure alcohol." She went on to cite the brand-new law, introduced a recording of the press demonstration with Gadget explaining that the car with her prototype carburetor would run on ethanol, then watching the car roar away from the curb. The lawyer stopped the videotape with a triumphant flourish of her remote, and said, "These statements to the press must surely be as good as a confession, Your Honor."

The judge managed to keep a straight face. There wasn't any jury, it being only a hearing.

Mather's lead attorney stepped out. "But the law specifies pure ethanol, and the fuel Mr. Smith developed for Ms. Farnum's carburetor isn't pure. He has added chemicals that retard combustion."

"Nonsense!" the prosecutor said with just the right amount of indignity. "The additives constitute less than one percent of the fuel. It's still virtually pure."

"Virtual isn't pure," Mather's lawyer retorted. "The law stipulates ethanol that is a hundred percent pure. The language doesn't admit of the slightest adulteration."

The judge nodded at the prosecutor, beginning to look as though he was enjoying the session.

"Less than one percent of additive surely still qualifies as pure under the intention of the law," the prosecutor maintained, "and the additive retarding the combustion rate to avoid dieseling certainly makes it significant."

"The additives were necessary to comply with the law," Mather's lawyer answered.

"Ah, but the second additive wasn't necessary until Mr. Smith had put in his first additive, which was there solely to make the ethanol undrinkable," the prosecutor maintained, "a clear attempt to circumvent the law."

"But it was that additive that made the fuel prone to dieseling," the defense countered, "which made it clearly an improvement in the fuel." She started to say something more, but hesitated at an urge that pressed suddenly into awareness at the back of her mind—almost as though a little voice was saying, *That's enough. Let her bring up intention.*

Sure enough, the prosecutor said, "But the purpose of that first additive wasn't to improve the fuel, Your Honor. It was there to make the fuel undrinkable, which clearly showed awareness of the intent of the law."

Charlotte opened her mouth with an indignant retort, but it seemed as though her tongue wouldn't move— and the little voice was urging caution again.

When Charlotte didn't jump in with a protest, the judge turned to her with a lifted eyebrow. "Counselor?"

"Yes, Your Honor?"

"No response on the matter of intention?"

Charlotte shrugged. "None needed, Your Honor. If the intent of the law was to prevent the sale of cheap, pure ethanol in order to make sure it wouldn't encourage alcoholism, then surely my client's adding a chemical that would make the fuel disgusting in taste, and cause regurgitation, shows a willingness"—and, at a sudden inspiration—"even a zeal to comply with the law."

"Ridiculous!" the prosecution exploded. "Your Honor, if the first additive made the fuel burn so hot that it induced dieseling, clearly the intent was to make it an even more effective fuel!"

The judge nodded at Charlotte, very obviously enjoying things now.

"The dieseling was only a side effect of making the ethanol impure and undrinkable," Charlotte maintained. It was nice to be able to state the simple truth for a change.

"Nonsense!" the prosecutor cried. "If the fuel was more effective, why add the second chemical to make it less effective?"

"To restore the original purpose of the carburetor," Charlotte said reasonably, "which was to make the fuel of benefit to existing engines in passenger cars with the changing of only that one part."

"Well, if they really wanted ordinary consumers to be running their cars on ethanol, why did they come up with an additive that made it work for commercial diesel engines?" the prosecutor demanded.

This time it wasn't a little voice so much as a temptation, and Charlotte gave in with glee. "To make it undrinkable and unpure, so it would comply with the law!"

The prosecutor started an angry retort, but the judge banged his gavel. "Enough! When the argument starts going in circles, we've heard everything that's going to make any difference. The court finds in favor of the defendant and rules that no law has been broken, nor was intended to be broken. The statute in question says nothing about any carburetor, modified or otherwise. It only prohibits the sale of pure ethanol as a fuel, and the defense has established to the court's satisfaction that the fuel in question is no longer pure. Besides, the law is in restraint of trade anyway and restricts the development of a system that may well prove vital to national welfare. Case dismissed!"

He banged the gavel. Gadget leaped up and hugged Charlotte, and I rose, grinning, to watch them. I still wasn't ready for it when Gadget whirled and hugged me, but I adapted.

And in the moist mauve corridor, Saint Genesius reached out through his hyperspatial window to shake Father Vidicon's hand.

"Masterful prompting!" the priest exulted.

"Who should know that skill better than an actor?" the saint returned, then waved as his window closed.

Father Vidicon turned to stride on down the throat of Hell, swelling with the delight of the latest victory, even if it hadn't really been his.

Two days before Christmas, Gadget and Charlotte sat at the bar clinking glasses with me. "To the wisdom of the court!" I toasted.

"And the good sense of a level-headed judge!" Charlotte sipped, then asked, "So how many millions are you going to insist on banking before you quit your night job, Nick?"

All that slowed the growth of the alcohol car was the speed with which the HOOCH stations could be built. Private enterprise took up the slack in its usual way— by thousands of filling stations converting at least one of their gasoline pumps to alcohol. After all, they'd already added high-voltage wiring for the recharging stations for the electric cars of forgetful owners, and methane cylinders for the other new kind of car on the market. Three years later, the filling stations had one gas pump at most, and the only people who used it were antique car collectors. Gadget and I were both rich from a flood of royalty money, and from our sugar company stocks soaring as the commodity market did booming business in futures of sugarcane, sugar beets, and every kind of grain that could be turned into ethanol. Detroit retooled very quickly, and in five years had cut out production of gasoline automobiles completely. When the electricity companies switched to ethanol too, petroleum sales dropped to only plastics manufacturers. Not that the big oil companies were hurting, of course—the minute the judge banged his gavel, they had started investing in farmland and building stills the size of office buildings. Rumor had it that the plastics companies were developing materials that could be made from plant fiber, and that Middle East terrorists were targeting their research laboratories.

All of which was pretty heady stuff for the two brand-new billionaires who clinked glasses at the Coq d'Or one night. Gadget was stunning in a hundred-dollar coiffure and a Paris gown. I only looked half as good in my tuxedo.

"To United Auto Parts and Biochemicals," she said.

"And to many contracts from Detroit," I seconded, and we sipped. I let the wine roll back against my palate and wondered if I would ever be able to tell the difference between this French vintage and the box of wine in my refrigerator.

"May our companies' merger expand all our markets," Gadget said with a smile.

"To conglomeration," I said, "as long as it's ours." Then I quieted, gazing into her eyes as I let my fingers stroke the bowl of my glass and wondered if I dared.

Gadget must have caught some hint of my intentions, because she only managed a half laugh before she swallowed nervously, never taking her eyes from mine. "What, Nick?" Her voice was short on breath.

Do or die. "I was thinking about another merger," I said.

"Really?" Gadget didn't sound as though it was any surprise. "What kind?"

"Between people," I said, "you and me. Would you run screaming if I proposed?"

Gadget reached out to catch my hand with warm fingers, and her smile was warmer still. "I'll scream if you don't."

But I didn't, not for a few minutes, anyway. I was too busy gazing into her eyes. Made sense—they were all I could see.

Tony envied Nick, of course, envied him like fury—but as long as he was hovering around them as a disembodied presence, he could share Nick's romance vicariously. After all, they were a lot alike—engineers, just in different fields—except that Nick had lucked into meeting Gadget. It was enough to make Tony think he should take up bartending, too.

Then the two young lovers seemed to grow smaller, the people at the tables around them began to become visible, and Tony realized that they were moving away. No, he was moving away—or his viewpoint was. The scene he was watching began to redden, then faded into the maroon that was becoming all too familiar. He looked up to see St. Vidicon watching him with a broad smile. "Success?"

"Double," Tony said. "Their ethanol car is legal, the world's dwindling oil supplies are safe, and they're about to become engaged."

"Wonderful." The smile turned into a grin. "I love happy endings."

"Then how about giving me one?" Tony asked.

"Ah! That, I fear, is up to you and Sandy," the saint

said. "I cannot guarantee the conclusion we both wish—but I can promise that, long though the day may be, you'll have more than enough energy to take Sandy dancing."

"But I don't know how."

"Oh, we can take care of that, too," St. Vidicon said, amused.

"Oh, good! An e-mail from Marge." Liza clicked on the link. "Wonder why she didn't have a subject, though?"

"No subject?" From the next desk, April looked up with foreboding.

"Yeah, she's kinda scatterbrained." Liza frowned at the screen. "That's funny, there's no message . . . oh, an attachment!" She clicked on the icon just as April lunged around the partition and yanked the network connector out of Liza's computer. "Hey, what did you do that for?" Liza protested. "You made my screen turn blue!"

"It wasn't being unplugged that gave you the Blue Screen of Death," April said grimly, "it was the virus in that attachment! Hope you didn't have anything important on your hard drive, Liza."

Liza stared, appalled. Then she asked, "Unplugging me caused it to wipe my hard drive?"

"No, unplugging it kept the virus from infecting our whole network." April picked up the phone. "Now we have to kill that virus before we dare plug you back in—and who knows? It may be cheaper to buy you a new terminal."

Liza blanched and prayed silently, *St. Vidicon, save me from Finagle!*

April punched buttons. "Hello, Business Systems Solutions? We have a virus . . ."

• • •

Only two more days till his date with Sandy. On the other hand, there were a whole two days left before he could see Sandy again! Tony went to work, hoping for distraction. Maybe the whole Internet would crash? That could distract him for a few hours.

He was idling through his e-mail thinking of Sandy when Harve stuck his head around the partition. "Pack up your old kit bag, kiddo!"

"Why?" Tony looked up, interested. "And isn't that supposed to be, 'Pack up your *troubles* in your old kit bag'?"

"No, the trouble's waiting for you: infected computer, but a savvy office worker managed to unplug it from the network before it spread—we hope."

"On my way!" Tony grabbed his briefcase and ran, pulse pounding with the delight of distraction. This ought to make the time pass a little quicker.

Harve handed him a slip of paper as he passed. "Monahan Securities. Here's the address."

Tony sat down at Liza's computer, called up the operating system's code, and ran his bug-detector. The screen sat immobile, but Tony knew the routine and waited.

Suddenly the code jumped, and Tony found himself staring at a highlighted section—one that seemed to be growing, digit by digit, even as he watched. He contemplated the whole screen, trying line by line to understand the context and figure out the gist of the anomaly. As his concentration grew, the code seemed to expand from the screen until it surrounded him completely.

It was terrifying at first, but Tony was getting used to it—the sensation of falling, this time into the screen.

The digits seemed to grow until they were taller than he, and he found himself wandering through a forest of ones and zeros. He picked his way through a huge loop, trying to find the section of code that had still been growing the last he had seen of it.

There it was, only the ones and zeros had been compressed into a tubular shape—tubular and writhing. With horror, Tony found himself staring at a worm.

An orifice opened at one end, and the worm swallowed healthy digits by the dozens—but its farther end excreted clumps of distorted code. Tony's gaze snapped to the garbage output; he was tempted to try to puzzle it out, but he already knew what it did—and the worm was coursing toward him. It reared, and the mouth at its front was rimmed with inward-pointing fangs: ones with points.

"St. Vidicon defend me!" Tony cried, and a clanging and clashing of metal answered him. Looking down, he was amazed to see he was encased in steel—armor, and as he lifted his head, a visor fell down to protect his eyes.

The worm struck; he lifted an arm to ward it off—and saw his own face reflected in the back of a shield. It rang like a gong, and the shock almost knocked Tony off his feet; he realized the worm had struck the shield. He raised his right hand to try to separate the ones and zeros that made up its body—and found he was holding a sword.

The worm struck again, but Tony pivoted, amazed at the lightness of his armor. The worm roared wrath and turned about to strike once more. Tony lifted his blade, crying, "Aroint thee, worm!" Then he stared, amazed at the medieval words that had leaped from his lips.

The worm pounced, gobbling them up, then froze. Tony frowned, not understanding—but he did realize his words had stalled the creature. He started talking, babbling, saying whatever came to mind. "Tomorrow and tomorrow and tomorrow creeps in this vicious worm from equation to equation, to the last byte of recorded code!"

The worm gobbled up the syllables as they fell.

Tony pressed on. "And all our technology serves but to enable fools to greater folly."

The worm froze, and Tony knew his words, and their lack of logic, were roiling within its innards. "Out, out, coded creature!"

The worm convulsed, then began to thrash about in aimless pain, toppling digits all about it.

"Thou art but a crawling shadow," Tony called, "a poor program that frets and hangs blue curtains upon the screen and then—is seen no more!" So saying, he fell upon the worm, chopping it into writhing blocks of digits, then prying apart the bytes to bits. In a few minutes, the worm had ceased to exist and was only a litter of ones and zeros lying in heaps about Tony.

"As goes the bit, so goes the byte." Tony sighed, sheathing his sword. Good or bad, it had been an amazing construct. Taking off his helmet and pulling off his gauntlets, Tony knelt to begin trying to reorder the digits into something harmless but useful—and found the armor evaporating, the shield and sword subliming into mist. He looked upward with a grateful smile. "Thanks, St. Vidicon." Then he got back to work.

"Time for coffee."

Tony's head snapped back; he looked up into Harve's concerned face. "Uh—what?"

"Time for a coffee break," Harve explained, then put a fatherly hand on Tony's shoulder. "They called me over when you wouldn't respond to anything they said. You okay?"

"Okay? Forsooth! Uh, I mean—yeah." Tony stood up, feeling as though he'd run a mile after a full-hour workout. "Got the system fixed, too."

"Really!" Somehow, Harvey didn't sound all that surprised. "How'd you get rid of it?"

"With a little help from a friend." Tony tried a step, found he could keep his balance. "And I could really use that coffee."

Of course, Tony didn't have the nerve to ask Sandy for a date every night. He felt presumptuous enough asking for Fridays and Saturdays. So after work every day, he stopped into his favorite coffeehouse for a cappuccino and a browse through the evening paper. He most pointedly did not go to an Internet cafe; he was content to leave his work in the office. So it was a bit of a surprise when the well-groomed stranger sat down at his table and asked, "Tony Ricci?"

Tony looked up from the paper, startled, then sat up straight. "I am, yes. And you are . . . ?"

"Jane Harr." The woman held out her hand. "I'm with Morgan, Baldwin, and Dallas."

Tony froze in the act of shaking hands, recognizing the name of the second most prestigious computer consulting firm in town. Then he finished the handshake, mustering his composure—which wasn't hard, since he could feel his defenses going up—and said, "Pleased to meet you."

"And I to meet you." Harr smiled. "We've been hearing quite a lot about you across town."

"I didn't do it," Tony said automatically.

Harr laughed. "On the contrary, we hear you *did*. The computer interrupted by some hacker's short story, the virus trashing the system, the worm at the securities company—oh yes, you're developing quite a reputation."

"Oh. Well." Tony dismissed the accomplishments with a wave of his hand. "Just good fortune, you know. Lucky hunches." He could almost feel St. Vidicon bridling at being called a "lucky hunch."

"But that's what we need," Harr said, "someone who happens to have lucky hunches about computer problems. You're not going to go very far in this industry staying with a small start-up company."

Stubborn loyalty rose in Tony—why, he didn't know. "They treat me pretty well at Bald and Chane."

"I'm sure," Harr said, "but does that include paying you what you're worth?"

Tony shrugged. "No complaints about salary."

"Other than that they have to pay you by the month because they'd go broke if they paid you by the hour," Harr said with a smile of amusement.

That rubbed Tony the wrong way, especially because it was probably true. He shrugged. "That's a pretty standard reason for putting people on salary—and there's no way to tell how long these lucky hunches will last."

"And no way to tell how long it will be before Bald and Chane is bought out by a bigger consulting firm," Harr said.

Tony stared, then shook his head, smiling. "They'd never sell."

"For two million dollars?"

Tony did some quick mental calculations that the firm was probably billing about half a million a year—and that was gross. "They still wouldn't sell." He raised his glass to sip as he asked, "Why kill the goose that lays the golden eggs?"

"To get a golden goose, of course," Harr said, "one

that lays nice little nuggets of regular payments. All right, so the buyout price might be higher, but they'll sell when they realize they can live very comfortably for the rest of their lives if they invest wisely."

Tony almost choked at the thought of Al Bald and Harvey Chane investing wisely. He set the glass down carefully, reminding himself that they would probably have the good sense to choose a sound mutual fund. "If I liked the new management, I'd stay on."

"If you could," Harr said. "New management usually wants to pick its own players. You'd be wiser to come to a bigger company now, for half again as much as you're earning."

That gave Tony pause; another thirty thousand a year was nothing to laugh at. But he remembered how Harvey had gone to bat for him when he walked out on the client manager who'd thought that hiring a consultant gave him the right to rant and rave at Tony. You couldn't put a price on that kind of support. "I'll jump that ship when it starts sinking."

"I hope you have a life raft when it does." Harr handed him a card. "Think it over; there's no rush. If you change your mind within the week, let me know." She smiled, rose, and left.

Tony breathed a sigh of relief. He would never have guessed that being offered a better job could be so nerve-wracking.

"One-two-three, one-two-three—that's right, a sort of swinging diagonal. Turn as you step . . . yes, that's it. One-two-three, one-two-three . . ."

Side by side, the systems analyst and the saint stepped off the classic pattern of the waltz. The ruby hall within which they danced certainly didn't provide the best footing for the project, but it had room enough.

"You don't really have to do this," Tony gasped. "I am taking lessons, you know."

"Yes, I know," Father Vidicon said grimly, "and I've seen how much progress you're making. Face it, Tony—we have to reprogram the motor skills in your brain, and the best way to do that is to practice while you're asleep. From the beginning, now—one-two-three, one-two-three . . ."

The saint drilled him mercilessly for half an hour. The bright side of it was that, being only his dream-self, Tony's legs wouldn't ache in the morning.

Finally satisfied with Tony's progress, Father Vidicon called a halt. "You'll do for the evening. Are you sure the band will be playing a waltz in a nightclub?"

Tony nodded. "It's the music for a really great dance sequence in the hit movie of the summer, Father. It probably won't last out the year, but it's back and very big at the moment, so every band has come up with its own rock waltz."

Father Vidicon shuddered. "If you say so, Tony. You can be sure you'll be competent. Remember, though, hold her no closer than six inches!"

At least Father Vidicon's errands kept Tony busy in the evenings and helped pass the time until he could see Sandy again. The days dragged, and it became harder and harder to keep his mind on his various minor fix-it tasks when visions of green eyes and a mischievous smile kept appearing on the computer screen.

Then, suddenly, it was Friday night.

Tony had to swallow hard as he rang Sandy's doorbell. He wasn't ready for this.

You're as ready as you'll ever be, a little voice said inside his head, and he was pretty sure he knew whose. He was very much afraid Father Vidicon might be right.

The tiny loudspeaker above the mailboxes asked in a tinny version of Sandy's voice, "Who is it?"

"Tony," he called in answer. "Ready for the Marinara?"

"Famished!" she answered. "Be right down."

Tony stood waiting, wondering where his question had come from. How had he known how to ask the right one?

He thought he knew the answer, but he tried to ignore it. Surely he could do his own talking! Not that he wouldn't appreciate whatever help he could get . . .

Then she was there, resplendent in an ivory dress with a subtle flower pattern, a strand of pearls, and a dark wrap draped over her arm, opening the door with a smile of anticipation.

"Wow," Tony breathed, and could feel his eyes bulging. Then, a bit louder, "You're lovelier than ever tonight."

"Why, thank you, sir." The roguish smile said she was pleased. "Ready to whisk me away on your magic carpet?"

"Why, yes, fair lady." Tony took the wrap, held it for her as she turned away, and slipped it on. As she turned back, he offered his arm. "I hope you don't mind yellow carpets with wheels."

"My favorite." She stepped down the stairs beside him and into the cab.

It was a good beginning for a wonderful evening. After dinner, Tony remembered that he had a couple of tickets to a jazz concert and, better yet, had them with him. After the jazz came a couple of drinks—one apiece, just enough to lower Tony's inhibitions so that, when Sandy glanced longingly at the hardwood, he actually heard himself asking, "Care to dance?"

"Yes, if you can dance with care," Sandy returned,

and held out her hand. They stepped out onto the floor and, wonder of wonders, Tony remembered the steps Father Vidicon had taught him. Even more surprising, he actually had some coordination. He knew he was out of fashion, but Sandy joined in enthusiastically. Tony had no trouble remembering the six-inch rule on the fast dance, but on the slow one, Sandy stepped right up against him, and the exaggerated shuffle everybody else was doing didn't leave much room for the box step Tony had learned. Nonetheless, he tried it, and managed to open up at least an inch between them on the turns. Sandy seemed surprized, but not really disappointed.

By the time she said, "No, thanks," to his offer of another dance, and by way of explanation, "I'm kinda tired," Tony was surprized to realize almost an hour had passed.

They chatted pleasantly on the way out the door and home in the cab; Tony discovered a knack for delivering straight lines with a straighter face, and Sandy was delighted to come in with the punch lines. He was in a happy daze as he opened the cab door for her—it was the first date he'd ever had that had gone really well. So, all in all, he shouldn't have been surprized when she opened her door, then turned back, and asked him, "Want to come in for a nightcap?"

"Uh . . ." Tony swallowed. "Uh, yeah! Thanks. Let me go tell the cab." He kept himself from running down the steps, handed the driver a ten and a five, and said, "Come back for me in half an hour, okay?"

"Sure, buddy." The driver winked. "How long do you want me to wait when I come back?"

"Oh . . . ten minutes," Tony said. "I'm sure I won't be late."

"Tough luck," the driver sympathized. "Step in the right direction, though."

As he drove off, Tony turned and went back up the stairs, reflecting that it was only the first of many probable steps.

"Thoughtful of you," Sandy said, still smiling, and opened the door.

"Cab drivers are people, too," Tony said, as they started up the inside stairs, "and you want them to remember you fondly."

"Boy, is that ever true!" Sandy said with a grimace. "The number of times I've stood on a street corner in the rain, wishing a driver I knew would see me and pull over . . ."

"I'm surprised even a strange cab driver wouldn't pull over after one look at you," Tony said gallantly.

"Why, thank you, sir," Sandy said with a mock curtsy.

They only had to climb one flight, and the lingering smell of cabbage told Tony that this wasn't a singles-only building. "Do you get to know your neighbors here?"

"Not really." Sandy unlocked her door. "I leave too early. But I do get to hear raised voices as they try to get the kids ready for school." There was something wistful about her tone, but before Tony could register it, she had opened the door and turned on the lights.

The table lamps were set low, illuminating a room that was decorated not to display good taste but to seem warm and cozy. Sandy stepped over to a stereo, hit a button, and the sound of strings murmured over the room. She hung her wrap on a hat rack, then went over to a console across the room. "Just hang up your coat and sit anywhere."

Hopefully, Tony sat on the couch.

Sandy opened the top of the console and took out a bottle. "Crème de menthe okay?"

"Yeah, thanks."

She brought the two miniature glasses and sat beside him on the sofa, not too close, as she handed him his. He sipped and nodded appreciatively. "This would be good first thing in the morning."

Sandy stared. "You're not an alcoholic!"

"No, but it sure beats my mouthwash."

The stare held a second, then dissolved in laughter. "Serves me right for taking you seriously."

"Well, I'm serious some of the time."

"Most of the time, from what I've seen of you." Sandy gave him a merry look over the rim of her glass. "But you did it with such a straight face! How am I supposed to know when you are and when you aren't?"

"Content," Tony said. "If it's important, I'm serious. For example, if I tell you you're beautiful, that's serious."

Sandy blushed and turned away to set her glass on the coffee table. "Don't, Tony."

Tony heaved a sigh. "You see my problem? People don't want to know what I really think unless I make a joke out of it."

"You'd better not be joking if you say something like that!" Sandy glared at him, her face scarcely a foot away.

"I'm not," Tony said.

They sat staring at one another for a few heartbeats. Then, slowly, Tony leaned forward and kissed her.

Her lips were soft beneath his, but nothing more—until he began nibbling. Then she gasped and began to return the kiss.

Tony was about to deepen the kiss and bring up a hand to touch when a voice inside his head said, very clearly, *No closer than six inches, Tony!*

Chapter 8

Tony leaned back from the kiss to gasp for air. "Wow," he said softly.

"Wow is right," Sandy said, a little breathless, and started to lean forward again.

Frantically, Tony glanced at his watch. "Blast! I told that cab driver half an hour!"

Sandy only stared at him in disbelief.

"I can't believe it's been that long." Tony stood up. "Thanks for the taste."

Outrage hovered about Sandy until she saw the glass in his hand. He drank it off, then set it down as he moved to the door. "Thanks very much. It's been magical."

"Oh!" Sandy paused in following him, momentarily confused, then said, "You can always call another cab."

"I could," Tony said, "but the half hour limit was a timing device."

"Timing?" Sandy was thinking about being angry again. "Why would you need it?"

"To make sure I don't ask for too much."

The anger evaporated; she smiled, stepping closer. "What if I wanted you to?"

"All the more reason why I shouldn't ask," Tony said, "the first time you let me in."

Somehow Sandy was closer than six inches. "How about the second time?"

"Ask me and find out," Tony said, and meant to open the door, but her lips were so very close, so soft and tempting, then brushing against his, he was exploring them with his own, tasting, savoring, and he felt her body against his own, printing its image, astounding, burning . . .

He lifted his head with a gasp, breathed, "Thank you," and slipped out the door.

He pulled it shut behind him, then sagged back against it until his knees were strong enough to hold him. As he went down the stairs, he knew this was one night he would never, ever forget.

When he got back to his apartment, Tony flipped through the day's collection of mail and found an invitation to a seminar about the latest operating system innovation, which made him wonder if that was how Sandy had learned computers. Then he made a hot drink, which reminded him of the coffee breaks he'd interrupted, which reminded him of Sandy, and watched an episode of a sitcom featuring ordinary young people (like himself) talking about inconsequentialities that mattered to people his age, all of which reminded him of Sandy.

In fact, that evening, everything reminded him of Sandy.

Sighing, he gave up and went to bed, expecting to dream about Sandy.

Instead, the moment he fell asleep, he found himself back in the moist maroon hallway walking beside Father Vidicon, who gave him a merry look and said, "You're drafted."

Tony's pulse leaped; he found himself grinning with anticipation. "Whose crisis is it this time?"

"The frame storer died?" Beth cried. "How am I supposed to put the phone number on the screen?"

"Use the character generator, of course." Bill was producing the pledge breaks and didn't see the problem.

Beth took a breath and a firm hold on her temper. "The character generator's down." It had suffered one of the thousand shocks that microprocessors are heir to and was writing squiggles onto the screen instead of titles.

Bill stared at her blankly. "Then use the graphics generator."

"Its title program crashed."

Bill stared, appalled. "Why didn't you tell me about this before?"

"Because I had the slides in the frame storer!"

Bill shook his head, mystified by the ways of directors. "They were all working this afternoon."

"Sure," Beth said, "before the engineers went home. How am I supposed to direct a pledge break without being able to put up the telephone number for the viewers to call?"

Finally, Bill was beginning to look rattled. "Call Jerry."

Jerry was the chief engineer. "I did. I left a message on his voice mail."

"I thought he had a cell phone!"

"He does. It's turned off. Angelica remembered that he said something about taking his wife to the movies."

"George, then!"

"George had to go to Springfield to fix the satellite transmitter. He won't be back until tomorrow."

Bill's face could have passed for the Mask of Tragedy. "Any of the other engineers?"

"Erin's in the orchestra in the middle of a concert. Joe's at a seminar. Ned has a hot date."

Bill threw his hands up. "I'll find a card and some paint. Meantime, tell Angelica to roll the blackboard over and write the number and the server address on it." Bill glanced up at the control room clock. "We'd better hurry—twelve minutes to the next break." He bustled off to the scene shop to hunt for a can of paint and a brush.

Beth sighed and turned back to the control room. With the overhead lights turned off, only the pin spots lit the desktops in the room. Recessed in the ceiling with only two-inch holes for their beams, they gave the impression that the crew stations were glowing by themselves. The reason, of course, was to avoid glare on the banks of television screens that lined the north wall. Ordinarily it was a tranquil sight, one that soothed Beth's nerves even when she was about to go on air. Tonight, though, they seemed to accuse her, with their pictures of the panel of volunteers ready to answer telephones; Dolores, the Director of Development, chatting with her guest of the evening about what kind of pitches they were going to make in ten minutes; and of the tally board with its list of pledges and their current total.

See, we're here, we're ready, the pictures seemed to say. *Why can't you put us on the air?*

Well, Beth would have to, and hope the viewers had paper and pencil ready to write down the phone number. Even as she watched, a volunteer came into the shot of the tally board and chalked up a new pledge.

Beth felt hot tears trying to push their way into her eyes and angrily shook her head. She wouldn't let the equipment defeat her! She'd just been promoted from crew; this was only her second time directing, and no matter how understanding the production manager was, he couldn't help but be influenced by the sight of a blackboard with phone numbers on it. And she had so wanted these pledge breaks to look really good!

She sat down at the switcher and ran her fingers over the buttons that each represented a camera or another picture-generating gadget. Deep within its innards, the frame storer thumbed its metaphorical nose at her, and it was all she could do to keep from slapping the blasted thing in hopes that a good sharp shock might jolt a loose connection back into place. That was only likely to make it worse, of course.

Sighing, Beth punched up the frame storer and made one more try at keying it over the shot of Dolores and her guest. All she saw were squiggly lines. Squinting, she decided they looked a little like Arabic letters. Maybe if they could find a Syrian engineer . . .

Or one who was a saint. Bits of her childhood religion classes came back to her, joined with the story she'd read about the video engineer who had died at his post in Rome, and she found herself praying, *St. Vidicon of Cathode, protect me from Finagle!*

Ridiculous, of course—but when you couldn't do anything else, you grasped at straws. It wouldn't do any good, but it made her feel better; the hot tears even receded from her eyes.

Tony sympathized with the poor kid even as he was trying to find his way through the tortuous turns of the printed circuit boards. The mist around him was silver this time, that being the color of the right-angled snail trails printed on the cards.

Tony felt a moment's exasperation. What did he know about video equipment? But he did understand microprocessors, and this switcher had its share.

Then he saw it—a tentacle trailing around a corner ahead. He was getting closer! He swam faster, his sodden pyjamas dragging against the fog, and spread his arms as he banked around the turn.

Tentacles whipped about him, binding his legs tight, as a dozen reedy voices cheered. By great good luck, he'd had his arms outstretched, so they were free. He tore at the tentacles around him, but dozens of the slimy things dragged his arms against his sides and pinned him there. They rolled him upright, and he stared at a dozen miniature beings with long torsos, little bandy legs, and four tentacles in place of each arm. Another four sprouted from each head above saucer eyes in noseless faces. Lipless mouths split in grins as the dozen homunculi cheered, "The engineer is bound, and the malfunction will endure!"

In desperation, Tony called out, "St. Vidicon, save me from . . ."

A tentacle slapped over his mouth, and Tony had to finish the sentence inside his head: ". . . from gremlkins!"

He seemed to hear a voice inside his head say, *Courage, troubleshooter,* and felt a sudden weight in his hand. He didn't have to look down to know what it was—the grip of a soldering gun was as familiar as the weight of his laptop. He squeezed the trigger.

A gremlkin yelped and a tentacle uncoiled from Tony's waist. The gremlkin blew on the burned spot, then sucked on it. Tony had a little more freedom of movement; he angled his wrist, hoping to hit another tentacle, and another gremlkin yelped and let go. Suddenly all the tentacles whipped away. Tony dived toward them, the tip of his soldering gun glowing.

Another tentacle slapped around his wrist, dragging aside the hand that held the soldering gun—but Tony only dived toward its owner, who squalled at the approaching glow and stiffened his tentacle to try to hold Tony away—but Tony angled the tip toward the tentacle, and the gremlkin let go with alacrity.

"Surround!" a voice called, and the gremlkins leaped to obey. Tony pivoted, seeing gremlkins wherever he looked, and his heart sank. He might turn about and about as quickly as he liked, but as soon as one group of gremlkins attacked him, the others would be at his back, tentacles binding his arms and legs. Sooner or later, one of them was bound to think of slapping the hand that held the soldering gun, and Tony didn't know if he could hold on to it.

But they weren't exactly geniuses, these gremlkins; with one massed shout, they all leaped in—and Tony shot up high where they couldn't reach. They churned for a minute slapping at each other, long enough for Tony to aim himself ready to singe any tentacles that came his way. He waited and wiped a drop of sweat from his forehead.

Sweat?

Now that Tony thought about it, this silver mist was heating up. With a shock, he realized why and let up on the trigger. The tip cooled, but Tony's brow squeezed out a few more drops, and he knew it would take the metal around him a little while to cool.

The gremlkins saw and cheered, even as they too started wiping away drops of sweat, and one of them called, "Let him be! He will melt this circuit, and our work will be done for us!"

Stalemate! But Tony had to try something. He squeezed the trigger again and dived toward the knot of gremlkins. They saw the glow zooming toward them and shot away, braying alarm.

Grinning, Tony let up on the trigger and chased them. One looked back, cried, "It cools!" and stopped. The others turned, thinking of making a stand—but Tony squeezed the trigger again, the tip glowed, and the gremlkins shot off and away, howling.

Tony swam after them, not so much because he wanted to catch them—certainly not!—but because he was trying to find out why this circuit board didn't work.

He found it. He rounded a corner and saw a chasm looming ahead. The gremlkins, instead of slowing down or skidding to a halt, sped up. In fact, by the time they reached the lip of the chasm, they were rocketing so fast that they leaped out into space, arcing high to land on the far side, then turned back to stick out their tongues and waggle their tentacles at Tony.

But Tony wasn't after them, he was after a repair. He skidded to a halt and scowled down at the chasm. This was what was wrong with the frame storer, then—metal fatigue, or a sudden shock, had cracked the circuit board, a hairline crack that was so fine he would probably have missed it if he'd been looking at the cards to check them. Since he was microscopic, though, it was very much apparent.

But being microscopic, there wasn't a whole lot he could do. He couldn't exactly pull out the circuit board and push in a replacement. He also couldn't fill it with solder.

Unless . . .

The gremlkins jeered, making rude noises, breaking his chain of thought. Irritably, he dismissed them, trying to concentrate—but one, determined to distract him, leaped high, disappeared into the gloom above—and didn't come down. Perched on a nut or bolt in the top panel of the switcher, no doubt—but its tentacle came swinging down, whirled in a circle, then slapped straight at Tony.

He saw it coming in the nick of time and ducked—then realized he was looking at opportunity. The tentacle came swinging back. Tony set the soldering gun's tip against the lip of the precipice and pulled the trigger, then caught the tentacle, wrapping its end between his feet as though it were a climbing rope in gym class. The gremlkin squalled in surprize, but its tentacle was already swinging back—and a trail of silvery metal followed it. The gremlkin tried to yank its appendage out of harm's way, but Tony was too heavy. Then he felt the tentacle slowing—the gremlkin had enough strength for that, anyway—so he let go, shooting feetfirst toward the far bank.

Gremlkins squalled, scrambling out of his way. Tony landed and spun to look back. Sure enough, on such a small (relative to his normal size) crack, the metal was strong enough to stretch, not break, under the heat of his soldering gun. Tony pressed it to the cliff edge at his feet, and it blended with the cliff. Tony looked out over his slender bridge and grinned.

Current flowed, heating the strand cherry red—but its heat melted both sides of the chasm, hotter and hotter until the lips of the cliffs turned molten and began to trickle out along the strand that joined them. Finally, it flared, burning through, but the waves from each side had enough momentum to flow together, making a thicker bridge—so both sides kept melting, slowly at first, then more and more until, with a roar, they both fell into the chasm. Molten metal churned, rising, until it reached the level Tony stood on.

Beth sat at the director's position with a feeling of impending doom. She put on her headset, and asked, "Okay, Ernie?"

"Everybody in place and waiting, Beth," the floor manager answered.

"Okay, then." Beth glanced up at the clock. "Going in ten." She looked up to see the famous tenor's face fade into a blank screen. "Going in five, four, three, two—cue her and fade in three!"

The screen brightened with the picture of Dolores and her guest side by side. "What a magnificent voice he has! Lena, tenors aren't supposed to sound so full, are they?"

"Not many," the voice professor agreed. "That man is very rare, with so rich a voice in so high a range."

"We're not so rich, though." Dolores turned to the camera.

"Zoom in to head and shoulders," Beth said.

Dolores's head and shoulders swelled to fill the screen as she said, "Here at WBEG, we operate on a very slender budget, and if we don't make our pledge goal, we won't be able to keep bringing you performances like these."

"Take two," Beth said, and she saw the music professor's face on the screen, saying, "Join me in making a pledge to our station. I have it deducted from my paycheck."

"Zoom out," Beth said, and the professor grew smaller on the screen as Dolores swam into it, telling the viewers, "If you don't work for the university, just call in and tell one of our volunteers what you're willing to pledge to keep these wonderful programs coming. Just call this number."

Beth's stomach tightened. "Ready one." She glanced at the monitor with the very amateurish numbers painted on it and knew she was headed back to working floor crew.

"Frame store is back!" Barry shouted.

Everybody turned to stare at the effects screen.

Chapter 9

Sure enough, the effects bank's screen showed Dolores and, along the bottom edge, a green banner with white numbers printed on it.

"Key title!" Beth's heart soared as she pressed the button. As the phone number appeared on the screen, she said, very softly, "Thank you, St. Vidicon."

Tony backed away from the heat, watching the ruddy glow turn dark and cease, and looked out with pride over the uneven but solid surface of the circuit, fully repaired now. He wiped sweat from his forehead and realized that his shirt was wringing wet, but that didn't matter. The break was healed, and that was all that did.

Then he looked up to heaven, where St. Vidicon certainly should be, lifted his soldering gun in salute—and was amazed to see it turn transparent, then disappear.

Of course—he didn't need it now. Grinning, he called out, "Thanks, St. Vidicon."

He was quite surprised when a huge voice echoed around him, saying, "Only Father Vidicon, Tony, please!" But as the voice spoke, the silvery mist seemed to thin and fade away, the voice reverberated less and less, and Tony found himself facing the good priest, who was saying, "I haven't even been declared a Beatus yet, let alone a saint."

"The Church's declaration doesn't send you to Heaven," Tony countered. "Your own actions have done that."

Father Vidicon smiled, amused. "Then my actions can't have been completed yet, for this certainly isn't Heaven!"

Looking around, Tony saw the familiar blood-red curve-sided hallway and knew the humidity wasn't going to do anything for his sweat-soaked shirt. He turned to Father Vidicon to ask, "What next?"

"Whatever I meet," the priest said, "but you have your own life to live while I keep searching for adventure—and be compassionate with that young woman; she's more fragile than she seems." He raised a hand in blessing or dismissal, Tony wasn't sure which, but before he could protest, the hallway seemed to dim, and he found himself staring at the reflections of the streetlight on the ceiling of his bedroom.

He sat bolt upright and called out, "All right, I know when I'm not wanted! But call me when you need me, okay?"

Then he realized the picture he must present, sitting up fully dressed in his bed and calling out to someone who wasn't even there. Maybe it was just as well he lived alone.

Why did Tony still feel nervous when he phoned Sandy? If only they worked in the same office . . .

"Hello?"

"Sandy?" Tony licked lips gone suddenly dry.

"Tony!" she said, delighted. "I wondered when I didn't hear from you over the weekend."

"Could I have called that soon?" he asked, surprised, then realizing how callow he sounded, rushed on. "Uh, I've got two tickets for *Two Against the World* Saturday night. I was wondering if you'd care to go with me?"

"Only if you ask me out Friday night, too."

Tony's pulse ratcheted. "Uh—yeah! Thanks. Great!" He swallowed. "Dinner and dancing?"

"Lovely!"

"Talking about yourself again?" Tony bit his lip. "Sorry—that just slipped out."

"Even better that way," Sandy said, amused. "But I can't think I'm pretty, can I? Not if beauty is in the eye of the beholder."

"Wish I were beholding you right now." Tony's thoughts raced, trying to find a topic. Then he remembered Father Vidicon's advice. "How could you ever think you're NOT pretty?"

"Bless you," Sandy said, her voice warm, "but not all of us made it to homecoming queen."

"Thank Heaven!"

"You didn't like the homecoming queen?"

"Oh, she was nice enough," Tony said, "but kind of . . . shallow, you know?"

"All too well," Sandy assured him. "You mean you didn't ask her out?"

"We didn't exactly run in the same crowd," Tony said, "but I did try to make conversation with her one time. Talk about uphill work!"

Sandy chuckled. "Easier talking to me, huh? At least I understand computerese."

"Yeah," Tony said with fervor. "I know why you took

your first course—but how'd you get interested in computers, anyway?"

"Why?" Sandy's tone hardened a touch. "Not very ladylike?"

"No, I've met quite a few women in the field," Tony said. "I always wonder how we stumble into it, though. With me, it was video games."

"Oh." Sandy sounded taken aback. "Well, I had one date with a computer nerd, and of course all he could talk about was his machines—but it sounded kind of interesting."

"And the rest is history, huh?"

"Scarcely." That warm chuckle again. "I'm still taking classes."

"Well, of course," Tony said. "Who isn't? Which one are you in now?"

Half an hour later, he hung up the phone, dazed to realize how easily the conversation had flowed. Maybe Father Vidicon had had some social experience, after all.

"What's the matter, Tony?" Harvey Chane asked.

Tony looked up from his e-mail in surprize—and guilt. "Oh, nothing, Harvey. Why would you think there would be?"

"When I see you staring at the screen for five minutes at a time between bouts of keystrokes, I'd guess you were preoccupied." Harvey sat in the chair beside Tony's desk. "Woman trouble?"

"No, not really." The thought of Sandy was a welcome relief. "She said she'll go to the opera with me Saturday night."

"Glad to hear it." Harvey fidgeted, apparently uncomfortable with the topic.

Tony waited.

"I heard Jane Harr had a chat with you last night," Harvey said.

Tony should have realized word would get back to his bosses. He wasn't the only one who stopped in there after work, of course, and the servers loved gossip, which meant they went through the serious topics very quickly and had to get picky to have anything to talk about. "She sat down while I was reading, yeah."

"Made you an offer you couldn't refuse?"

The thrill of guilt amazed Tony. "Oh, no. I refused it."

"But it's open, huh?" Harvey's mouth tightened. "How much did she offer?"

"Uh . . . no definite figure . . ."

"Percentage, eh? Well, whatever it is, Tony, we'll beat it. How much did she say?"

"Uh . . ." Tony felt his face growing hot. "Well . . ."

"Come on, tell old Harve! We don't want martyrs here."

Tony thought of St. Vidicon and felt even more guilty. "Okay, she offered me fifty percent."

Harvey leaned back and whistled. "Ninety thousand!"

"I said no," Tony reminded him.

"And I appreciate it," Harvey said slowly, "but I did say we'd beat it. Okay, Tony, you just got a raise to an even hundred thousand a year. Think that'll hold you?"

"You don't have to . . ."

"Oh, yes I do," Harve said. He stood up and managed a grin. "Can't have you working at a loss, can we? And we sure don't want to lose you." He held out a hand. "Congratulations, Tony."

Tony shook it, in a bit of a daze—but not so deep that he didn't remember to say, "Thanks, Harve." Then, as he watched Harvey walk back to his office, he muttered, "Thank you, St. Vidicon!"

*   *   *

"I had nothing to do with it, Tony!" the saint assured him.

Tony was physically in his bed, but his dream-self was in the maroon hallway with St. Vidicon.

"Well, you did, sort of," Tony said. "You arranged for the companies to call Bald and Chane for a trouble-shooter."

"Fortunately, their computer people were listening."

"I can't really take credit for those repairs," Tony said, "when it was you who gave me the power to go inside the circuits."

Father Vidicon shrugged. "That would be like giving your high school physics teacher credit for your trouble-shooting, because he's the first one who taught you anything about computers. I may have sent you there, Tony, but it was you who outsmarted the gremlkins."

Tony felt warm at the thought. "Well, I wanted to thank you, anyway. Guess I'll say good night, now."

"No you won't!" Father Vidicon looked up, shocked. "I've had another call for help!"

"And you've got your hands full here." Tony nodded. "After what you've done for me, it's the least I can do. Who and where?"

"His name is Tom and he's in the control room of a nuclear power plant. None of his controls are responding and he's afraid of a meltdown."

Tony swallowed thickly, but before he was done, he found himself floating ten feet off the floor in the nuclear control room.

Tom was alone on duty, but he was on the phone. "I don't know what's gone wrong, but the water's pouring out, and the controls won't respond . . . Oh, there's definitely power, my board's lit up well enough. It's just that none of the controls will do anything, that's all!"

Tony didn't have much doubt that he would be able to fix the controls, just as he had in the television studio. In fact, he suspected he'd find little gremlkins in its circuitry just as he had inside the television switcher—but first things first. He drifted through an inner wall and found himself looking down into the reactor chamber. The water was indeed flowing out and the fuel rods were beginning to glow.

Childhood conditioning took over—if it was radioactive, it had to be dangerous—and Tony winced, then reminded himself that radiation couldn't hurt a soul.

On the other hand, how could an immaterial soul close a valve?

The same way an electrical current could, of course. Tony jumped into the valve to trace its controls.

"What do you here, mortal?" the glowing creature asked. "This is no place for your kind."

Tony squinted against the glare and made out a shape that was more or less human, bald and with huge eyes, shaped more like a baby than an adult. "What are you?"

"I am the Spirit of Entropy, and only your fellow mortal Maxwell had the sense to think of me—though he did term me a 'demon,' which I most certainly am not," the creature answered.

Tony could understand why, and he felt a chill. Maxwell's Demon was a force for chaos, whether it knew it or not. "Why are you letting the water flow out?"

"Because it and the fuel rods were both merely warm," the Demon answered. "Water should be cold and plutonium hot. I seek to restore the natural balance."

"If that plutonium gets too hot, it's going to blow up and take the whole island with it!"

"It would not have done so," the Demon countered, "if you mortal folk had left it in the ground where it should have been. Indeed, it would not have existed if you had not tinkered with the uranium from which it came."

Tony frowned. "You can't think you're trying to restore the natural order!"

"The natural state, aye," the Demon answered, "which you foolish mortals have sought to reshape into forms more convenient for you."

"There's a paradox here." Tony frowned. "By restoring what you think of as order, you're making chaos."

"Order emerges out of chaos, as some few of your scholars are beginning to note. I govern that process—but you have interfered with it."

Tony watched the water running through the valve and felt sick at the thought of the dropping level in the pool and the heat the fuel rods must be generating. "If you let the plutonium explode, you're not exactly going to be creating order!"

"On the contrary, I shall," the Demon said, "after a few centuries."

"But you'll kill hundreds of people with it! Thousands, as the radiation cloud settles!"

"The earth will absorb it all." The Demon seemed quite happy about it. "The land will regenerate, the waters flow clear again."

"Yes, in a thousand years or so!" Tony's mind raced; he knew there was no use in fighting this creature by physical force. It could turn any form of energy into any other.

Come to think of it, though, he wasn't physical at the moment—and a soul wasn't energy, though it could certainly generate a lot of it. He dived at the Demon, crying, "I can't let you kill all those people!"

He cupped his hands to close them around the Demon—but just as he swung them together, the creature disappeared. "You cannot think to imprison me," its voice said from above and behind him.

"No, but I can do some work while you're out of the way." Tony seized the metal and began pulling.

A blow rocked him, and he shot back against the side of the valve. "Foolish mortal," the Demon scolded. "Did you think to staunch the flow so easily?"

"Seemed logical, yes." Tony picked himself up and braced himself for another try at making moving parts move.

"You cannot," the Demon said, "for I've welded metal to metal, and you would have to exert enough force to break the weld."

Tony felt sick. How could a virtual ghost wield that kind of power?

By strength of spirit, of course. Tony felt himself warming at the thought. He might not be a strong man himself, but he had St. Vidicon behind him, and the saint drew on the greatest source of strength in existence. Tony stood up, straightening his necktie. "What do you expect to get out of this?"

"Get?" The Demon's tone was confused. "Why should I 'get' at all?"

"Everyone does. If they didn't, they wouldn't do anything."

"I am not human, foolish mortal."

"You don't have to be," Tony said. "Everything living works to gain something—otherwise there's no point in doing anything. A wolf chases a deer to get food. The deer runs to stay alive. Two bucks fight to try to scare each other away from a doe. To live is to strive—strive to gain."

"But I am a spirit, not a living creature," the Demon reminded him. "I do what I do because I wish to."

"But why do you wish to?"

"For satisfaction," the Demon answered, "satisfaction at seeing the world as it should be."

"Forest fires? Floods? Creatures burned or drowned?"

"Even so," the Demon confirmed. "All things die. It is better that they die as they naturally would. Water and fire balance one another. All the world seeks balance."

"And you, being part of the world, find satisfaction in that balance," Tony said slowly, "even if it comes after horrendous destruction and suffering."

"The trees and grass will triumph."

Then Tony had it—genetic mutations. "Yes, but what kinds of trees and grass will those be? For maybe my kind shouldn't have made plutonium, but we did, and if you let it explode, its radiation will cause so many mutations that the plants will never return to their natural forms!"

But the Demon had the answer to that one. "Eons are nothing to me, and over thousands of years, the mutations that weaken the species will disappear as their owners die young, and those that strengthen the species will prosper."

"And create a whole new species?"

"Thus has it ever been," the Demon assured him. "Thus will it ever be. What if a few roentgens of radiation hasten the process by a few thousand years?"

"And the deaths, the suffering and destruction of those weaker ones, doesn't bother you?"

"Destruction is progress toward balance," the Demon said. "Suffering is part of existence."

"Well spoken, for a creature who doesn't suffer."

"I suffer most shrewdly, when the world is askew."

"But here there is harmony," Tony argued. "The heat of the plutonium balances the coolness of the water. They share that heat and turn a turbine, which makes electricity to do work for people. If it didn't balance, there would be fires and explosions."

The Demon was silent, energy snapping in a corona around it.

Inspiration struck. "Here, I'll show you." Tony strode over to the shaft. He put his arms around it and pulled. Of course, it didn't yield. "Give me a hand here, will you? I can't turn it alone."

"To what purpose would you move it?" the Demon asked slowly.

"To restore the balance within the tank," Tony said. "Radiation is a small thing, but it can throw others out of balance amazingly."

"That is why I shall remove this generator."

"No you won't," Tony said. "You'll unleash an unholy amount of radiation, vastly more than Nature supplies. But fill the tank again, and the power plant will keep that radiation in balance."

"But when it is spent? When the fuel is exhausted? What then shall you do with the residue? How shall you prevent its radiation from contaminating the world?"

"By burying it deep in the earth where it came from," Tony said. "That's where you think it should have stayed, don't you?"

"Indeed."

"Then you shouldn't have any problem with its being returned there. First, though, we have to soak up the worst of its radiation and make it safe to return." Tony threw his weight against the valve. "Want to give me a little help?"

The Demon hovered, silent except for the snapping of its corona as it watched him.

Chapter 10

Finally the Demon moved. "Perhaps there are more ways of letting things work than those of the centuries," it said. "Stand aside, mortal. Nay, begone completely, for the heat I shall expend in melting that weld would be quite unpleasant for you."

Tony stepped aside, as far aside as he could—in fact, out of the valve, out of the radioactive water (and he had to remind himself again and again that he wasn't vulnerable to it in spirit form) and up to the control chamber. He didn't stop there, though—the sensation of upward movement went on even as sight went away and brightness surrounded him, as though he rose through a sunlit cloud. It darkened, though, to a deep ruby, then dissipated, and he found himself walking the maroon hallway next to St. Vidicon, who clapped him on the shoulder and laughed. "Well done, Tony! You led the creature in a circle back to its own original assumptions!"

"Did it work?" Tony asked anxiously.

"Look and see." St. Vidicon pointed to a mirror on the wall; it clouded over, then cleared, showing a close-up of a meter with its colors receding down from red through yellow toward green—but as Tony watched, it grew smaller and he saw more and more of the control panel which housed it, then saw Tom watching it and trembling with relief. "You can take off the suits now, guys! Somehow we have control back."

The mirror clouded over again, and St. Vidicon said, "They will have to troubleshoot the circuit, of course. It might be polite of you to create some minor misconnection for them to find."

Tony sighed, beginning to relax—and suddenly realized he was exhausted. "Tomorrow night, okay? I'm kinda shot right now."

"Don't worry, your body will wake up fully rested," St. Vidicon assured him, "with more than enough energy to take Sandy dancing."

Dinner was lasagna at Marinara, then drinks at Bandillero. Tony had kept up the dancing lessons, which proved to be a good thing, because the band played a samba, and Sandy was delighted to find he could dance well enough for her to enjoy it. On the way home in the cab, she sat very close, so Tony held her hand and enjoyed the pressure of her shoulder and thigh against his as he asked where she had learned Latin dancing. This time he didn't ask the cab driver to come back. After all, he had a cell phone.

He also had cognac, and Sandy sat very close again. The stereo was playing the music from *Carmen*, and his heart pounded in time to the beat of the "Habenera" as he kissed her, then kissed her again.

Her lips were soft and moist and warm, and the tip of her tongue traced sparks across his lips. He drew a shuddering breath; then, since his mouth was open, he tried touching her lips with his tongue and was amazed at her answering gasp, even more amazed, when he explored further, that she went rigid.

Only for a moment—then she melted, and their mouths fused together. When she lifted her head to breathe, her eyes were wide with surprise. Tony's probably were, too, but he wasn't aware of himself at all, only of her, as he lowered his head and began nibbling her lips. She stiffened again, then caught his hand and lifted it to cup her breast.

Tony froze for a moment, startled, then began to caress. She squirmed, murmuring into the kiss. Then he felt her fingers light upon his chest, felt her undoing buttons, then her fingertips against his skin.

He was aware only of her mouth, her breast, and the tingling on his own chest. Then he lifted his head to gasp, and say, "I'd better go."

"Go?" Sandy stared at him, shocked, then darkened with anger. "This is a hell of a time to say good night, mister!"

"It would be worse a little later," Tony said. "You don't want me to do anything you'll regret."

"Oh yes I do!" Sandy pressed against him, churning, and her fingers danced. "But I won't regret it."

"I don't want . . ."

"Yes you do." Her fingers searched for proof, and it was Tony's turn to gasp. "And don't try to tell me you're gay—I have evidence to the contrary."

"Oh, I want sex, sure enough," Tony said, "but not until we're married."

Sandy turned into a staring statue. Then she said, in a very stiff voice, "You can have sex. You don't have to con me."

"I don't want to," Tony said. "I don't want to take advantage of you."

"I could say no," Sandy said through wooden lips.

"If you did, you'd be really glad we hadn't gone further than this." Tony held up a palm. "Don't get me wrong, I'm not proposing yet—only giving you fair warning. After all, we really have to know each other a lot better before you decide to let me ask."

Desire seemed to slacken as Sandy frowned and looked down, brooding. "Asking is nice," she said. "I don't know about asking if you can ask, though." She looked up again, and desire came roaring back. "And I don't know if I want to wait that long."

"I don't know if I *can*," Tony said.

Sandy stared into his eyes for a minute, then said softly, "Maybe that's one of the things we need to find out."

"You mean if I really can stop if you say to?" Tony smiled. "I think I can. It'll be difficult, though."

"It is already." Sandy's voice shook as she said, "But if you're going to say good night, you'd better go."

"Okay then. Good night." Tony brushed his lips over hers in what he meant to be a chaste kiss, but it made her shiver anyway. She went to the door with him, and the kiss there was anything but chaste. When he came up for air, he found he was on the other side of a closing door.

Tony went down the stairs, his head feeling curiously light while a sudden bright energy went coursing through him. It almost made up for the frustration.

That week, Tony could scarcely keep his mind on business long enough to get started. Fortunately, in his line of work, people were used to programmers who sat staring at computer screens for long periods of time. Sooner or later he'd remember why he was at that particular office and get back to analyzing the problem he'd been sent to solve, and once he could manage to make a start, he could block out the rest of the world as he had always done and become fascinated with the malfunction.

"Computers are so much easier to understand than women," he complained.

"That may be true," said Father Vidicon, "but they're nowhere nearly as fulfilling."

"I could debate that," Tony grumbled, "but I suppose you're right. No matter how much you love a microprocessor, it can't love you back."

"But a woman might."

"Might," Tony echoed. "There's no guarantee she will, is there? Or that the love will last."

"Nothing in life is certain," Father Vidicon reminded him.

Tony started to answer, but Father Vidicon frowned suddenly, head cocked as though listening.

Curiosity roared in Tony, but he held his peace, afraid to interrupt whatever the saint was hearing, until Father Vidicon sighed and turned to him. "Another stressed soul who could use a bit of help."

The floor shook, and from somewhere deep below them came a muffled laugh, so deep that they felt it as much as heard it.

"I don't think I'd better leave this place just now, though," Father Vidicon said slowly, "even simply by concentrating on the plight of someone on Earth."

"After all you've done for me, the least I can do is volunteer. Where to this time, Father?"

"An army encampment just outside Shanghai, China," the saint said, "in 1863. You're going to join the army, Tony."

Tony stared, then said, "It doesn't seem to matter what time people are calling you from."

Father Vidicon nodded. "I hear appeals from people who were born twenty years before I was. That foolish author . . ."

"I thought you said 1863! That's a little farther ago than . . . let's see, you died when you were thirty-eight, in 2020 . . ."

"The man you're helping is a time-travel agent," Father Vidicon explained. "He was born in 368 in a village between Beijing and Tientsin and was left on a hillside to die because he had a harelip. The time-travel organization sent an agent to wait until everyone was out of sight, then scared away the wolf who'd been attracted by easy prey, picked up the baby, and took him forward to the 1980s, where they had a surgeon who could fix his lip and cleft palate. When he grew up, he decided to join the organization—after all, it was his home. He's based in the 1950s, but some of the agents he knows travel hundreds of years into the future, so he knew about me and is calling for help."

Tony frowned. "I don't think a computer programmer is going to be much use in 1863."

"No, but somebody who knows logic and has a gift for working with technology could be just what he needs," Father Vidicon replied. "You see, he's caught in a time loop."

The roar of musket fire drowned out any other sounds as Chang Chu-Yi marched around the circle of musketeers, loading his musket as he went, but with quick glances over his shoulder at the ridiculous mongrel army that charged the T'ai-Ping line of marching circles. It was useless, for how could a few hundred Chinese and Europeans hope to prevail against the disciplined T'ai-Ping soldiers who kept up a continuous field of fire? Somehow, though, they were managing it, and as Chu-Yi came up to the front, he saw the slender dark-haired young man at their head, waving a rattan cane as though it were a secret weapon and shouting encouragement to his men. They responded, charging madly into the T'ai-Ping fire and, incredibly, losing only a few along the way. It was unnerving, so unnerving that the fire wavered as, here and there, a T'ai-Ping soldier fled from the impossible sight and the howling foreign devil who led. More fell with European musket balls in their chests and bellies as the Ever-Victorious Army came closer and closer until, on the verge of panic, the circles flattened into a ragged line, and the T'ai-Ping soldiers levelled their muskets in a single shattering broadside. It was their worst mistake, though, for as they all struggled to reload, the mercenary army bowled closer and closer.

Through it all, that ridiculous young Englishman came charging and yelling. Musket balls whistled past him, grooved his hair, tore his shirt, but none ever wounded him, and his soldiers shouted with triumph, for they followed an invulnerable leader with a charmed life whom no Chinese weapon could touch.

Then, suddenly, he shuddered, throwing up his arms and arching his back—then crumpling as blood gouted from his chest. Shocked, his soldiers jolted to a halt, staring in disbelief—but their young commander's body jerked twice where it lay, then went limp.

The T'ai-Pings saw and howled victory, charging the tattered little army that turned and ran for the river boats that had brought them there, courage fallen with their stricken leader.

The absurd little cannon on the boat's rear deck roared, giving the T'ai-Ping soldiers pause—and giving

Chu-Yi the chance to blunder into a thicket of reeds that hid him from view. "Okay, Doc, reel me in!"

The scene around him wavered and grew dim, then faded and bleached into stark white walls—and Chang Chu-Yi stepped out of the time machine with a sigh of relief as he let himself go limp.

"Bad?" asked the twisted little man in the white lab coat.

"Battle always is." Chu-Yi tried to shrug off the nightmare sight. "You were right, though—a T'ai-Ping musket ball definitely did kill Gordon a month after he took command."

"And the Ever-Victorious Army stopped being victorious." Doc Angus nodded.

Chu-Yi frowned. "What difference does that make to us? General Li has the real army, the one with tens of thousands of Chinese soldiers instead of two hundred guttersnipes. It's he who won the war and put down the T'ai-Pings, not Gordon."

"But the European reporters made it seem as though it was Gordon who was the architect of victory," Doc answered.

"Why should we care?"

"For the same reason General Li cared enough to go to bat for Gordon and talk him into coming back to lead the Ever-Victorious Army after the prince dismissed him," Doc Angus said. "Li knew he needed European support, and it was Gordon who was bringing it for him."

"They didn't need support! They were doing just fine without England or any of the other European powers!"

"Li was." Doc turned away to lead Chu-Yi out of the time machine bay and into the hubbub of the common room. "The Manchus were in trouble, though, and Li knew what was going to happen when they fell."

"Anarchy," Chu-Yi said. "There was always anarchy

when the barbarians came charging in and brought down a dynasty."

"Only this time," Doc said, "the barbarians weren't Mongols or Turks or Manchus—they were English and German and French."

"You forgot the Americans."

"So did the Manchus." Doc pulled out a chair at a cocktail table. "Sit."

Chu-Yi wavered, months of abstinence in the T'ai-Ping army warring with his desire for a civilized drink. Then he sat with a sigh of delight.

"Wallow in luxury while you can." Doc Angus sat with him.

"I know—I have to go back and save Gordon's life," Chu-Yi said. "I still don't understand why."

"Sure, General Li could easily win the war without him," Doc Angus said, "but he's clever enough to know that Gordon attracts good publicity, and considering how chowderheaded that incompetent young emperor is and how quickly his mandarins alienate the Western ambassadors, China needs all the publicity it can get if it's going to take its rightful place as a leader in the world community."

"Ridiculous," Chu-Yi said. "China already *is* the leader of the world community, everyone knows that—at least, everyone in China. It's the oldest, most cultured country on earth, and those insolent barbarians are mere flyspecks."

"Li knows better," Doc said. "Li knows that those ignorant barbarians could make the empire suffer, and suffer very badly, if China can't pull itself together. That's why he's fighting a native Chinese rebellion for a Manchu emperor—and that's why he needs Gordon and his favorable publicity."

"And that's why I'm going out to kill some poor T'ai-Ping soldier before he can kill Gordon." Chu-Yi sighed.

"Also to save the people from the anarchy that will follow the fall of the Manchus," Doc said. "Li doesn't want hundreds of thousands of people to die from starvation and disease, or in the battles between the warlords who always crop up when a Chinese dynasty falls."

Chu-Yi frowned. "And with the British already talking about bringing in an army to enforce the concessions the trade treaty gave them, the Manchu emperor is going to look as though he can't hold China together."

Doc Angus made an impatient gesture, then looked up as the waiter brought their drinks. "Thanks, Joe." As the waiter turned away, Doc Angus turned back to Chu-Yi without taking a sip. "The current emperor is an idiot. Well, okay, not an idiot, but not exactly a genius, either—only a very ordinary man who's been spoiled rotten from birth and hasn't the slightest idea how to govern a country."

"Then it's a good thing his advisors don't let him do it—because they can run China by themselves."

"They could, if they weren't each concerned with seeing how much money he can pile up and hoard," Doc Angus said, "and with carving China up into their own petty kingdoms—and when the British burn the Summer Palace, all China will realize how weak the Manchu dynasty has become."

Chu-Yi froze as the implications trickled in. Then he said, "So even if Li does succeed in putting down the T'ai-Ping Rebellion, thousands of individual soldiers will run for their lives and still be around—and when 'Emperor' Hung Hsiu-Chien commits suicide, they'll simply say they have an ally in Heaven."

Doc Angus nodded. "So if the Manchu government folds fifty years early—which it will, without European support—all it will take will be one defeated leader coming out of hiding and raising the banner again, and the rebellion will be back on. Do you really want to see China united while America is still building its railroads—and united under a bizarre sort of government that's willing to adopt European weapons and European army discipline at the same time that it rules its citizens with a fundamentalist zeal that makes the Puritans look liberal?"

Chu-Yi shuddered at the thought.

"The T'ai-Pings are Christians, after all," Doc said. "Very weird Christians, but Christians—and European preachers were ranting that England and Germany should support them against the pagan Chinese, until the reporters started telling the West just how distorted T'ai-Ping Christianity was."

"And Gordon is a Protestant fanatic." Chu-Yi nodded. "He thinks the T'ai-Pings are blasphemous."

Doc shrugged. "With their self-styled emperor and prophet claiming to be the younger brother of Jesus? You bet he thinks they're blasphemous."

"So General Li needs him for propaganda value." Chu-Yi nodded, resigned. "If Gordon lives, the reporters who follow him will convince Europe that the T'ai-Pings are the worst threat since Genghis Khan—and when the Manchus fall, they'll help anybody but the T'ai-Pings."

"There won't be any of them left, if Gordon lives," Doc Angus said. "The Empress Dowager will take over and keep the Manchus in power until all the T'ai-Ping survivors are dead of old age." He gave a bleak smile. "Of course, that doesn't mean their grandchildren won't band together to overthrow her successor."

"The Kuomintang." Chu-Yi nodded. "Okay, you've convinced me. Gordon has to live." He finished his highball and stood up. "Time for a haircut."

Chapter 11

When the Manchus conquered China, they made the Chinese men shave their heads except for a pigtail down the back. When Hung So-Chien declared the advent of the T'ai-Ping Tien Kwoh, the Heavenly Kingdom of Great Peace with himself as emperor, and his troops conquered most of southern China, he banned the pigtail as a badge of Manchu oppression. For his masquerade as a T'ai-Ping soldier, Chu-Yi had only had to let his hair grow—but now, as a Chinese fighting for the Manchu Emperor, even though he was supposed to be a blatant mercenary working only for Gordon's pay, he would still have to wear the pigtail—and no makeup would do when he would have to maintain the appearance for several days, sleeping and waking and in battle—so the barber shaved his head except for the small round of hair in the back, which he plaited into a queue. So, shaved and dressed in traditional Chinese costume,

Chu-Yi stepped into the time machine to enlist in Gordon's Ever-Victorious Army.

"This foreign devil is crazier than the last one!" Po Chao grumbled as he cleaned his musket.

"Maybe, but he wins the battles." Chang Chu-Yi ran the whetstone along the blade of his knife. "I thought he was a fool, naming us the 'Ever-Victorious Army' when we'd never even won a skirmish."

Chao shrugged. "It sounded good to the merchants, and they're the ones who pay us to keep Shanghai safe from these crazy T'ai-Pings."

"Assemble!" the sergeant bawled.

Po Chao came to his feet with a sigh and shoved the ramrod back into its holder. "At least he waited until I'd finished cleaning. What is it now, I wonder?"

"Probably another of this foreign devil's 'parades,'" Chu-Yi said, resigned. "Well, I don't mind his checking our gear as long as we win."

They trotted down to the bare, beaten ground fringed by the bulrushes and reeds of the river and fell into place in the line, and the sergeants bawled, "Atten-*hut*!" in the finest English style as they stiffened into brace. The lean young Englishman stepped out between them and began to prowl along the front rank, his ludicrous rattan cane stuck under his arm.

It was typical of the Western ethnocentrism of the time, Chu-Yi thought, that Gordon regarded the English form of drill as the only acceptable one. The Emperor's troops knew how to line up, of course, but they didn't have to subject themselves to the ludicrous postures Gordon called the Manual of Arms. Still, Chu-Yi stood at attention like the rest, musket slanted forward at ten degrees from the vertical, and waited for Charles George Gordon to find some miniscule fault in his uniform. Not his musket, of course—Chu-Yi made sure it was immaculate. He didn't want Gordon inspecting it too closely, gazing down the barrel or such. He might have noticed the rifling inside.

Outwardly, the piece looked like any of the others in the hodgepodge of arms Gordon's soldiers had managed to assemble, but the rifling made it far more accurate. It had to be, because Chu-Yi was going to have to shoot a poor T'ai-Ping soldier with it—not just any T'ai-Ping, but the one who would shoot Gordon in this battle.

Gordon finished rebuking a German mercenary for the speck of dust on his boot. The Ever-Victorious Army was a mongrel accumulation of the gutter-sweepings of every band of soldiers that had ever visited China. Most of them were Chinese, but there were also Germans, French, English, Americans, and a few others. Chu-Yi felt right at home, for he had been reared Western-style in Dr. Angus McAran's time-travel complex inside the Rocky Mountains. The Chinese, ironically, were more alien to him than the Westerners, never mind that he had himself been born in China of Chinese parents. But he had been rescued from exposure on a hillside, and the only other Chinese he had known were the few dozen who were his fellow time-travel agents—until his tutors had started bringing him back for a tour of China's history. Chu-Yi had visited Chang-An, the T'ang Dynasty capital; had been a soldier on the Great Wall when it was brand-new; had been a water-carrier in Canton drafted into the fabled exploring expedition that sailed as far south as the admiral could (he had escaped at the last minute from that one); and had played a dozen other roles at various times in China's past and future. He had known even before he joined as a time-travel agent that he would be assigned to missions in China.

Why else would Doc Angus be rescuing Chinese babies who were fated to die? He needed Chinese agents to help finance his time travellers by bringing back lost treasures from ancient days, and as troubleshooters to visit Chang An and Annam and Shanghai and Hangzhow, to keep historical accidents from changing the world in which he lived.

At least, that was his excuse. The real reason, as everyone knew but nobody said, was because Doc Angus was outraged at the idea of letting babies die and children be exiled simply for being different. Since his own body wasn't exactly an example of normality, he sympathized with the maimed and lame and twisted—and being a scholar, he had just as much sympathy for the ones whose ideas got them into trouble.

Yesterday, Chu-Yi's mission had been simple—to spy out the soldier whose bullet had killed Gordon as he led the Ever-Victorious Army in its third attack with no weapon but that silly rattan cane—Gordon the invincible, whom bullets never touched.

Well, this bullet had—but Chu-Yi was going to prevent that.

Of course, it was tempting to kill the Englishman himself, and right now, because Gordon was drawing himself up in the manner that meant he was going to give an inspirational speech. Chu-Yi sighed and braced himself for boredom.

Gordon spoke to the sergeants, who bawled, "At ease!"

Chu-Yi took a half step to his left and slapped his left hand against the small of his back. This was supposed to be more relaxing?

Gordon raised his voice and called out in English; his sergeant spoke in Chinese half a sentence behind him, translating. Chu-Yi, able to understand both the original and the translation, had to give the sergeant credit—he might not have been all that accurate, but he was fast.

"Men," Gordon was saying, "rejoice! Your time of waiting is over! Today we go to attack Hangzhow!"

The men to either side of Chu-Yi stiffened. Battle hadn't been exactly what they'd desired.

"Of course, there will be no looting, no . . . unmentionable and ungentlemanly activities," Gordon went on.

The sergeant was more blunt. "Usual rules—no looting, no raping, no beating up civilians."

The soldiers looked grim.

"But we will win, and there will be a bonus for each of you!" Gordon exulted. "Now take ship, and may Heaven speed our enterprise!"

"Fall out!" the sergeant bawled. "Board ship!"

The gong sounded and Chu-Yi relaxed with a sigh. So did Po Chao, grumbling, "I never did like boats. Why can't we march there, like ordinary people?"

"Because the streams that run through this giant marsh are faster than walking," Chu-Yi told him, "and with those little cannon in front and in back, they're a lot less likely to attract T'ai-Ping ambushes than we would be on the march—especially considering that we'd probably blunder into a bog every dozen feet."

"I know, I know!" Chao said. "I can't complain about something that keeps me alive—or, for that matter, saves me work. May I see you tonight, Chu-Yi."

"And I you, Chao." It was their homemade good luck charm, for they would both have to be alive to see one another that evening.

They filed aboard the *Hyperion*, Gordon's "flagship," with the rest of their half of the Ever-Victorious

Army and braced themselves as the little steamer pulled away from its dock.

Li had kept the T'ai-Pings boxed up in Hangzhow for a month, so they were running short of supplies and had to try to break out. Gordon had kept his troops out of sight with only a picket line to guard the gate, so it would look to the T'ai-Pings as though this side of the city was weakly enclosed. Now his sentries had heard men gathering and had sent word.

As the *Hyperion* pulled up to the bank, the western gate opened and the T'ai-Pings came charging out. "Form up!" Gordon shouted, and the sergeants repeated the order in Cantonese. The soldiers came off the boats at the double and formed up in ranks and columns.

The T'ai-Pings, seeing them, formed their line of marching circles and began to lay down a field of fire.

The sergeants bawled their translation, but Chu-Yi heard Gordon call out the original. "They're weak from hunger, but you are well fed! Only a little courage and we'll have them surrendering! Forward—MARCH!"

Gordon turned his back and set off toward the city at the double. Firing as they went, the Ever-Victorious Army followed him.

Chu-Yi followed more closely than any, firing, reloading, and firing again until he was close enough to make out the features of the man whose shot would kill Gordon. Levelling his musket, Chu-Yi aimed at the man's leg and fired.

He could tell from the way the man fell that he had missed and hit the soldier in the chest. The T'ai-Ping was dead.

Then the whole world seemed to shift subtly, and Chu-Yi was looking at the man through his musket sights again. Somehow, incredibly, he had another

g, who therefore *had* tripped his fellow soldier, sav-
Chu-Yi's life so Chu-Yi could shoot him, thereby
ning his own death warrant . . .

Or, rather, dooming them both to keep living and
ing again and again, in that same loop of time—un-
ss Tony could figure out a way to stop the paradox.

Tony pulled out of the man's head, dizzy with the
circularity of it, trying instead to figure out how to solve
the paradox and break the time loop. He knew the basic
principle, of course—step outside the terms of the paradox—but how did you do that in this case? It was one
thing to do it when you were only solving a puzzle in a
classroom—then you could reassign functions—but
this paradox was happening in the middle of a battle,
and he couldn't change Chu-Yi's grandson into someone else's descendant, nor persuade Doc Angus—he'd
never even met the man, and probably never would—to
assign a different agent for this job.

But he could spike Kuo-Feng's gun.

He flashed back in time a few minutes, hovered beside Chu-Yi's grandson long enough to get his bearings,
then plunged into the lock mechanism of the musket.

It was a flintlock, considerably more primitive than
the kind of technology Tony was used to working with,
but he thought he could grasp the general principles
anyway. He started rearranging subatomic particles,
stripping electrons off atoms and making them flow
through the lock mechanism in a circle.

Sure enough, a diminutive head popped up, and a
remlkin glared at him over the hammer's spring. "Be-
ne, mortal! This is my meat, not yours!"

Tony was only too glad to oblige.

Kuo-Feng tripped the T'ai-Ping, then pulled his trig-
, and the hammer drove the flint into the pan—but
gremlkin had done its work, so the spark made a

chance to save the fellow's life. He raised his aim and
squeezed off another round.

Again, the man clutched his chest and fell.

Again, the world seemed to shift suddenly.

Again, Chu-Yi raised his aim and fired.

As the man clutched his chest and fell once more,
Chu-Yi realized, with a sense of despair, that he was
doomed to repeat the same action forever, and that not
even starvation would come to stop him. In desperation,
he dropped his aim—but the T-ai-Ping fired, Gordon
fell, the world shifted, and somehow Chu-Yi was staring through the sights of his disguised rifle at the same
blasted soldier.

Tony hovered unseen over the battlefield, appalled
as he watched men die and saw the blood spreading. It
was raw, it was gruesome, it wasn't at all the way Hol-
lywood would have done it.

Then he felt the world shift and saw Chu-Yi drop his
aim, saw Gordon jolt backward and fall, felt the world
shift again. The problem wasn't with Chu-Yi's musket,
then. In fact, there wasn't anything on this battlefield
that was of a high enough level of technology to attract
gremlins.

But there was a time machine—maybe not here, but
behind the events he was watching. Even Tony had
learned in world history that Gordon had only been
wounded once during the T'ai-Ping Rebellion, and he
hadn't let it keep him from the next battle. Indeed, he
had survived to become a hale and hearty old maverick
of a general who'd died in the Sudan, facing the
Mahdi's army of desert marauders at Khartoum. What
did a computer programmer know about time travel?

Well, it was an exercise in logic, wasn't it? Handi-
capped without a keyboard, without even a piece of

paper, Tony tried to trace the sequence of events in his mind: Chu-Yi had killed a T'ai-Ping soldier and Gordon had survived. But somehow, that soldier's death had wiped out Chu-Yi's shooting, and the soldier had lived after all, to fire the shot that killed Gordon. But if Gordon had died, then the earlier Chu-Yi who had been watching from the T-ai-Ping side had lived to go ahead in time to become one of Gordon's soldiers and protect him by shooting the T'ai-Ping—but the soldier's death had negated Chu-Yi's actions, and so on around and around in a neat little circle.

A feedback cycle.

A logical loop.

Why?

Tony flashed over to the T'ai-Ping side as the world wobbled again. He sank into the T'ai-Ping soldier's head for a few moments, long enough to read his memories and learn his biography.

His name was Chang Kuo-Feng, and he was a time traveller. Not only that, he was Chu-Yi's grandson.

He was one of Dr. Angus's agents, to be specific. He was stationed in 2047, which was why Chu-Yi had never met him. Kuo-Feng had just finished a scouting trip, living through this section of time to find out whose musket ball had killed Chu-Yi. He had seen the T'ai-Ping soldier shoot and seen Chu-Yi die. Then he had gone back in time a few minutes and tripped the T'ai-Ping before he could fire the musket ball that would have killed Chu-Yi. Instantly Kuo-Feng had fired a wild shot for camouflage—but had unwittingly killed Gordon.

Then he had found himself reliving those few minutes again, but this time, before he could shoot Gordon, pain had exploded in his chest, and the world had faded into darkness.

Then, suddenly, he was alive agai[n] firing their muskets all around him, and [real]ized more clearly than he ever had that [he had put] his life on the line. Duty was duty, thoug[h, and] a sentimental attachment to his grandfath[er] tripped the T'ai-Ping before he could fire [the] ball that would have killed Chu-Yi. Then Kuo[-Feng] fired his next wild shot for camouflage—bu[t un]wittingly killed Gordon.

Then the world had shifted, and Kuo-Feng h[ad] tearing pain in his chest, and the world had gon[e] again . . .

So why was he on his feet in the midst of men f[iring] muskets again? This time, though, he was dazed eno[ugh] so that he forgot to trip the T'ai-Ping, and Chu-Yi h[ad] fallen with a musket ball in his chest.

Now, under normal conditions, watching your grand-father die is shortly followed by ceasing to exist—bu[t] because Chu-Yi had started a time loop, his descendan[t] had found himself reliving the last few minutes ov[er] again. This time he did remember to trip the man n[ext] to him, the soldier who was aiming at Chu-Yi, [who] fired a shot himself to seem innocent, not knowin[g the] musket ball would go through Gordon's ribs—bu[t Chu-] Yi had come back in time to shoot his fellow age[nt,] not knowing the man was:

a) one of his own band,
b) saving his life, and
c) his grandson.

So Kuo-Feng had died before he could [fire the shot that killed Gordon,] after all—but he also hadn't been there [as the sol]dier whose shot had killed Chu-Yi. So C[hu-Yi had lived,] but having died, he hadn't been ther[e] pretty flash but did absolutely nothing else. Kuo-Feng frowned and looked down at his musket, then shrugged and sprinkled on new priming powder.

Tony grinned; he'd been pretty sure a flow of electrons would attract a gremlkin. After all, before the invention of electric lights, before the invention of radio, during a time when the only technology using electricity was the telegraph, there had to be a huge number of unemployed gremlkins looking for a chance to work mischief. Tony flashed over to the Ever-Victorious Army and saw Chu-Yi hesitate with his rifle levelled, wondering why the T'ai-Ping hadn't fired at Gordon. When the man did fire, his musket was pointed ten feet away. An American soldier spun about with blood streaming from his thigh and fell.

Chu-Yi, very confused, lowered his musket. He didn't know why the time line had changed, but he knew it had and was wary of doing anything to change that change.

Tony grinned, rising above the battle to watch grandfather and grandson for a few minutes until the T'ai-Ping line broke and the soldiers ran for cover. Kuo-Feng plunged into a thicket of bulrushes and never came out—but he did step out of a time machine in 2047. Chu-Yi, ostensibly chasing fleeing enemies, dashed into another clump—and promptly disappeared, back to the time lab in the mid-1950s.

That left only a horrible scene of men hunting down other men. Tony's stomach churned, and he gratefully shot back to Father Vidicon.

As the ruby tunnel formed around him again, he wished he could be in Doc Angus's time lab to hear Chu-Yi trying to make sense of the events. But Gordon had lived, that was all that mattered to history—and Chu-Yi and his grandson were out of the time-loop trap, and that was all that mattered to Tony. Sure, it would be nice if they knew what he had done and could thank him for it, but this was definitely one case in which the work would have to be its own reward.

"You've taken her on twenty dates," Father Vidicon said, "first Saturday nights, then Friday nights too, and now you're seeing each other on Sunday afternoons and one or two other evenings into the bargain."

"Those aren't really dates," Tony protested, "just hanging around together—and they don't always end with going back to her apartment. I mean, well, they do, but most of the time just to drop her off."

"I'm glad that petting hasn't become a required part of your agenda," Father Vidicon said. "When it becomes obligatory, it can start becoming boring. But you're together that often, your relationship's been growing through five months, and you wonder that she expects it to become more intimate?"

"I'm ready to propose," Tony objected.

"But she's not ready to accept." Father Vidicon shook his head with a sigh. "Your generation! Expecting the final intimacy as a step toward marriage rather than the culmination of a courtship! But the young woman does have some right to expect a deepening of the relationship. It won't remain static forever, you know. It can't—it has to grow or wither, like everything else that lives. Besides, it would be very imprudent for her to tie herself to you for life and have you turn out to be a lackadaisical lover. Much though it grieves me to say it, your generation does seem to have grown to expect a trial marriage."

"You're not saying I should have sex with her!"

"Of course not—no priest would ever say that. I am, however, trying to understand her viewpoint." He lifted his head, turning to look at his protégé. "Perhaps it's time to fish or cut bait, Tony. If you're going to insist on being steadfast in virtue, as indeed you should, perhaps you should free her to seek out another."

The thrill of horror that froze Tony amazed him. He hadn't realized how much he'd begun to count on Sandy being part of his life.

Chapter 12

"You need distraction," Father Vidicon advised, "and I have a plea that needs answering."

"Oh, yeah?" Tony asked, immediately interested, then was amazed at his eagerness. Maybe he did need a break from worrying over his future with Sandy. "Who's in trouble how?"

"A company of actors," Father Vidicon said. "They're on the road, touring a comedy through the Midwest, and things are going wrong—inexplicably, I might add."

"Of course," Tony said. "If they were explainable, they'd fix them instead of calling on you."

"You *are* learning this business," St. Vidicon said, with an amused smile. "Go unsnarl them, Tony, would you?"

Sometimes you get a bad feeling about a show. I mean, you aren't even on the road when you realize things are going to go wrong—little things, nothing huge or life-threatening, but so many of them that it's going to take the gloss off every performance and make everybody miserable. The electrician will miss a cue or two, nothing that the audience will notice but enough to give the actors a bad feeling; an actor will get confused and repeat a sequence of lines; a stagehand will leave the stairs six inches out of true, and they'll trip the unwary actor and leave a gap between two "flats," two fake walls, that the audience won't see but will bother another actor on a level so low that he won't even realize it—or a spotlight will come crashing down in the middle of a performance.

Now, that requires two mistakes—neither terribly hard to make, especially considering that, when you're touring, the crew have to hang lights all over again every time we come to a new town, which is every week and sometimes twice. The good side of such a routine is that they get to know the light plot so well that they could hang the lights in their sleep. The bad part is that is that they sometimes come perilously close to doing exactly that. After all, they have to take down the lights after one performance and drive hundreds of miles overnight to a new city where they have to hang the lights all over again, which doesn't give them much time in bed—they nap in the truck and are sometimes pretty groggy when they start climbing ladders again.

Still, for a spotlight to fall means that the electrician not only forgot to tighten the clamp that holds it to the pipe over the stage, but also forgot to fasten the safety chain—a piece of steel cable that loops around the pipe and the yoke, the spotlight's "handle." Mind you, I'm not saying it can't happen, as the gouge in the floor of the theater in Indianapolis will attest. Fortunately, the spotlight fell two feet away from Lon as he was sternly lecturing the young roommates. Unfortunately, it threw him off for the rest of the performance. Worse, he couldn't even chew out the lighting crew because they were union—IATSE—and he was Actors' Equity. He couldn't complain to the director, either, because she was back in New York.

He could, however, complain to the stage manager, which he did, loudly and at great length, with the whole cast joining in, and when I'd finally managed to calm them down, I had to go talk to the union shop steward. Of course, my union is Actors' Equity, as is theirs, but I'm one of the rare ones who has his IATSE card, too. Even without it, union rules allowed me to "communicate" with the IATSE shop steward about making sure his people got enough sleep.

"Enough sleep?" Joe gave me a hoarse laugh. "We'd just driven eight hours, put up the set and hung the lights, then managed a two-hour nap while you guys were rehearsing, and I'm supposed to make sure they get enough sleep?"

I felt as though I could walk under a canary with plenty of headroom. "Yeah, I know, Joe," I said, "but we're gonna be here for two days. Maybe your folks could catch up on the Zs?"

"Which we intend to do," Joe said, "if some smart-alecky stage manager doesn't keep us up all night with asinine gripes."

He said it without rancor; he knew I had to complain to him because the actors had complained to me, and he knew I knew why his crew hadn't been as careful as they might have been if they'd been fully conscious.

"Sometimes the stage manager has to pay lip service to trying to keep the show in shape."

"Yeah, I know, kid." Joe gave me a commiserating

slap on the shoulder. "It ain't the world's easiest job for any of us. At least you're a grown-up."

I appreciated that. At thirty-two, it was nice to think I had finally come into adulthood. On the other hand, I no longer felt young. To Joe I was still a kid, of course—he was in his fifties. "Sometimes I do kinda feel like the chaperone on the high school Washington trip," I admitted.

"Don't we both!" Joe rolled his eyes. "Only way I can still make it through setups is because I let them drive."

I knew he had rigged a sort of bed in the scene truck—a slab of foam in the "loft" over the cab. "We better not let them unwind too long," I said. "Right now, they need sleep more than beer."

Joe bristled. "You talking about your kids or mine?"

"Yes," I agreed. "'Scuse me—I gotta get down to the bar and see which actress Al and Will are going to fight over tonight."

"Good luck, kid." Joe grinned. "I'd rather be chief electrician than stage manager any day."

Stage manager? I don't manage the stage, I manage the people!

I made sure everything was ship-shape backstage— picked up a few props and put them back on the table, made notes to warn Lon and Arlene that once more leaving their pipe and gun, respectively, in their dressing rooms instead of on the prop table would result in a fine, then checked to make sure the ghost light was on—really the job of the local IATSE crew, but it could be one of my actors who became the ghost if it hadn't been left on and he or she tried to cross the stage in the dark. People have fallen through trapdoors carelessly left open, walked off the edge of the stage into the orchestra pit, and tripped over props and hit their heads on stage pegs, so I made sure the single work light was lit to let the ghosts of old actors know they were welcome to come back—and headed off toward the nearest tavern to join the kindergarten set.

On this tour, by some fluke, everyone was under thirty, even the actress playing the mother—Arlene may have been twenty-five, but she had the right facial shape and the right build so that she could play older. When she wasn't made up to look fifty, of course, her figure seemed voluptuous, not matronly, and her face looked slumberous and seductive, but onstage I could have sworn she was ready to sit in with my grandmother's bridge club. Only part of it was makeup, of course—the gal could really act. Character actors generally can. Ingenues, juveniles, and leads can at least look the part.

Even at that, Arlene was the senior citizen of our onstage set. The rest of them were just out of college and still working on their Equity points. I came in the door to find my charges had commandeered a table, but that Arlene, Britney, and Debbie had already attracted a small group of standees, all for some reason male, who were giving my boys challenging looks. Farther down the table, the stagehands were giving those looks right back.

Some companies, the actors won't even sit with the techs and don't realize the stagehands are snickering at them behind their beers. At least I had them both at the same table, even though it was IATSE at one end and Equity at the other. Sometimes I could even pull them all into the same conversation.

Tonight, however, looked to be brewing up a different kind of solidarity. One of the locals leaned down for a closer look at Ashley's neckline, and Jory asked, "Need glasses?"

"Shut up, kid," the local said, not even looking at him.

"He talks," Jory said in tones of exaggerated wonder. "Gary, did you hear that? It talked!"

The local looked up with a frown. "You want your teeth fixed?"

"At least I still have them," Jory answered.

The local rumbled anger and came for him.

Jory stood up, grinning.

I caught the local's arm as he passed, shoved it up behind his back, grabbed his shoulder with my left, and said, "We take it outside."

His friends shouted and started for me, but two of the stagehands stood up behind Jory. Mike and Al were each well over six feet and bulky with muscle. The locals hesitated.

"Thanks, guys." Jory swerved past them and came after me.

For some reason, the other locals between me and the door didn't try to interfere—they let us pass, then followed us. That blocked Jory from catching up, unfortunately. Well, maybe not so unfortunately.

I frog-marched the loudly-protesting local into the parking lot and spun him as I let him go so that he ended up against a wall. Snarling, he stepped away, bringing up his fists, and the crowd muttered appreciatively, forming a semicircle.

I kept my fists on my hips. "You don't want to fight with my boys," I told him. "They're all black belts except Jory, and he used to spar with a kid who made Golden Gloves."

That gave the local pause, but he had to save face. "All you actors are gay," he snarled. "Everybody knows that."

Well, not all—but a substantial percentage of my fellow showmen are indeed homosexual. Theater is one of the few professions where they won't be hassled for it, where a man's talent and skill count for more than his sexual orientation. "Not every actor," I told him, "and even gays have to learn how to fight these days."

"Yeah, sure," he sneered.

"Aw, hell, Jack," said one of the stagehands' voices, "I thought we were going to have some fun."

"Just an exercise in practical education, Lyle," I told him without looking away from the bellicose local, "and I don't think he's going to need a tutor."

"Yeah, and what do you think you could teach him?" Another local stepped forward toe-to-toe with Lyle.

My local stared past me, gawking. I swung around beside him with a wary glance out of the corner of my eye, but he was all rapt attention, watching the big man who was no doubt the local champion challenging the invader. That quickly, he had shifted from boxer to spectator.

The champ was every inch as tall as Lyle with, I could have sworn, the same black hair and beard. They were both muscular and had the kind of thickened belly that looks like fat but is all muscle.

"I could teach him street fighting," Lyle said with a lazy grin. "Maybe you, too."

"Might be you'd learn a little more than you wanted." The local leaned in nose to nose.

"Phew!" Lyle stepped back, waving his hand across his face. "Your buddies really oughta tell you about that breath."

The local grinned wider. "You got a problem with my breath?"

"No," Lyle said, "you do. Really oughta try cleaning the chitlins before you eat them."

An ominous silence fell, and my heart rose to block

my throat. Indy is close enough to the Mason-Dixon line that you don't tell a Good Ol' Boy he eats chitlins.

With a snarl, the local charged—but Lyle pivoted out of the way, and it was dark enough that nobody could have said for sure that he kicked as he turned, but the local did trip and fall. He scrambled to his feet just as the siren wailed, and the parking lot lit up with flickering blue-and-red lights.

The spectators disappeared like butterflies in autumn, but Lyle and the local still stood toe-to-toe, neither willing to give in before the other. Neither of them seemed to be daunted by the thought of a night in jail. I, however, had the reputation of the company to consider, not to mention trying to shift the scenery tomorrow night without Lyle's help. I stepped up to the two Goliaths and hissed, "Indian wrestle!"

They both turned to me with blank stares, but the doors of the patrol car slammed, and they spun toward each other, locking hands and setting shoe against shoe. They strained against each other's pull in perfect, rigid stillness as the patrolman stepped up. "What's going on here?"

"Just a friendly test of strength, Officer." I stood hands on hips, watching.

The policeman took the sight in with one sweep of his flashlight and grunted. "What're you doing here?"

"Somebody has to referee," I said, "or they'll start arguing about whose back foot moved first."

The local champion yanked hard, but Lyle was ready for him and yanked too. The local lunged forward, trying to throw Lyle off-balance, but he'd played this game often enough to know that the yank would probably be followed by the lunge and shoved hard.

Stasis.

The cop was still, watching.

Lyle yanked to the side, then shifted and pulled back. The local wavered.

The cop laughed. "Almost had you there, Bull."

"Almost," Bull grunted, and executed a sudden pull-twist-shove maneuver. Lyle whirled his free arm, striving for balance and managing to keep it, but his back foot shifted an inch.

"Score!" the cop declared. "Moved your back foot, stranger."

"Only an inch." Lyle relaxed. "Only one fumbling . . ."

The local yanked—but Lyle, readier than he looked, yanked back too, with a laugh. "Round two?"

"Game's over," the cop said firmly. "Settle for winning, Bull."

"Awright, then." Bull straightened with a grin. "You owe me a beer, stranger."

"The best the house has got." Lyle slapped him on the shoulder and turned away. Back inside the bar they went, trading friendly insults having to do with their ancestry. As I remember, Bull was denying any relationship to the orangutan Lyle was hypothesizing as his grandfather and countering by claiming descent from a buffalo.

"Nice maneuvering," the cop said.

"Looks like Bull has played this game before," I answered.

"So have you," the cop said. "I had a call about a barroom brawl that had moved outdoors."

"Must have been some other tavern," I said.

"Yeah, it must," the cop agreed. "Make sure it stays that way, okay?"

I did my best.

●　　●　　●

Nobody minded if Lyle seemed a little hungover the next day. Everybody was looking well rested when they showed up for makeup call. The stagehands ran through the preshow light check, sound check, and scene check while Maryann made sure everything was where it should be on the prop table, then reluctantly admitted to me that no one had to pay a fine that night. I went back to the makeup room, telling myself that one of these days I was going to let Lon and Arlene know how much they owed me for picking up after them. As usual, I decided that day would come when we were all safely back in New York and the tour had closed.

As I came in, Lon stood up, glaring down at Johnny, and demanding, "Who says I did?"

"It's your kind of sense of humor." Johnny glared. "And you haven't exactly shown respect for other people's makeup before."

"You think I want to get pink-eye from your infected eye shadow?"

I sidled a little closer to see what the problem was. Johnny's makeup kit was open, and a lump of nose putty lay in the bottom. My eyebrows shot up when I saw how it had been shaped.

Chapter 13

It was a very artistic job, actually. The nose putty had been carefully modelled into the shape of a fist with the thumbnail protruding between the first and second finger. That wouldn't have been a problem if Johnny's birth name hadn't been Gianni, and if he hadn't been Italian. As it was, I only knew what "the fig" was because I'd been in a rather authentic production of Romeo and Juliet and found out why one of the young bloods took offense at another "chewing his thumb."

"Nice work," I said in my best tone of admiration.

Johnny swivelled to glare up at me. "You call that nice?"

"It's good modelling." I looked up at Lon. "Didn't know you were a sculptor."

"Me?" Lon stared. "The only chisel I've ever held was a slice of cheesecake!"

"I could believe that," Johnny said, with an acid glare.

"Then do," I said. "Lon didn't do this."

Johnny swung around to stare up at me, disconcerted.

I sighed. The juvenile and the leading man—a natural antagonism if there ever was one. In most companies, the juvenile would nonetheless defer to the leading man's maturity and experience, but not when they had both graduated the year before.

Johnny recovered and turned back to glare at the nose putty fist. "It's not that great. I could do that well whittling."

"With a jackknife and a stick, maybe," I said, "but with nose putty? I mean, you do a pretty good fake nose for Act Two, but I wouldn't think they covered fists in your makeup class."

"They didn't," Johnny admitted.

"So somebody in the cast has unsuspected talents," I said, "but it's not Lon."

"No, I suppose not," Johnny said. Then, as though it were dragged out of him, "Sorry, Lon."

Lon stared in surprize, then grinned and said, "'S okay, Johnny," and went back to putting on his own makeup.

Not to lose too much face, Johnny glared up at me again. "It could have been one of the crew!"

"I suppose," I said. "I know a couple of them were acting majors before they saw the light."

"Saw the light?" Johnny's glare hardened, and every actor in the room looked up, taking offense.

"Well, I'm technically a techie at the moment," I explained. "The pitfalls of being a stage manager, halfway between onstage and off. When I'm acting, I knock the stagehands, but when I'm stage managing . . ."

"You knock the actors," Dulcie said, amused. "Just don't try to knock on me, Jack."

"You mean adore?"

"What else would you knock on?"

Everybody groaned and went back to their makeup. I made a mental note that I owed another one to Dulcie.

We were trying out a new comedy, hoping we'd get a big enough box office and good critical reviews to justify opening in New York. If we didn't, we might have to stay on the road until the production broke even—assuming we weren't running in the red on every performance. The plot, if you can call it that, was about a group of roommates who get fired from their various jobs and try to make a living by opening their own computer consulting business. They fall afoul of Finagle, of course, but the only flesh-and-blood antagonist is (predictably) the landlord, Mr. Cassandro, who is continually predicting doom for the enterprise and chivvying all the roommates to get honest jobs again, to which they reply, "We're trying!" again and again, until you're expecting the audience to join in with them. For an ending, Cassandro comes storming in to claim that one of the kids has parked in another tenant's space, and, when they deny it and refuse to move the car for the simple reason that none of them has the keys, Mr. Cassandro says he'll hot-wire the car and goes storming out.

JESSIE: Whose car do you think it could be?

ORIN: A sporty little red model? Isn't that Alice, down the hall?

NANCY: Oh no, it couldn't be! You know how paranoid Alice is.

BARRY: So?

NANCY: Well, she thinks her ex-boyfriend has booby-trapped her car, so she's afraid to start it until the bomb squad gets here.

ORIN: Bomb squad? (HE GLANCES AT THE WIN-
DOW) Maybe it's a good thing they've been
making cars you can't hotwire these last ten
years.

BABS: Oh, Alice's car is older than that.

(AN EXPLOSION IS HEARD OFFSTAGE.)

ORIN: You don't suppose . . .

Sure enough, Mr. Cassandro stumbles in through the
door, face smudged and clothing torn with a steering
wheel hanging around his neck (and you can bet that
Gertie, our costumer, had a lot of fun with *that* quick
change!). Of course, we had to build the steering wheel
out of soft plastic so that Lon could pull it apart, fasten
it around his neck, then lock the ends together again. All
in all, I was hoping we never missed that last cue. Carl
had a backup laptop in his sound booth (assuming whatever theater we were in HAD a sound booth) just to
make sure.

This theater did have a sound booth. Well, okay, it
was a projection booth, the theater having been converted for movies in the thirties. Fortunately, the conversion had consisted of hanging a movie screen from
the flies and walling off the back of the balcony to make
a projection booth. When the movies moved out to the
malls with twenty-screen "theaters," the community
had made renovating the old theater part of its campaign to save the downtown. They had remoted the
lighting controls back to the projection booth and even
installed an audio board at one end with a separate window for the audio operator to watch the stage.

They hadn't bothered modernizing the fly system, of
course, so the drops and electrics were still being held
up by rope and sandbags. It wasn't the only hemp house

left in the country, but it had to be one of a very few. We all felt as though we were on a field trip for Theater History class.

But because it was an old vaudeville house, we actually had real dressing rooms—old and rickety, but real. And a greenroom, believe it or not, even if the walls had been whitewashed and you could hear the other actors' footsteps overhead. It was right under the stage, and looking up, you could see the grid of beams with heavy bolts holding the floor in place. Those beams cut the stage floor into squares, and each was numbered—A through E, one through four. They'd been trapdoors once; a touring company could open any one of them for a dramatic exit or entrance. Ophelia's grave could be anywhere onstage you wanted it. The statue could stomp Don Giovanni down to Hell anywhere within that grid. The financiers could follow the directions of the Madwoman of Chaillot down to the sewers from any point onstage.

That had been one of the abilities they'd lost with the conversion to a movie theater. When travelling troupes stopped coming through, who needed trapdoors in the stage? So they had bolted them all closed to prevent accidents.

Of course, the stairs down to the basement, where all this was, were old, worn, steep, and uneven, but even actors can be careful when the occasion calls for it.

I studied all this carefully, I assure you. As stage manager, I was definitely going to need to know who was in which dressing room, or supposed to be, just in case I needed to send someone to track them down for a late cue—the stage hadn't been updated any more than was strictly necessary, so there was no PA system into the dressing rooms and greenroom.

At the moment, Dulcie, Britney, and Arlene were in

the women's dressing room while Andy, Lon, and Johnny were in the men's. There were smaller dressing rooms upstairs, presumably for the stars in whichever 1920s road shows had come through, but they were mercifully filled with old curtains, seats somebody had pulled out to make room for wheelchair access, and a set of antique electrical dimmers—mercifully because their being unusable spared me the sizzling catfight that would have erupted over who got which dressing room to his- or herself, if they'd been available.

I confess to having spent ten minutes gazing at the old dimmers, in awe of the generations of stagehands and stage managers who had gone before me—and shuddered at the thought of electricity ever having gone through those immense old open wheels. Of course, their wires hadn't been so badly frayed when they were being used—at least, not when they'd been new.

I was down in the actors' territory on a legitimate errand, of course. "Ten minutes till places!" I called as I went through.

"Who've we got in the house, Jack?" Dulcie asked as I sped by, so I put on the brakes and leaned back to look through her doorway long enough to answer, "Bluehairs, Dulcie. It's a matinee." Then I was off, leaving a trio of groans behind me.

All for effect, of course. The actresses knew our afternoon audience was most likely to be senior citizens. Who else has time to come to the theater on a Thursday afternoon? The high school kids would be here on Friday, of course—perfect thing for the teachers to do with the little blighters on the day when all their energy is directed toward getting out for the weekend. There would be wolf whistles at each actress's entrance and a muted roar like a minor earthquake when Dulcie (as Lettie) kissed Andy (as Jerry), and all of us would be fighting the urge to turn to the audience, and yell, "Get over it!"

It was enough to make a fellow call on St. Vidicon. I hadn't done that—yet. So far, everything could be explained as an accident, and there hadn't been enough of them to call for saintly intervention. Well, okay, there had, but it still didn't seem like the decent thing to do. I mean, things do go wrong—right?

They could also, of course, be the result of sabotage, but I didn't want to even think that one of my cast or Joe's crew could be trying to make it seem as though the production was jinxed.

Today, though, was going to be problem enough. "Ten minutes till places!" I called as I sailed past the men's dressing room, then went up the narrow stairs, holding tight to the handrail every inch of the way, and settled down on the high stool behind the stage manager's desk. There had been one built in; I'd noticed where it had been ripped out to make room for a cabinet in the 1940s. Fortunately, we brought our own folding model.

I turned to the house stagehand (have to have at least one local around—union rules, but a good one; you need to have somebody available who knows the theater), and asked, "Has the asbestos gone up?"

"Half an hour ago," she said, with the requisite thinly-veiled contempt of the person who knows the local fire laws.

I nodded. Most shows don't use curtains at the beginnings and ends of performances anymore, so they don't use fire curtains, either—but this was a traditional play in everything except the amount of innuendo. When the fire curtain had gone up, it had revealed only the grand drape—one that probably hadn't been replaced since movie theaters actually opened a curtain as the movie started. The set was a very realistic living room with a railed balcony to indicate a second floor. I went through my precurtain checklist—all actors in costume and makeup, preset props in place, all actors present and sober, stagehands at their stations and so forth—then put on my headset, and asked, "Ashley, you there?"

"Of course," the electrician answered, bored and slightly resentful (even when she's running the lights instead of hanging and connecting them, she's an electrician).

"How about you, Rally?"

"Yeah, I'm here, Jack."

I frowned; our audio tech's voice sounded funny. I was trying to phrase a delicate inquiry when I heard a cavernous yawn right in my ear. My blood ran cold; a sleepy sound op is not what you really want five minutes before curtain.

Make that two; I glanced around and saw Andy, Dulcie, and Britney standing by the door in the fake wall, waiting for their entrances. "Warn the audience," I told Ashley.

Through the crack between curtain and proscenium pillar, I could see the auditorium lights dim, then brighten again. Anybody in the lobby would be hurrying in. I counted off the next hundred twenty seconds, then said, "Houselights out," and the sliver of light darkened completely. The audience's noise stopped, except for a faint murmur of anticipation; the community might have had amateur theater, but a professional production was rare.

Professionals? Sure we were! We were being paid, weren't we?

"Curtain up," I said. Lyle hauled on a rope, and the act curtain rose.

The rising curtain revealed a luxurious living room.

The audience murmured in appreciation, and I started feeling optimistic. They were on our side, for a change.

And they stayed on our side. This was an audience who had come to be entertained and were old enough to know that they had to pay attention to get the most out of the performance. The cast felt it right away; Dulcie made her entrance, coming down the stairs in her slip, saying, "Darling, where did you put my pills? I missed today's dose."

The look of horror on Andy's face was priceless—in fact, he couldn't have bought it if he'd had money. The audience roared, and you could almost see Dulcie and Andy expand.

That's the way the performance went, from one laugh to another. Somebody even hissed when Lon told the roommates they'd have to move. Whoever it was hissed on his second entrance, too, and you could see him picking up energy. His character started exuding twice its usual amount of slime.

It was the perfect feedback loop, the kind you never get from the movies or TV, the kind that makes you realize live theater will always survive, one way or another. The actors drew energy from the audience's reactions, and the audience got a better and better performance.

The only thing that worried me was the lateness of the sound cues. Nothing serious, mind you—but the first one, the doorbell, was right on time, the telephone ringing was maybe half a second late, the car backfiring in the street was a full second. No big deal, you may think, but the actors were building unbelievable energy with the most perfect timing they'd ever had, and the late cues were throwing them off. At the act break, I stayed on the headset long enough to tell Rally to confirm my warning for every cue. He grunted, which I as-

sumed was affirmative, so I took off my headset and
went to check on the actors.

They were in high spirits indeed; you would have
thought the ginger ale they were sharing was champagne. "Did you ever see such an audience?" Dulcie
asked, as I came into the greenroom. "The old dears
really love us!"

"It helps that Sinjun gave us such good dialogue,"
Andy said, "but we've never had this many laughs from
it before!"

"We're brilliant!" Dulcie bubbled. "They've got me
convinced that we're absolutely brilliant!"

And on it went. I grinned and went back upstairs to
give the five-minute call. No need to worry about anybody being late for Act II—with an audience like that,
those actors would be so eager to get back onstage that
I might have to physically restrain them from jumping
their entrances.

They were lined up in the wings a full two minutes
early—not just the pair who were supposed to be in
place when the curtain went up, but all of them, hovering within earshot of the audience and panting for a sip
of applause. Andy's first line, "Who was it, then?"
wasn't at all funny, but the audience wanted it to be, so
they chuckled anyway —— and Dulcie's answer, "The
tack-counter," gave us a roar you could have heard a
mile away.

But the knocking was late.

I know—how can knocking be late? Actors do it
live, on the back of the set—but this knocking had to
come from the sound booth, because it was supposed to
start onstage, then travel out into the house and all the
way around before it came back to the stage, when
Andy was supposed to say, "Does he have to tap them

as he counts them?" Only this time, the tapping didn't start.

"Go Cue Thirty-three!" I snapped into my mouth-piece.

Silence.

"Rally! Go!"

Finally, the tapping started.

I swung the mouthpiece away from my lips while I cursed in my softest tone. I was going to have to have Rally's hearing checked.

Right on cue (though the cue had been horribly late), Andy demanded, "Does he have to tap as he counts them?"

"She," Dulcie said. "The tack-counter is a woman."

"Well, go knock on the door where she's working and ask her to ease up on the tapping, would you?"

"It's not bothering me that much," Dulcie said. "You go knock her up, then."

The laugh was surprised, a little shocked, and totally delighted—much more than the line deserved. What can I say? You had to have been there—and this audience would be glad they had been.

At least we were back on track. We would have stayed that way, too, if Rally hadn't kept missing cues. Well, not missing them, really, but late every time and getting later. I could tell it was bothering the actors, but the audience gave them a huge laugh after every late cue, and they relaxed again.

Then came the ending.

Mr. Cassandro went out the door, the roommates talked about the car being booby-trapped, and Dulcie said, "Oh, Alice's car is older than that."

"Go Cue Sixty-four," I said into my mouthpiece.

Silence.

There was supposed to be an explosion. There was silence.

"Go Cue Sixty-four!" I hissed—even now, I had to make sure the audience didn't hear me. "Rally! Go Cue Sixty-four!"

Nothing.

I groaned. I sweated. I finally broke down and prayed. Not a very long prayer, mind you—only a simple, "St. Vidicon, protect us from Finagle!" Then once again, "Rally, go Cue Sixty-four!"

Dulcie went to the window to look out. The others took the cue and crowded around her. They waited.

And waited. And waited.

Now, time stretches when you're onstage and things go wrong—a second seems like five minutes—but even so, it was an unholy wait, with me hissing into my headset, "Go Cue Sixty-four! Rally! Snap out of it! Go Cue Sixty-four!"

But the explosion still didn't happen.

Tony's disembodied presence hovered over Rally, where he lay with his head on his forearm, eyes closed, headset askew—which was why Tony could hear Jack calling, "Go Cue Sixty-four!" No denying it—Rally was firmly and irrevocably asleep. But why? He'd had a good eight hours the night before—his first in three days; he'd been surviving on catnaps since they closed Cincinnati, but even so, he should have been able to stay awake. So Tony dropped down into the dregs at the bottom of the glass beside him and filtered through the molecules there. Admittedly, he didn't know what champagne molecules were supposed to look like, not even ginger ale molecules, but he did recognize the smell of a well-known sleeping tonic—the kind that was only supposed to be given at night and had a very light taste. Add that to a glass of champagne on top of a full meal with three nights of little sleep, and you had . . .

Sound cues coming later and later.

In fact, the amazing thing was that Rally had been able to come out of his stupor long enough to hit any sound cues at all.

Tony had a choice—he could slip into Rally's mind and try to wake him up, or he could drop into the computer and try to close a connection without tapping the space bar.

The mind wasn't really Tony's area, so he dived into the keyboard.

Without a body, he couldn't tap the spacebar, but he could shunt an electron across a gap—he had enough strength for that. He found the connection and the electrons piled up against the contact—if they'd been human, they would have been straining for release when the circuit closed. Tony jumped on the contact. He didn't have any mass, but he did have energy, and he only needed to move it a thirty-second of an inch.

It gave a little under the energy of his spirit, but not enough.

Chapter 14

In a panic, Tony jumped up and down on the contact. He may not have had any mass, but apparently he was gathering energy, because the contact finally moved— not enough, but it moved.

"May I help you?" asked a rich, resonant voice.

Tony started so violently he nearly leaped out of the circuit. Turning, he saw a distinguished-looking gentleman in a top hat and opera cape over a tuxedo, silver-headed walking stick in hand. His hair was silver, too, and so was his neatly-trimmed mustache.

"Who," Tony squeaked, "are you?"

"Horace Astin at your service." The old gent swept off his hat for an elaborate bow. "Member of the resident company of this theater back when it had one, in 1912. Collapsed in the wings right after my finest performance as Old Hamlet's Ghost. Perhaps that is why I prefer to haunt. Couldn't leave the theater, you know."

Tony didn't, but he did grasp the fact that there were

now two spirits instead of one. "Think if we both jump on the contact, it might move?"

"It might," the ghost conceded, "but I have a simpler solution." He flipped his cane over and jammed the silver head between the contacts. With a snap, electrons flowed. Astin yanked his cane out.

Okay, the contact sprang up again, but it had only had to close once. Tony froze, listening to the horrendous noise of the car bomb that went on and on far longer than any explosion really could have—and when it had almost died away, boomed again. The audience roared at the sound cue itself.

Trembling with relief, Tony wiped sweat from his imaginary forehead. "Thanks very much, Mr. Astin."

"Not at all, my good fellow. The show must go on, you know."

Tony didn't, but he wasn't abut to say so. "'Scuse me—gotta check on the action."

"Of course," Horace Astin said agreeably, and waved his hat as Tony sprang out of the laptop and peeked around the screen to see the stage. He was just in time to see Cassandro stagger back in through the door with the steering wheel around his neck—and the audience went wild, rocking the walls with laughter, hooting and cheering.

Rally slept blissfully through it all.

When the laughter began to slacken, I said, "Go Cue Sixty-five—curtain down!"

The curtain fell and the applause crashed on my free ear. I glanced at the stage, saw the actors lined up trembling with eagerness, and said, "Curtain up."

The applause grew even louder. The cast all bowed, straightened up, waited a second, then bowed again.

"Curtain down," I said.

As soon as it touched the stage floor, Andy was gesturing at me to raise it again. I waited a few seconds to build audience desire, then said, "Curtain up."

Another wave of applause hit, and the actors bowed again.

After five curtain calls, I decided enough was enough and called, "Go houselights."

The applause slackened, and the murmuring began as the audience gathered up their purses and hats and started for the door.

The actors came running to berate me, everyone sure they could have milked the applause for one more bow at least, but I wasn't there to tell them that the audience would have realized it was being milked and would have resented it. No, by the time they got to the stage manager's desk, I was halfway to the light booth to see what was the matter with Rally.

He was sound asleep.

Rally was sitting slumped forward with his head on his arms, a laptop to either side and a plastic cup knocked on its side next to his forearm. I picked up the glass and took a sniff. That definitely wasn't ginger ale. So the whole cast had been drinking champagne during intermission—just one very small glass, apparently, or it would have thrown their timing off—and one of them, not wanting to be selfish, had brought Rally a glass. I had a notion that if I could have afforded a chemical analysis, I would have found more in it than fermented grape juice.

Lyle edged in the door—sideways was the only way he would fit, and even then he had to duck—and stared at Rally. "What happened to him?"

"We'll never know," I said, "and neither will he, I suspect. You want to grab his shoulders, Lyle? We oughta get him to bed."

Lyle took Rally's shoulders, and I took his feet. As we went out the door, Lyle said, "There's a pile of old curtains in one of the stage-left dressing rooms."

"Flame-proofing," I warned. "If it's old enough, traces can get in the dust."

"So we throw a tarp over them," Lyle said. "I'll take first shift."

"Yeah, Rally shouldn't wake up in a strange place alone," I agreed. "Who's gonna cover for him tonight?"

"The local hand," Lyle grunted. "Let her do something while she's watching. Doesn't this count as a criminal offense, Jack?"

"What, slipping him a mickey? It's not enough to call the cops in for. Besides, the last thing I want is for us to get bogged down with the local law."

"Yeah, they might make us stay around for a couple of days." Lyle looked up at me. "Who do you think did it, Jack?"

"I don't know," I grunted, "but suddenly I'm beginning to suspect that all those 'accidents' that have been happening, may not have been so accidental after all."

Lyle was silent as we eased Rally out of the door to the balcony lobby and started down the main stairs. Then he said, "That almost-fight last night—you could say Jory got us into it . . ."

"What, by trying to get that local to quit drooling into Dulcie's neckline? Might as well say Dulcie started it by being so desirable."

But he had a point. I was going to have to review all the accidents and see where Jory had been a few minutes before.

Tony hated to leave Jack to his detective work alone, but he had a date with Sandy that night—at least, he hoped he did. Besides, St. Vidicon must have had him on

a bungee cord or something, because the theater lobby
grew redder and redder until Tony seemed to be swimming in wine. Then the wine developed lumps that
turned into shapes, and he found he was walking down
the maroon hallway again by Father Vidicon's side.
"Thanks, Father. We got 'em through that one, anyway."

"The rest is their own concern," Father Vidicon said,
"that is, until they call upon us again."

It was nice of the priest to include him, but he knew
nobody was going to call upon Saint Tony. Besides, the
way he was feeling toward Sandy was scarcely saintly.
"I'd better wake up," Tony said. "Don't want to be late
for work."

"Perish the thought," Father Vidicon agreed. "Remember, Tony—no closer than six inches."

Sandy and Tony were quite well behaved for several
weeks after that, going to the theater and the ballet and
the movies and spending Saturdays and most of Sun-
days together, roaming the city. Once she asked to see
his apartment, which of course ended with a little light
cuddling before they resolutely went back out to see if
they could find any new sights.

There were minutes of very agreeable silence, staring into each other's eyes or gazing at the scenery in the
park while they held hands, but most of the time, they
were talking—sometimes serious, sometimes not, sometimes reducing each other to bundles of laughter. At
work, Tony found it hard to concentrate on the latest
problem he was trouble-shooting—images of Sandy
kept popping up over the screenful of code.

After each date, though, he did see her home, and
she always invited him in for brandy, and the chats always turned into cuddling sessions, which Tony usually

managed to end before they turned into outright fore-play.

Finally, one night when he managed to stop, and said, "I . . . I'd better go," she turned cold as ice. "If you do, don't come back."

"What? I . . . I don't understand."

"You can't keep doing this to me! You can't keep getting me all worked up, then run out on me!"

"I don't mean to . . ."

"Don't mean to frustrate me? Don't mean to leave me hanging? But you do it."

"Only respect . . ."

"Or cowardice? What are you afraid of, anyway, Tony? Are women really all that frightening?"

"Not at all. You're wonderful creatures, you more than any."

"And your idea of proving that is to walk out on me?"

"You haven't said 'yes' yet."

"What do you think I'm saying now?"

"Not to the right question! If this doesn't work out between us, I don't want you doubly hurt!"

"It's gone too far for that already," Sandy said, her voice shaking. "Why? Are you *planning* to run out on me?"

"No, of course not! I want it to work out, want it to last forever! But you only want it for the moment!"

"Enough moments add up to a lifetime," Sandy returned, "and if they don't, I might as well have gotten something out of it. If I'm going to suffer the agony, I damn well want to have the ecstasy first, don't you think?"

A sudden stillness came over Tony, a sudden certainty. "I don't think you should have to suffer at all." He stood up. "Let me know when you're ready to hear me ask the right question." He caught up his jacket and went to the door.

Sandy caught up with him before he turned the knob and pressed it shut. "What if I don't believe in marriage?"

"It exists," Tony said.

"Oh sure, people get married, but I've never seen it work out the way it's supposed to! A lifetime of wrangling and quarreling, or some really bitter fights before a divorce—why take the chance?"

"Because I have seen it work out," Tony said. "Okay, not with joy and symphonies every step of the way, but I've seen couples in their sixties still together, still loving each other."

"Loving each other *again*," Sandy corrected, "And I notice you don't say still *in love*."

"No," Tony said. "The priest doesn't work magic when he says the words. There are rough spots, sometimes rough years, but people can make it work, and when they're in their sixties, they're awfully glad they did."

"After they fell out of love but had to keep living together," Sandy said. "I'm sorry, Tony, but I don't want to wait until I'm sixty-five to be happy."

"I don't want to wait either," Tony said softly, "but I will if I have to."

Sandy stared in surprize, and her hold on the door weakened enough for Tony to open it. She made a wild grab, but he stepped toward the opening, and she jolted into him, face-to-face. He kissed her, sweetly, sadly, then leaned back to gaze into her eyes, and whispered, "Good night."

He stepped out into the hall before she snapped, "Good-bye!" and slammed the door behind him.

• • • •

Of course Tony knew he'd been really stupid, turning down an invitation like that. Any man in his right mind would have leaped at the chance to jump into bed with a beauty like Sandy. Did that constitute getting serious or just taking advantage? Or did all those dates with no sign of anything more than petting constitute taking advantage? He supposed sex could be interpreted as a sign of getting serious, though he'd known a lot of men for whom it was anything but.

"This is all your fault, you know," he told Father Vidicon in a dream that night. "I never thought of sex as a sin until I met you."

"Ah, the sad state of Catholic education!" Father Vidicon sighed. "I see that Finagle is afoot even in popular culture."

"Probably more there than anywhere," Tony said glumly. "Our TV sets tell us 'Go, go!' but the schools and the preachers tell us, 'Don't, don't!' "

"There is good sense in it," Father Vidicon said. "Sex should involve emotional commitment, Tony, and does when a woman is young. The heartbreak of the first break-up is far worse if bodies have been involved."

"I suppose so," Tony said, "but that's what a priest is supposed to say."

"Tony! You don't think I'd mislead you?"

"Not willingly," Tony said, "though you haven't been entirely forthcoming either."

"Me?" Father Vidicon cried in genuine surprize. "What information have I withheld from you?"

"Now that you ask," Tony said, "I've found myself wondering what you're doing while I'm off fighting little gremlkins."

"Those interludes do have their interesting sides."

"What about that run-in you had while I was convoying Gadget and Nick? You were fighting the minion who lay behind all their troubles, weren't you?"

"In a manner of speaking," St. Vidicon admitted.

Tony counted five paces, waiting for the priest to go on. When he didn't, Tony prodded, "You going to tell me about it?"

"Why bother?" Father Vidicon asked. "You can read about it on your computer."

"Hey, I've earned the right to hear about it from the horse's mouth! I mean . . ."

Father Vidicon laughed. "No offense taken, Tony. Well, enough; if you really want to know what happened, I'll tell you. Let's walk while we talk, though, shall we?" He set off down the hall, and as he told the story, his voice began to fall into the Renaissance rhythms and patterns of King James's scholars.

Saint Vidicon strode bravely onward through the throat of Hell. He was newly martyred, having died in place of a resistor, that the word of His Holiness the Pope might reach unto every corner of the world for the saving of its souls—but even ere he had come to Heaven, he had found himself pitted against the Imp of the Perverse, that he might achieve governance over the spirit of self-defeat, for the glory of God and the salvation of all who labor with video or keyboard. Yet having routed the Imp, he did not seek escape, but strode ahead in answer to the call he felt, the new vocation the Lord had given.

As he went, the crimson of the walls about him darkened down toward ruby, then darkened further still, toward purple. Protuberances began to rise from the floor, each taller than the last, excrescences that did stand upon slender stalks as high as his waist. Then did their tips begin to broaden and to swell until he saw that, every few paces, he did pass a glowing ball that stood by his hip. And he did see a strip upon the ceiling that did widen, with decorations that did glow upon it, curlicues and arabesques. It sprouted chandeliers, and square they were, or rectangular, and they did hang down from chains at each corner. Yet neither were they chains, but cables or, aye, rods. "These are like to tables," Father Vidicon did murmur. "Tables inverted." Then he did notice that a bulge, extruding from the ceiling, did broaden out, then sprouted upon a side. The good father frowned and bethought him, " 'Tis like unto a chair." And it was, in truth.

Thus did the saint realize that he did pace upon the ceiling of a hallway with a strip of carpet oriental, and with chairs and tables hanging above his head. And Lo! He did pass by a mirror set into the wall that did glow with the maroon of the wall across from it, and as he did step past, he saw himself inverted, with chest and hip vanishing upward. He squeezed his eyes shut and shook his head to rid himself of the sight, and when he did ope them, he did see that the walls now did flow past him toward his front; indeed, the mirror did slide past a second time, from back to fore. With every step he took, the walls went farther past, and dizziness did claim him. Then did thrills of danger course through his nerves, for he saw that he had come upon a region of inversion, where all was upside down and progress turned to regress, where every step forward took him two steps backward, and all was opposite to how it should have been. "I near the demon," the saint bethought himself, and knew that he came nigh the Spirit of Illogic.

Yet Saint Vidicon perceived that he could not approach that spirit unless it chanced that he might discover some way to progress. He stopped; the motion of the wall stopped with him, as it should; and Father Vidicon did grin with delight, then took one step backward. In truth, the wall did then move from front to back. He laughed with joy and set off, walking backward. The mirror slid past him again, going from the front, then toward the back, as was fit and proper. So thus, retreating ever, Father Vidicon went onward toward the Spirit of Contrariness.

And Lo! The spirit did come nigh.

The spirit approached, though he moved not; for he stood, arms akimbo, feet apart, sailing at Father Vidicon as he watched the good saint come; and the spirit's eyes were shielded behind two curving planes of darkness. From head to foot he was clothed in khaki, aye, even to his shirt, where it did show between lapels, and his necktie was of brown. Clean-shaven he was, and long-faced, smiling with delight full cynical, crowned with a cap high-peaked with a polished visor, and insigniae did gleam upon his shoulder boards.

Then Father Vidicon did halt some paces distant, filled with wariness, and quoth he, "I know thee, Spirit—for thou art Murphy!"

But, "Nay," quoth the spirit, "I am someone else by that same name."

Father Vidicon's face did darken then. "Deceive me not. Thou it is who hath enunciated that fell principle by which all human projects come to doom."

"No mortal man or woman declared that phrase," the spirit replied. "It sprang to life of itself among the living, and none on earth know why."

Father Vidicon frowned. "Dost thou say thou art a Form Platonic, an essence of that source within humans that doth enunciate perversity and doom?"

"The doom's within the doer," the spirit answered, "How may I exorcize it? Nay, 'tis they who bring it out, not I."

"Thou speakest false, fell foe!" Father Vidicon did cry. "Well thou dost know the wish to fail is buried deep in most and, left to lie, would sleep quiescent. 'Tis thou dost invest each mortal, thou who doth nurture and encourage that doom-laden wish!"

But the spirit's smile remained, untouched. "If I do, what boots it? Wouldst thou truly blame me for encouragement?"

"For nurture of foul folly, aye! As thou wouldst know, if thou didst not look upon the world through the fell filter of Inversion!" Thereupon did Father Vidicon leap forth to seize those darkened lenses of the spirit, to rip away the shadow's shades, crying, "Look not through your glasses, darkly!"

They came away within his hand, yet not only those dark lenses, but all the face, peeling off the spirit's head like to a shrivelled husk, exposing there within a mass of hair.

Father Vidicon gazed on the coiffure, stunned.

Slowly, then the spirit turned, hair sliding aside to show another face. Hooded eyes now gazed upon the saint, darkened indeed, but not in frames; for his eyes were naught but frosted glass, and his twisting mouth a grinning grimace.

Father Vidicon did swallow thickly and looked down into his hands, where he beheld the back side of the empty mask. "Truth," he cried, "I should have thought! Thou has backward worn they wear!"

But the spirit chortled then, "Not so! Behold my buskins!"

Then Father Vidicon looked down and found that the spirit spoke in sooth. The heels of his shoes were there, and his toes did point away upon the other side. "Alas!" the good saint cried, "What boots it?" Then up he raised his gaze, and did declare, "Thy head's on backward!"

"In sooth." The spirit grinned. "Wouldst thou expect aught else?"

"Nay, surely!" Father Vidicon now clamped his jaw and folded all his features in a frown. "I should have known! Thou art the jaundiced Janus!"

"Two-faced in truth," the spirit did agree.

"That thou art not! Truth there cannot be in him who's two-faced. Thine hinder face was false!"

"What else?" The spirit shrugged. "Yet canst thou be sure? Mayhap another countenance doth lie beneath my hair, and I have truly eyes behind, as well as those before."

"Nay, that sight must be seen," the saint then said, and looking up to Heaven, he did pray: "Good Father, now forgive! That in my false pride and folly, I did think myself so fit for fighting such ectoplasmic enemies. I pray Thee now Thine aid to give, and send me here a weapon to withstand this Worker of our Woe!"

But the spirit chuckled. "What idle plea is this? What instrument could thy Patron place in thy palm that could reverse the perverse?"

A spark of light did gleam within the good priest's hand, glaring and glowing into glass, and Father Vidicon held up a mirror.

His foe laughed outright. "What! Wilt thou then fight the Spirit of Defeat with so small a service?"

"Aye," quoth Father Vidicon, "if it shows truly."

"Nay—for 'tis 'DARKLY, through a glass.' Dost thou not recall?"

But Father Vidicon held up the mirror to reflect the spirit's face into his eyes.

"Nay, I have another, then!" it cried. One arm slipped backward into its inner pocket and did whisk out another glass, a foot or more in width, and opposed it to the plate the good saint held, reflecting back reflections into the Reverend's regard.

"It will not serve!" the good priest cried, and even as he spoke, his mirror grew to half again the size of the spirit's, throwing back into its eyes the sight of its own face with a glass beside it, within which was his face, with a frame, within a face. The spirit shrieked and yanked his own glass aside, away, but its image held within the priest's reflector. "'Tis too late to take away!" the good priest cried. "Dost thou not see thou hast begun a feedback uncontrolled?"

And so it was.

"It cannot serve!" the spirit wailed. "No feedback can sustain without a power input!"

"I have the Input of the greatest Power that doth exist," Saint Vidicon explained with quiet calm. "All power in the Universe doth flow from this one Source!"

The mirror grew still brighter within the view of each—brighter then and brighter, white-hot, flaring, burning up the image of the Imp, and as its image burned, so did the spirit itself. For, "In truth," quoth Father Vidicon, "thou art naught BUT image."

Thus with wailing howl, the spirit frayed and

dwindled, shimmering, burned to tatters, and was gone.

"So, at bottom, he was, at most, a hologram," Father Vidicon mused, "and what was formed by mirrors can by them be undone."

He laid the glass that had swallowed the spirit most carefully on its face and, folding his hands, cast his gaze upward. "Good Lord, I give Thee thanks that Thou hast preserved Thine unworthy servant a second time from such destruction! I pray Thee only that Thou wilt vouchsafe to me the strength of soul and humility that I will need to confront whatever adversary Thou wilt oppose to me."

The mirror winked, and glimmered, and was gone.

Father Vidicon gazed upon the place where it had been and sighed "I thank Thee, Lord, that thou hast heard me. Preserve me, thus, I pray, 'gainst all other hazards that may hover."

So saying, then, he signed himself with the Cross, and stood, and strode on farther down toward Hell.

But as Tony had been reading, Father Vidicon's words had been turning into print, scrolling upward— and by the time they had turned into letters on a computer screen, he had been too much engrossed in the story to complain. Now that it was finished, he was too happy with the ending to feel cheated. After all, that was one fight every engineer wanted to win.

Anyway, it had taken his mind off Sandy for a little while.

A little. Now all he could think about was her, again.

"Sandy, honey, what's the matter?"

"Oh, nothing, Rachel." Sandy dabbed furiously with her hanky, blotting the tears.

"Nothing?" I find my friend crying in the bathroom and it's nothing? Tell Rachel what it really is."

"Just a mood." Sandy took out her compact and started trying to make repairs. She froze for a moment, repulsed by the tear-stained face in the mirror, then patted on more foundation with renewed vigor.

"What's his name?"

Sandy froze again, then went back to her makeup.

Rachel's eyes widened. "It's that computer guy, isn't it? The one I saw you with at Nepenthe the other night! What's the matter, honey? Did he dump you?"

"No, no, it's not *his* fault!" Sandy cried in alarm.

"So it is him!" Rachel came forward, arms wide. "Oh, poor Sandy! What did he do?"

"Nothing." Sandy's voice broke on the word. She tried to ignore it, tucking her compact away.

"Oh," Rachel said, and her tone spoke volumes. "That's too bad, honey. He seemed like such a nice guy."

"He is." Appalled, Sandy felt the tears starting again. "Oh Rachel, I think I did something really stupid."

When Tony was about worn-out with writing letters he didn't mail and moping in the doldrums, he acknowledged that his fascination with Sandy wasn't going to wear off and felt doom settle over him. He headed for bed, hoping things would look better in the morning, and finally managed to drift into sleep in spite of the images of Sandy that kept flashing and fading before his eyes. It wasn't much, as sleeps go, so he wasn't all that surprised to find himself walking down the maroon corridor next to Father Vidicon.

"You did as your conscience told you, Tony," Father

Vidicon said. "You knew you'd be taking advantage of her, and you refused to."

"Any man in his right mind would have taken advantage of her!"

"Then it's a good thing you're not in your right mind." Father Vidicon clapped him on the shoulder. "Cheer up! If she's really in love with you, she'll bolster her courage and marry you."

"So if she doesn't want to marry me, she must not really be in love with me," Tony said glumly "That's not all that reassuring, Father Vidicon."

"And you think that if you accepted her offer, not to say blackmail, it might grow into a marriage?"

"In fact if not in name?" Tony shrugged. "There would be a chance, at least."

"Have faith in the young woman, Tony—and have faith in yourself. Give her a while to think it over before you do anything drastic."

"Give her a while. Yeah. Sure. Just how am I supposed to keep from going crazy while I'm waiting?"

"Well, as to that," St. Vidicon said, "I did have something in mind."

Chapter 15

Nancy loved the Merchant Marine—the long watches where a person had time to think, away from the noise and crowding of the cities and the prying and gossiping of the small towns. And it wasn't lonely; there were three other people on the crew, so she always had two others for company at dinner and, if she wanted, a chat over the intercom during her shift. Since they rotated watches, it wasn't always the same two, either—one week it would be Bruno and Sylvie for her companions, the next it would be Sylvie and Aubrey, the third it would be Aubrey and Alice. Of course, if there had been a larger crew, the way there had been back at the beginning of the Twenty-first century, rivalries might have cropped up, maybe even that old superstition against having women on board—but in the year 2052, automation was so advanced that one person alone could supervise the day-to-day running of a factory and a crew of four could navigate a tanker the size of three football fields.

Of course, if those four hadn't gotten along with each other, it could have been a minor hell—but in 2052, the company psychologists did a good job matching people, and since they all had sex-drive suppressant shots before they boarded ship, the ugly possibilities of jealousies and rivalries never arose. All in all, it was a very good life—as long as all the equipment was working.

Truth to tell, Nancy would have vastly preferred to be aboard a ship that was hauling bananas, or cargo containers, or virtually anything but oil. Fortunately, biofuels had reduced the need to ship the stuff, but some countries who didn't have their own oil still did booming business manufacturing plastics, so here she was steering a million barrels of petroleum from the Persian Gulf across the Atlantic Ocean.

Tonight, though, the satellite navigation system had gone out.

Nightmares of the horrendous oil-tanker wrecks and petroleum spills of the last century haunted Nancy as she ran the diagnostic program on her navigation computer.

"Is it something we can fix?" the intercom asked in Bruno's anxious voice.

"Doesn't seem to be." Nancy bit her lip. "The computer says it's working fine. Must be the antenna coming in, or the satellite itself."

"We can check the antenna, anyway," Sylvie's voice said.

"Not at night, please," Nancy said firmly. She went around in back of the console. "I'd just as soon not lose one of you and have to blame myself . . . No, the antenna connection's in and solid." She didn't tell them her nasty sneaking suspicion—that if the computer could malfunction, so could its diagnostic program. Admittedly, the chances of that happening had to be a million to one, but she was beginning to feel that somebody in there had it in for her.

And her shipmates.

"So what do we do?" Sylvie asked, dread echoing in her voice. "Drop sea-anchors and call for help?"

"The calling for help part sounds good," Nancy agreed. "Bruno, drop anchor."

"Right," Bruno said.

The "anchor" was only metaphorical, this far out at sea; in 2052 it was really a program that adjusted the ship's screws to hold the massive tanker more or less in one place, as much as you could measure "place" in the middle of a trackless expanse of water.

"Uh-oh," Bruno said.

Nancy's stomach dropped. "I know what the 'uh' was, but what's the 'oh'?"

"The sea-anchor isn't holding."

Nancy's stomach hollowed. "Run the diagnostic program."

"Will do."

Nancy waited, biting her lip and hoping—but her stomach was so hollow that a cuttlefish was thinking of taking up residency.

"The diagnostic program is hanging,"

"Hanging?" Sylvie cried. "That computer's guaranteed against hanging or locking up!"

"I think the warranty just ran out," Bruno told her. "Okay, Nancy, you're the navigator—what do we do?"

"We'll have to steer by the stars."

"Do you know the stars that well?" Bruno asked, voice heavy with doubt.

"Second thing they made us learn in navigator school," Nancy assured him.

"What was the first?"

"How to use the old tools—sextant, compass, clock, even cross-staff."

"Oh." Bruno packed massive relief into one word. "So as long as you can see the stars, we're okay."

"Okay," Nancy agreed, "but I want to stay well away from the coast until daylight." She looked up at the stars through the transparent ceiling. "We're headed west southwest." She glanced at the wall clock that said "GREENWICH" under it in big letters. "Sixty-three degrees east longitude." Back up at the stars, guessing Polaris's angle above the horizon, at 2:00 A.M. local time . . . "Can't be sure of the latitude, but we should be about twenty degrees northward."

"That puts us out in the middle of the ocean, doesn't it?" Sylvie asked, relieved.

"Far enough out that there shouldn't be a problem," Nancy agreed. "Bruno, I'll have to call you course corrections to hold us in place."

"Will do."

Nancy felt the throbbing of the great engines slacken, almost die. "Maintaining headway?"

"Screws turning over just enough," Bruno assured her. "I'll cut in the nose screws just a little to make sure our bearing doesn't drift."

Nancy felt the high-pitched vibration begin, though she didn't hear anything, of course—the insulation was too good for that.

"Uh, Nancy," Sylvie said, her voice full of foreboding.

"What is it, Sylvie?"

"You're not gonna like the weather."

Nancy looked up just in time to see Polaris disappear. The cuttlefish in her stomach wrapped its tentacles around her spine. "I'll get out the compass."

"Maybe it's just overcast." Bruno was forcing the optimism.

"I don't like the odds," Sylvie said.

"Me neither," Bruno agreed. "What are the chances of a storm blowing up just when our GPS system goes out?"

"We can still hope those clouds aren't bringing a storm," Sylvie answered.

Nancy did more than hope—she knew what improbable coincidences meant. As she opened the emergency closet and hauled out the compass, she muttered, "St. Vidicon, protect us from Finagle!"

The sensation of being sucked down a drain was familiar to Tony now. What wasn't, was where he would end up. As the location stabilized, he looked around him and discovered he was in his element—silicon. "Inside a computer again," he breathed, and relaxed.

But the silicon turned translucent and he saw tentacles waving. As they came closer, the silicon turned transparent, and he saw two huge baleful eyes follow the tentacles. Tony stared—what was a squid doing inside a computer?

Of course—more hands to twist potentials wrong.

"Who are you?" Tony demanded.

"I am the scuttlefish," the squid answered in hollow tones.

Tony began to develop a very bad feeling. "Scuttle" meant sinking a ship. "I take it we're all at sea."

"You surely are," the scuttlefish answered. "What do you here, small and soft one?"

Yes, definitely a very bad feeling. "I'm going to keep this tanker from driving ashore and being wrecked on a rock."

"Oh no, you must not do that," the scuttlefish chided.

"The tanker must crash and the oil must spill—worse than any oil spill your kind have wrought. Only then will the people of the world rise in protest; only then will governments band together to outlaw the shipping of rock-oil. No, this ship must lose its way and shiver upon the rocks."

Tony shuddered. "What a horrible thought!"

"I find it delightful," the scuttlefish returned.

"But the death! The misery! The birds who won't be able to fly because the oil will glue their feathers to their bodies! The otters and other sea animals who will die slicked with slime!"

"Indeed," the scuttlefish agreed. "It is for their sakes that the governments will unite."

"But all the fish who will be poisoned, the fishermen who will starve from empty nets!"

"Oh, not starve, surely," the scuttlefish said. "Your kind is adept at keeping their own from starvation when they want to. No, they may lose their boats, may lose their houses, but they shall not starve."

"They won't lose anything if I can help it!" Tony pushed himself upward, swimming through silicon, twisting and turning through the trails of circuits.

Something caught his ankle and pulled him back. "You shall not go. The rocks must wreck the ship."

Looking down, Tony saw a tentacle wrap around his ankle and another arrowing toward his other ankle. "Let go!"

"Begone," the scuttlefish retorted. "You have the power to disappear, to go back whence you came. If you do not, I shall hold you here—or draw you in."

Other tentacles lifted, and for the first time Tony saw the glistening beak at their center—but the squid had given him an idea. "The disappearing part makes sense, at least." And he did.

He reappeared on the surface of the chip. Here, there was no illumination of electrons rushing through conductors—but Tony seemed to be emitting a glow of his own. By it, he searched the circuit board. The first thing to check, of course, was the antenna dish's connection. He oriented himself by the glimmer of microwave radiation and went toward it.

"Forfend, foolish mortal!"

Looking back, Tony saw tentacles slap onto the edge of the chip and the arrow-shape of the scuttlefish's top rise. He didn't wait to see the eyes but ran toward the antenna signal's glimmer.

"I have ten legs! I can move more quickly than you!"

"They're arms." Tony came to the edge of the board and looked over. "I don't know about you, but I can't walk on my hands too well."

"I can! Disappear while you may!"

"Got to finish my job first." Tony saw that the connection from the dish's lead seemed solidly connected. He dived into it to investigate—and heard a bellow of anger behind him.

He swam through silicon, following the glow of electron flow, knowing he would have to be quick, because once it was back inside the chip, the scuttlefish would be able to move faster than he—at least, if its jet worked the way its real cousins' did, in water.

Suddenly he was in darkness.

Tony could have shouted "Eureka!" because found it he had—the source of the malfunction, or rather its site. He traced the circuit flow backward until he saw light again, and saw that it stopped where another chip was plugged into the board. He ran from chip to chip, figuring out the logic of the circuit board, and realized that the darkened chip was the one that converted the incoming signal from microwave frequency in gigahertz, down to something the rest of the circuit could handle more easily—megahertz, the frequency range of FM radio. He knelt to peer at the base—and saw that the chip was halfway out of its socket. Something had jarred the GPS receiver hard enough to loosen this component.

Or something wedge-shaped had driven in and pried it loose—something very slender at the tip but that thickened amazingly, something that was very strong—or both.

"Foolish mortal, I come!"

Turning, Tony saw the squid slithering along the surface of the board. Sure enough, if it couldn't swim, it couldn't move very fast.

Fast enough, though. Tony would have to think of some way to jar this chip back into place, and he'd have to do it quickly.

Very quickly.

"Nancy, do you hear a moaning?"

Nancy looked up in alarm, then ran to look at the night-vision screen. She cranked up the gain, zoomed in to the limit—and saw spray rising into the air. "It's waves crashing on a reef! Bruno, what's the report on the sea-anchor?"

"It's doing the best it can." Bruno was silent a moment, checking his screen, then said, "No, we're holding steady. Sure, the current's been carrying us north-northeast at six knots, but we're holding our place in it."

"We must have been a lot closer to shore than I thought."

"What shore?" Sylvie's voice asked.

"I don't know!" Nancy cried. "I thought it was the Canaries, but they shouldn't have been this close!

Bruno, turn the helm seaward one hundred eighty degrees—south-southwestward! And give us full power!"

"Will do." But Bruno's voice was strained. "Don't know if we can counter this current, though—it's pretty strong."

Nancy felt the whole ship come alive with the throbbing of the huge engines, and the spray stopped growing larger in the scope.

Well, it almost stopped.

"That's good, Bruno, that's a lot better, but we're still drifting shoreward!"

"That's all the power I've got, Nancy."

Nancy felt as though she were shrivelling. At least it would take them a lot longer before the tanker broke open on the rocks.

Maybe until daybreak. If there were light, a rescue tow could find them—if she could tell their position to the Coast Guard of whatever country they were approaching. And she could, if only the GPS would kick back in.

"St. Vidicon, protect us from Finagle!"

Tony reminded himself that at a quarter of an inch in height but with ordinary human proportions, he had a lot more strength than he was used to—probably even stronger than an ant, proportionately. He gathered himself and leaped.

The scuttlefish cried out in anger as Tony soared through the air and landed on top of the wayward chip—not that it did any good; his disembodied self was a spirit, after all, and might have had a great deal of energy but also had absolutely no mass.

All right, use energy. Tony ran to the higher edge of the chip, the one whose pins were actually out of their sockets, and jumped. He couldn't leap very high, of course—the cover of the unit was only half an inch above his head—but he landed sitting on the edge.

No result—nothing—as far as he could tell, his energy hadn't done anything, not without mass to give it downward force.

Something made a slapping sound.

Tony leaped up, turning, and saw a tentacle tip hooked over the far end of the chip. Another slap and another, and five tentacle tips had lined up beside it. The fleshy arrowhead of the scuttlefish's end rose into view—and Tony realized what he was going to do.

The scuttlefish's eyes came into view. "Foolish fellow! Do you not know you are spirit only and can do nothing here?"

"Maybe," Tony said, "but if I really believe I have a form, maybe I can have the characteristics of that form—such as strength and weight!"

"Ridiculous!" the scuttlefish snapped, but perhaps too quickly, too angrily. "You are nothing but an idea and a small one at that, not a bonfire but a candle flame, and as such can be quickly snuffed!" It lowered its arrowhead and launched itself at Tony.

The surf moaned on the rocks, and Nancy glanced quickly over her shoulder. In the predawn half-light, she could see the spray shooting high as the waves crashed on the reef, now only a quarter of a mile away. In minutes the surf would lift the tanker high, then drop it on the reef; it would break open, spilling a million barrels of oil into the sea, killing fish, killing kelp, slicking marine mammals with oil . . .

And probably killing herself and her shipmates with it. "St. Vidicon," she cried, "if you're going to do anything, please do it fast!"

"Who's St. Vidicon?" Sylvie's voice asked, but

Nancy didn't have time to tell her. A huge wave rose under the tanker's bow, lifting it high, bearing it toward the reef.

Tony stood tall, a clear target for the scuttlefish, waiting as the fleshy arrowhead shot toward him. At the last second, he leaped high. The scuttlefish hissed in anger and swerved up toward him.

Tony shot through the casing and emerged into the darkness of the bridge but didn't have time to notice; he heard a faint but distinct "bong" and dived right back into the receiver. He shot past the slanting bulk of the scuttlefish, jammed between chip and casing, on down to its tentacles. One great circular eye stared at him as the scuttlefish thrashed its tentacles, trying to reach him—and in the process, started to straighten. Tony thumbed his nose at the monster; the scuttlefish roared in anger and thrashed its tentacles in an effort to grab the insolent mortal who dared defy it—and jammed its length more and more solidly between casing and chip. As it thrashed, its body pushed the chip downward ever so slightly. The scuttlefish was so intent on its prize that it didn't notice, but Tony did—noticed the glowing trails of electron flow, and knew the GPS system was working again.

"Mayday, mayday!" Nancy called into the radio. "USS oil tanker *Fortune* is stranded without navigation!"

"Coast Guard here," answered an accented voice. "Can you see any landmarks, *Fortune*?"

Nancy couldn't restrain a shout of joy. It almost drowned out the mellow tone of the GPS system coming back on-line. She whirled to stare, then grinned, and said to her screen, "Correction—we have our navigation system back." Then, remembering that the fix might not last, she read the Coast Guard her position, reading off the GPS screen, then added, "We have our engines at full power, but we seem to be caught in a rip tide that's driving us onto . . ."

"Onto Fortress Reef!" the radio answered her. "Do the best you can to hold your position, *Fortune*—we'll have a tug to you as quickly as we can."

Nancy went limp with relief. "Thank Heaven—and thank you, Coast Guard."

"You're welcome. We want your oil in our refineries, not on our beaches."

Slowly, bit by bit, the current pushed the fighting tanker toward the reef. Nancy held her breath and hoped the Coast Guard would be there in time.

The chip jolted into place, creating just enough room for the scuttlefish to free itself. Realizing it had been tricked, it plunged toward Tony with a shriek of rage.

Tony leaped high, hands joined above his head to dive out of the GPS receiver. The scuttlefish was right behind him, both of them diminutive, both of them pure energy. Neither would have been visible in daylight, but the bridge was darkened, only a pool of light on Nancy's console, so out of the corner of her eye, she noticed a mite shooting past her and swung at it irritably, her attention on the receiver. Her palm missed Tony but swatted the scuttlefish, and it gave a high, thin shriek as it passed through her skin into the muscles of her palm.

Nancy frowned, wondering what the tiny noise had been, but she had other things to worry about—worry a lot. What if the tug didn't get there in time? Maybe she should just get it over with quickly, turn the ship's bow toward the reef and let the engines drive them onto the rocks . . .

She gave herself a shake; what was she thinking of? The tug would get there in time, they would live, and so would the fish that swam off this coast. Relief gave rise to joy, and joy drowned out the momentary urge to self-defeat. She frowned, thinking she heard a high, thin sound again, then decided that it must have been the wind past the corner of the bridge.

Tony, however, heard the scuttlefish's wail of anger as it drowned in a rising tide of optimism, and knew that its last attempt to scuttle the ship, by shooting a suicidal impulse into the navigator's brain, had failed. He grinned, wishing Nancy well even as the darkened bridge seem to turn red, deep red. A floor of sorts pressed up against the soles of his feet, and he found himself walking on the yielding surface next to Father Vidicon.

"Well done, Tony!" The priest clapped him on the shoulder. "You saved a great many lives that time!"

"Yes, but only four of them human." Tony savored the taste of triumph.

"A life is a life," Father Vidicon said. "You also saved Nancy from her own private purgatory of self-blame, which she did not deserve."

"She didn't," Tony agreed, "but I'm afraid she'll have a small pessimistic streak running through her for the rest of her life."

"Nothing that her natural common sense can't overcome," St. Vidicon said, "something you might want to remember yourself, Tony. After all, it is time for you to wake up and rejoin the world of the living."

"Yes," Tony said, "the living, and Sandy! Good night, Father Vidicon."

"Good morning, Tony."

Tony woke up, feeling amazingly rested, considering what his spirit had been doing that night. He swung out of bed, debating how best to renew contact with Sandy. After all, a week and a half had gone by without seeing her, and Tony decided it was do-or-die time. He'd try once more to renew the relationship, but if she didn't want to, he'd have to stop and get used to life without her again. There was, after all, a very thin line between devotion and harassment. What was the worst that could happen?

Well, the worst was that she might tell him to get out of her life and stay out, but the way he was feeling now, even that would be an improvement. At least it would be something definite, even if it was only a definite ending.

He would just have to tell her that this would be his last attempt to get in contact, if she didn't want him to—but how best to say that?

Clear the way, Tony.

Tony frowned; the voice inside his head sounded suspiciously familiar—and it was also suspicious that, calm though it was, he could hear it over the city traffic as he walked the block from the subway to the office.

Still, the voice had a point—and Tony suddenly realized he could check and see how to phrase his next contact. He stopped into a florist's and ordered a dozen red roses. It helped knowing where Sandy worked.

Chapter 16

"Ms. Clavier?"

Sandy wrenched herself out of her unseeing trance and looked up at the delivery girl with Rachel hovering behind her.

The teenager handed her a long white box with a grin, but all she said was, "Sign here, please."

Sandy signed in a daze, then remembered to say, "Thank you."

"You're welcome, lucky lady." The kid popped her gum and went out the door.

Rachel was still hovering. "Come on, open it! I'm dying of curiosity!"

It didn't even occur to Sandy to tell her friend to mind her own business; she untied the ribbon with fingers that felt like sausages. The roses glowed at her like life restored.

"Oh Sandy, they're beautiful!"

Other co-workers looked up from their desks and exclaimed approval and envy as Sandy lifted the bouquet out of the box.

"Hold on, I'll find a vase!" Rachel bustled off.

That was fortunate—at least she wouldn't see Sandy open the card. She slid it out of the diminutive envelope and read:

I'm very sorry, but I can still hope.

Love,
Tony

Sandy's knees gave way; she sat down harder than she had intended. Maybe it wasn't over, after all.

"Nothing today, Tony."

"Nothing?" Tony looked up at Harve in surprize. He had to quell a moment of reflex panic, the feeling that no work meant no pay. He was on salary now, and okay, he might not be earning a commission for fixing someone's system today, but he wouldn't exactly go broke, either. "Good!" he told Harve. "I'm behind on correspondence and way behind on filing."

Harve grinned. "Have fun cleaning up your desk."

Tony did. He spent the morning pushing documents into folders and shoving them into his filing cabinet drawers. Then, with his desk mostly clear, Tony glanced at the clock, remembering Sandy and wondering if it was time for the next step in his campaign to win her back. It was—lunchtime. Now he could go scouting.

Tony went by Sandy's office building during lunch hour with a special eye toward the trash cans in the alley. He didn't notice any roses, so he dared to hope.

Of course, that didn't mean his roses weren't sitting in a wastebasket somewhere inside the building; but if she didn't mind having them in sight, there was a chance.

As soon as he arrived back in the office, Tony turned to his computer to check his e-mail.

There it was at the top of his inbox, Sandy's name next to the word "Roses." Heart suddenly hammering, he clicked on the link, then read,

Dear Tony,

The roses are lovely—thank you so much. I can hope, too. Let's get together for coffee after work today and see if we can work something out. At Nepenthe?

Tony's pulse rocketed; for a moment, he felt as though he were floating. Then the words on the screen came into focus again and he tapped out a confirmation and sat back to bask in the glow of achievement.

When the glow faded a little, Tony reminded himself that all he'd achieved was a new start. If he really wanted Sandy back, he'd have to work out a campaign—but the way he felt right now, if she insisted on sex, he'd agree, scruples or no.

And of course, his whole body thrummed with desire at the thought; he felt as though he were a guitar tuned for her playing.

How about if she had come over to his side and was ready to say "yes"? Or even to keep dating without sex?

An unaccountable wave of depression hit Tony, but at least he knew its cause. He would just have to soldier through and be as good as his former word—and he had enjoyed going to the theater much more with her, than by himself.

But the reminder of the routine they'd shared also reminded him that he was in the office and should at least go through the motions of earning his paycheck. He turned back to the screen just as a window opened, filling the center of the frame.

Only this one didn't feature a beautiful woman exhorting him to buy something—it showed him the maroon hallway with which he had become all too familiar.

Well, there wasn't much that had to be done on the job today, anyway—and he needed somebody to share his triumph. He let the image on the screen become more and more real to him until he found himself walking down that moist and infirm corridor beside the reassuring bulk of the stocky priest.

"I've got another date, Father," he said, straight out.

"Very good, Tony! I couldn't be more pleased for both of you."

"Well, I don't know about being pleased for her," Tony said. "She's not getting as good a bargain as I am."

"Oh yes she is—and I do indeed think highly of the young woman. Your opinion of your own worth, Tony, is far lower than the reality."

"Maybe someday I can believe that."

"Do! After all, your experiences combatting Finagle and his minions should convince you of some of your abilities."

"They're helping a little," Tony admitted, "but those aren't the traits that make for a good fiancé, let alone a good husband."

Father Vidicon smiled. "It takes courage and perseverance to make a marriage succeed, Tony."

"A marriage, maybe," Tony said glumly, "but how about a romance?"

"How about it?" Father Vidicon gave him a quizzical look. "Why don't you ask the young lady?"

Courage and perseverance, Tony reminded himself. He reached out, picked up the phone, and dialed.

It was ten minutes to four when Sandy's phone rang. She answered it with more caution than hope; after all, she'd had a dozen calls that day, and none had been from Tony.

"Sandy?"

It was his voice.

Sandy sat up a little straighter and felt a smile coming on. "Hi, Tony." Her voice came out high and thin, and she cursed mentally.

"Hope you had a good day."

"Well, it was better after a long white box arrived. You're a dear! You didn't have to, you know."

"No, I don't," Tony said. "You deserved them. We still on for Nepenthe after work today?"

Sandy tried very hard to rein in her exultation. "Yeah . . . I think I could manage that . . ."

"Okay, then." Tony sounded massively relieved. "I'll be there by quarter after for sure."

Awkward pause.

"That'll be great," Sandy said through wooden lips.

"Yeah, it really will," Tony said in a rush. "See you then."

"Nepenthe," Sandy said. " 'Bye."

She hung up the phone and Rachel pounced. "Well? Was it him? What did he say?"

"I'm meeting him at the coffee house right after

work." A wave of dread swept Sandy. "Oh Rachel, what if he wants to make the break-up official?"

"What if he wants to make sure it hasn't happened?"

Tony couldn't concentrate, his whole body was quivering with elation. He was so filled with energy that he felt he would burst, felt he could go out and build a skyscraper just to let off tension.

Still, he had to go through the motions of work. He turned to the screen and, for want of anything better to do, clicked on his Internet icon. Its home window opened— but another frame opened on top of it.

Another dratted pop-up ad! Well, he'd at least see what the topic was before he closed it. He gave it a quick glance—then glanced again and read the words the funny little man in the monk's robe was pointing to:

Want to save the world? Well, you can—or at least, the duty engineer at Interworld's earth station!

Then, as though he knew Tony had finished reading, the little monk turned to point at a button that said, "Start."

Tony felt a minute's burning resentment. Wasn't it enough that he give the ghostly priest his nights without having to give up his days, too? But he remembered that he might want to be keeping his nights to himself in the near future—well, to share with only one other person who was far from being a monk—and that Father Vidicon just might have been instrumental in smoothing things over with Sandy. For the first time, it occurred to him that he might not be the only living person helping out the saint.

So he leaned back in his chair and let his eyes lose focus as he clicked on "Start." The picture inside the frame changed to a long room lined with screens that centered around a console, a long room that seemed to

become longer as Tony gazed, until it wasn't on the
screen any longer, but all around him, and Tony knew
he was inside the earth station, watching invisibly as a
ghost.

Ben had had an absolutely lousy morning. The dog
had knocked over his food dish, the cat had started in on
the drapes, then the dog had taken his own sweet time on
his morning walk. So much for the pleasures of house-
sitting to escape his narrow apartment for the week.

Then, of course, his car had refused to start, and it
had taken the tow truck an hour to get there—pretty fast,
for rush hour, but it hadn't seemed so at the time. Then,
of course, it only took the driver a few minutes with
jumper cables, and one quick signature later, Ben was on
his way, blessing his auto club—but that had axed the errands he'd been planning to run on the way to work, not
to mention the leisurely breakfast. He'd had to settle for
a biscuit sandwich and a large coffee at the drive-
through, both of which would probably be cold by the
time he got to work. Then, as he'd driven under the
shadow of the huge old satellite dish, he'd heard the roar
of heavy equipment and had had the good sense to brake
as he came out of the curve, to see the backhoe digging
a trench just past the line of smaller satellite dishes. It
was going to be a jolly day, all right, with that thing bellowing right outside his window. He turned right at the
power company's transformer that supplied the electricity that ran his earth station and braked as his car rolled
down the drive to the double gate in the chain-link fence.

Of course, the lock didn't want to turn when he put
his key in. He jiggled and twisted, though, and it finally
gave, grumbling at having to move. He shoved the gate
open, went back to his car and drove in, got out to close
and lock the gate, and turned to survey his hurricane-

fenced enclosure. From this angle, the satellite dishes had turned their backs on him and the long one-story control cabin at his right—a converted house trailer, actually—did leave the view clear for him to look out over the college campus to the island of Manhattan, there on the skyline.

The sight was inspiring, of course, but it was also the reason Ben was here—or that Interworld had its ground station on top of this old mountain (big hill, actually). They had leased the site from the college so that they had a clear microwave path to the Empire State Building, where Interworld had its distribution control center. Stations in New York City piped their signals into the Empire State Building by fiber-optic cable, and there on the Eighty-third floor the signals were converted to microwaves so that they could shoot out here to the earth station. The little microwave dishes on the tower picked up those signals and sent them down long strands of cable into the control cabin, where Ben would punch buttons and turn dials to change those signals back into microwaves and send them through other cables into the feed horn of the big satellite dish, where they would spray into the metal umbrella to be beamed up to Interworld's satellite twenty-two thousand miles above the equator—and, of course, that satellite and several others would send their signals down to these same dishes to be gathered into the feed horns and piped back into the control cabin to be microwaved to New York, so the people in Manhattan could turn on their cable TVs and see what was happening all around the world. In the early fifties, "Window to the World" had meant dollying a camera over to a window to look down twenty stories onto Forty-second street. Now it meant seeing what was happening on a street in Tokyo—or New Delhi or Baghdad, wherever the news of the world was happening that day.

The thought lifted Ben's spirits, as it always did—lifted them enough so that the backhoe didn't seem quite so annoying anymore. He slipped back into his car and parked it outside the cabin. It had taken a lot of convincing to keep the college's development committee from building the new dormitory between the earth station and Manhattan. In fact, it had taken some pretty strong persuasion to make them realize that Interworld wasn't just concerned about their spoiling the view—but reason had finally prevailed, and they were building the new dorm over to the side.

Ben stepped out of the car into a blast of summer heat and humidity. He winced and trotted over to the cabin. He closed the door behind him, blessing electronic equipment's need for air-conditioning, and raised a hand toward the intern he was relieving. "Hi, Gloria."

"Hi, Ben." Gloria stood up, slapping her pen down onto the log sheets on the clipboard. "Everything's boring."

Ben grinned; for Gloria, "boring" meant "normal." "Glad to hear it. Hot date tonight?"

"On a Thursday?" Gloria gave him a strange look.

"Hey, anything you do tonight is going to be hot."

"Sorry to hear it." Gloria went to the door. "Well, everything's set for the three o'clock feed. Want me to run it?"

"Nah, I'm here in time." Ben went to the operator's chair and sat down to scrutinize the log. "Not that much is set to happen, anyway."

"Looks like a good documentary coming at 7:00 P.M.," Gloria said. "Enjoy it."

"You too," Ben said absently, and managed a wave just before the door closed. Then he went back to perusing the log. He had two minutes before he had to start the feed, and the dish was already aimed at the Interworld

Three satellite. All he had to do was punch two buttons. He looked up at the clock, tracking the sweep second hand with his fingers ready. As the hand hit the top of the clock, he pushed the buttons, then glanced at the monitor—then stared. All he saw was "snow," the randomly-dancing dots that meant there was no signal coming through. Wildly, he glanced at the meters and saw their needles bouncing merrily—so the signal was going to the dish as it should. Why wasn't it going up to the satellite?

The telephone rang. Ben snatched it up, snapped, "I know. I'm working on it," put down the receiver, and ran to the window. One glance at the dish showed him why; it was still set for the horizontal transponder. He hit the manual key to rotate the great bowl to the vertical. Usually he would be able to hear the chain drive clanking, but not with that backhoe's roar, so he looked—and saw the chain stock-still. It didn't move, so neither did the bowl. It stayed set on horizontal. The dish was frozen in the wrong position.

Why?

Then he saw the backhoe swinging its shovel around for another bite at the ground—right between the power company's transformer and the dish. "St. Vidicon, protect us from Finagle!" he called on his way to the door. He yanked it open and pelted out into the summer heat, yelling and waving his arms. Of course the backhoe was making so much noise that it drowned out his yelling, but the driver saw his frantic signals and cut the motor. "What is it?" he called.

"You cut the cable!" Ben called back.

The driver stared, then looked back at the trench and swore.

"Didn't you see sparks?" Ben panted as he came up to the backhoe.

"Thought my shovel had hit flint," the driver answered.

"Good thing you have a padded chair," Ben said, "or you would have found out the hard way. I'll go call the power company." He ran back inside, but before he called, he was going to have to figure out a way to get the three o'clock feed up to Interworld Three. He suffered a brief vision of soap opera fans all over the country staring at the snow on their screens and cursing. He would have indulged in it himself, but he prayed to St. Vidicon instead.

Satellite communications weren't exactly Tony's forte, but he certainly knew the basics of circuit design, so it only took him a glance or two, and a little eavesdropping on Ben's frantic thoughts, to realize that if you can't get a signal where it's supposed to go by its usual route, all you have to do is figure out a different path. However, that meant he was going to have to put his thoughts into Ben's head—well, not into, exactly, just around his head where he could pick them up. He hovered unseen next to the racks of equipment, focusing his thoughts on Ben.

They coruscated off like a meteor shower, and a small ugly flat head lifted from Ben's hair, hissing, "Avaunt, interloper! This brain is not yours."

Tony froze, staring as the creature's skin opened to spread a hood behind its head—and conveniently over Ben's, blocking him from Tony's thoughts. "What manner of creature are you?" he demanded.

"I am the Serpent of the Single Mind," the cobra hissed, "and I have filled hisss with one thought and that one thought only—that he must find a way to make the great sssky-facing bowl rotate. Begone, interloper— I'll not have you dissstracting him."

"Distracting is scarcely the term," Tony said. He had

already figured out another solution to the problem—
but how to get it through to Ben, with the cobra's hood
blocking the way? "St. Vidicon, I could do with a little
inspiration here!"

Obligingly, the idea surfaced from his subconscious.
Grinning, Tony asked the snake, "How did you get here?"

"Why, by hisss choice," the cobra answered. "From
hisss youth, thisss man ssought to avoid dissstractions
when he concentrated his thoughtsss upon a problem—
and out of that wish, I grew to sshield hisss mind from
any other influence."

"But only when he's solving a problem," Tony reminded the snake. "When he is not, don't you think you
should be letting alternative solutions in?"

"It isss hisss choice," the snake returned. "If he had
wished for solutions that did not follow from a train of
thought, each step in its proper order, I would not have
arisen."

"But you know he's not going to be able to solve this
problem by logic."

"I know nothing of the sssort."

"Well, take my word for it." Tony began to move to
his right, heading toward Ben's face. "He's going to
have to think outside the terms of the problem, or he
won't find a solution."

"What iss that to me?"

Tony stared; then, still sidestepping, he asked, "You
don't care whether or not he solves the problem?"

"Not a bit," the snake answered. "I exissst to ssshield
his mind from distractionss while he thinksss, nothing
more. I care only if an unwanted thought should enter
hisss mind."

"How about if the thought is wanted?"

"It issss not."

"But if it's an alternative solution to the problem, he will want it."

"I sssee no evidence of that," the snake answered. "Ssstop sssidewalking, man! Do you think it will do you any good to ssstand before his eyesss? I assssure you it will not!"

Tony stood in front of Ben. The snake reared up above his forehead, its hood spread, making him look for all the world like an ancient Egyptian pharaoh. Tony reached out to touch the control panel, reached into it, and jiggled a contact.

Ben frowned as the tally light that showed the transponder link from the Japanese news agency blinked. All he would need right now would be for that link to go dead too! The Japanese network paid well to keep a transponder illuminated to carry the signal from its New York bureau to its Tokyo headquarters twenty-four hours a day whether there was any program to carry or not, just to make sure they weren't late with a story. Ben didn't want to think about the rebate Interworld would have to pay if that link went dead. A second's disruption in the signal now and then wouldn't be a tragedy; it could be sunspot interference or even just . . .

The tally blinked again; then the dark one next to it blinked on for a second but went dark.

Ben frowned. How could the tally for Interworld Four's number six transponder light up? It wasn't scheduled for now. In fact, the dark jewel showed that it wasn't in use; how could the tally have . . .

His eyes widened as the thought penetrated, and he whirled to check the schedule.

"Wicked man, you have bypasssed me!" the snake hissed, and struck at Tony, fangs dripping.

Chapter 17

Tony leaped out of the way and the snake crashed into the panel—well, not crashed, really, since it went right through, being only an idea. The lights on the panel went crazy for a second before the cobra slithered back out. "You have defeated me in my duty! You must pay!" It reared up, hood spread, fangs gaping.

"But you've deserted your post," Tony pointed out. "What kind of alien thoughts are entering his mind while you're here trying for revenge?"

"Then I shall slay you quickly!" the snake hissed, and struck again.

Tony sprang high, and the scaly body swished past— only this time, he landed on Ben's head. "I'm going to put a thought into his brain," Tony said, "a thought of a pretty girl!"

The snake hissed in rage and struck.

Tony leaped aside, but not quite fast enough; fire scored his ribs. Then he was down on the panel again, the snake was coiling protectively around Ben's head, and Tony found himself puzzling how to rid Tony of the serpent for once and for all. Then he remembered that wasn't what St. Vidicon had sent him here to do and watched anxiously as Ben frantically punched buttons.

The signal was still coming through from Manhattan and transponder six wasn't due to be illuminated for four more hours. Ben only had to receive that signal, not send it, and its link was one of the smaller dishes. That might be time enough to restore power to the main dish. One way or another, it was the only way to get this program through to its destination. Ben punched buttons, routing the signal from Manhattan through to transponder six; the tally glowed, confirming the connection, then Ben picked up the phone and dialed the number for the earth station in California. "Hi, this is Ben from the New York link . . . Yes, I know you've lost *The Guided World*; we've had a disruption here. No time to explain—just look to Interworld Four, transponder six vertical . . . yeah, it's there, okay, take it. I'll send a full report as soon as we're done." Then he sat back and blew out a long shuddering breath, nearly limp with relief. The crisis was past.

But only temporarily. Reviving, he picked up the phone again and called the power company.

Tony paced the maroon corridor beside Father Vidicon. "Okay, the country is now receiving their favorite soap opera. Tell me I did the right thing."

"You did the right thing," Father Vidicon said, amused. "If they hadn't watched that soap opera, they would have watched another, and at least *The Guided World* isn't glorifying premarital sex or organized crime."

"I suppose there's that," Tony admitted. "Of course, it could be more important that I saved Ben's job."

"Yes, we do have to balance society's needs against the individual person's," Father Vidicon agreed, "say—Sandy's."

Tony looked up, startled. "You don't mean I'm ignoring her needs!"

"It may seem that way to her at the moment," St. Vidicon said. "You made a good beginning sending roses, Tony. Be sure you follow it up."

"I will," Tony said, then realized that he had said it out loud to a computer monitor. He glanced around, face burning, but no one seemed to have heard him—no faces were prairie-dogging over the partition to see what he was talking about. He turned back to the screen just in time to see Father Vidicon wink before the screen cleared.

Tony glanced at the clock, remembering Sandy and wondering if it was time for the next step in his campaign to win her back.

Sandy waited in an agony of impatience before she left the building; she knew it would take five minutes to walk to Nepenthe, and she didn't want to get there first.

She needn't have worried; Tony was sitting at their usual table against the wall, staring morosely into a cup watching the foam settle. Sandy felt her self-confidence renewing and sauntered over to him. "Hi, hacker."

His head snapped up, his eyes locked on hers. His mouth moved once before sound came out, and it was hoarse and strained. "Hi." Then, a bit stronger, "Hi, beautiful."

Sandy tried to hide her glow. "Mind if I sit down?"

"No, not at all! I mean, please! Uh . . . what can I get you? Raspberry mocha?"

He'd remembered. "Yeah, thanks."

"Coming right up." Tony darted away.

Sandy sat by herself, realizing that she was in a stronger negotiating position than she'd thought. Well, actually, she hadn't thought—she'd just been ready to agree to anything he wanted so long as they were dating again.

Even marriage.

Now, though, it looked as though she could make a few demands, such as not accepting a ring yet.

She suddenly realized that wasn't a priority. Maybe the folklore she'd grown up hearing was true, maybe she should find out how good a lover he was first.

The mocha appeared in front of her. She looked up from it to see Tony's anxious gaze as he sat. "You, uh . . . have a good week?"

From anybody else that would have been a probe, but she knew Tony was only trying to make small talk. "Things have been pretty quiet. Yours?"

"Just the usual." He thought of telling her that "the usual" had included a company of actors that was about to self-implode and a frantic earth station operator, but decided against it. Honesty didn't mean answering questions she hadn't asked, after all—especially if they might make her think he was delusional.

"So life as usual, huh?" Sandy lifted her cup.

"I can hope," Tony said softly. "I'd like 'usual' to include going out with you—except that life is never 'usual' when you're in it."

Sandy took a breath; the boy was definitely improving. "I think that could be arranged," she said carefully, "but there'd have to be some after-show activity."

"Anything you want!"

He was so earnest, so forlorn, that Sandy realized she could make whatever demands she wanted—and that made her realize she should keep them moderate. It would be wrong, very wrong, to take advantage of the poor guy.

But it was wrong to take advantage of her, too.

"All I want is for nature to take its course," she said slowly.

"And hope that it passes?" Tony asked, heartened.

Sandy looked up at him in surprize, then smiled with affection. Tony might have been callow and naive, but he was so *real*.

Cute, too.

And he was the only guy who hadn't dated her just because he wanted sex. "Let's hope nature gets an 'A,'" she said.

"Even if it has to plagiarize?"

Sandy stared in surprize, then felt her smile grow into a grin. "I have no objection to your reading the occasional book," she said. "Found any good ones lately?"

The topic shifted into literary gear without a tremor— and that easily, the relationship was back on.

Even as he climbed into bed—his own, and alone— Tony was still marvelling that the evening had gone so much better than his usual dates. The conversation hadn't lagged, not a single awkward pause, and Sandy had actually seemed to enjoy his company. Must be her generous nature.

Then another possible explanation occurred to him, and he stiffened, staring up at the lights on the ceiling. *Thank you, St. Vidicon*, he thought.

There was no answering admonition, no booming voice, but he did feel an aura of amusement and satisfaction that quickly passed but left in its wake the conviction that he wasn't alone.

•　•　•

Tony dreamed, of course—dreamed that he was walking down that humid hallway that was beginning to feel more and more organic, and Father Vidicon was saying, "So I've faced three of them now, and can only wonder when I'll confront Finagle himself."

"Sounds pretty busy." Tony frowned. "How can there be people claiming you've worked miracles to protect them from things going wrong?"

"There's time for the occasional rescue while I'm walking down this hallway waiting for the next ambush," Father Vidicon said, "though I must admit you have helped considerably."

"Quid pro quo." Tony grinned. "Thanks for helping me with Sandy."

"Me?" Father Vidicon said with exaggerated innocence, but when Tony chuckled, he admitted, "Well, I might have put a thought or two into your mind. Which reminds me—how are the dance lessons going?"

"Me? The original two-left-feet fool? I tried to learn when I was twelve and tried again when I was sixteen, and the best I can say of it was that I didn't trip anybody *else*."

"Perhaps, but your midteens are ten years in the past, aren't they? You may find your coordination has improved considerably—and I asked how you're doing *now*."

Tony sighed and confessed.

"Don't think of your legs as having to hold up your body," the dancing teacher advised. "Think of it as supported by invisible wires from above you—that's it! Back straight, shoulders square—posture is very important. Now, step, rock, back, and step!"

The music started, and neither Tony nor his partner spoke, concentrating fiercely on getting the steps right. He felt vaguely disloyal to Sandy, dancing with another woman even if it was just a dance class. He consoled himself with the thought that she wasn't very pretty. None of the girls here were.

But, truth to tell, neither were the women he passed on the street, which was strange, since only a few months ago, he had been amazed how many beautiful women there were on his way to work. The traitorous thought crossed his mind that having met Sandy, only the most dazzling of women would seem beautiful to him, but of course that couldn't be true.

"Step - rock - back - step!"

Tony did.

Gail stepped into the studio to wave before she left the radio station. "See you, Gordon."

Gordon looked up in surprize. "You're leaving early. It's scarcely drive time."

"Came in early, too," Gail said. "My little girl's in a grade-school pageant, so I knew I'd have to bow out at four."

Gordon shuddered. "Better you than me. Good luck."

"You too, Gordon. Station's all yours. See you tomorrow."

"Tomorrow, Gail." Gordon gave a quick wave, then hit the program button and began talking into the mike. "That was the Everly Brothers with 'Wake Up, Little Susie.' We'll have another twelve in a row up for you in just a minute here on Rollin' Oldies One-oh-one, but first, let's check the traffic report. How're things at Twelfth and C, Carmen?" He toggled the "remote" and eased in the sound of helicopter rotors. After all, everyone knew Carmen prowled the back streets in a Bugmobile and hiked to the intersections from a parking place, and they hadn't actually said she was in a helicopter, so what was the harm?

"Well, Gordon, we've hit a snarl here," Carmen's voice said. "Only a fender-bender, fortunately, and the officers are here taking the accident report, but it's slowing westbound traffic to a snail's pace. I'd recommend you homebound people try Church Street all the way to Eighth Street, then double back to Avenue C after the snarl. I'll talk to you from Second and Avenue K in . . ."

A raw, monotonous beat crashed in, bass drum and snare with some sort of string, and a driving nasal voice chanted,

> "School's a waste
> And job's a paste,
> And cops'll watch
> Your every move.
> So leave . . ."

Gordon made a frantic dive for the studio monitor and yanked it down to a bare mumble. "What the hell?"

The phone rang. Gordon grabbed it and pasted on the smile. "Rollin' Oldies One-oh-one! Sorry, no requests just now, gotta little problem . . ."

"It's going to be a really big problem really fast if you can't get that racket off our station," Josh's voice said. "What the hell got into you, playing that teenage garbage during drive time?"

The boss, of course! "I ain't playing it, Josh." Gordon swept the board with a glance. "It's not coming through the board at all."

"You kidding? *Everything* comes through the board."

"Yeah, I know." Inspiration struck. "Everything except . . ." Gordon turned to the automation computer and saw the activity light fluttering. "Josh, it's the computer! It kicked in early!"

"That kind of music on *our* computer?"

"It's a computer, Josh, and we're hooked into a music service. It feeds all kinds of music."

"You mean somebody actually broadcasts that sludge?"

Gordon froze, listening to the music. That repetitive beat, inhumanly regular, and the teenage lack of resonance . . . "Josh, that ain't coming from the music service. If that's a pro band, I'll eat the hard drive!"

"A garage band?" Josh sounded confounded. "How could they be on our station?"

"Because they hacked into our computer, that's how! Haven't you heard the kids around town griping because none of the stations plays their kind of music? Get our computer consultant down here fast or we'll lose every listener we've got! 'Bye, now—I've got a few phones to answer." He hung up, rolled his eyes up to Heaven for a brief "St. Vidicon, protect us from Finagle!" under his breath, then punched another line and picked up the phone again. "Rollin' Oldies, but not our usual style . . ."

"Hey, Tony!"

Tony looked up at Harve, feeling the thrill of the call to battle. "Something come up?"

"Just your cup of coffee! Get down to WOLD-FM right away—some kid has hacked into their automation computer!"

Tony didn't stop to ask how they knew it was a kid, just grabbed his laptop and headed down to the garage and slipped into a company car. Once outside the steel box of the building, he turned on the radio and realized why they were sure the hacker was a teenager.

•   •   •

Bells were ringing, and they weren't on Santa's sleigh. Gordon took a quick look at the phone and saw every line glowing. "Send an engineer, St. Vidicon! 'Scuse me, now—I've got phones to answer." He hit another line. "Rollin' Old . . . yeah, I know it's a shock. Wires crossed somewhere; it's not what we're playing . . . How? Well, we think some kid has hacked into our computer . . . Thanks, I'll need it. I've got it turned way down low, but I have to keep an ear on it, and I'm out of ibuprofen . . . No, you don't really need to bring me any; why should my problems be your problems? Don't worry, I'll get it off the air as soon as our engineers figure out how to disconnect it. G'bye, now!" He hit another line. "Rollin' Oldies One-oh . . . Yeah, I'm real sorry about that, ma'am, but there isn't a whole lot I can do about it yet—the wonders of modern computers, you know? We'll get back to the British Invasion as soon as we . . . Yeah, you too, thanks." He punched another line. "Rollin' Oldies One-oh . . ." The doorbell rang. He looked up in relief, and said, "Lemme put you on hold just a sec. The repairman has arrived." He punched hold and ran to let Tony in. "Thank heavens you're here! There's the computer! Good luck!"

Tony almost said he wouldn't need it but bit back the show of arrogance and only grinned as the DJ hurried off to answer another call. Tony patched in his laptop, powered up, and gazed at the screen, letting his consciousness drift into the circuit, trying to do as St. Vidicon would as his fingers flew over the keyboard. He knew St. Vidicon was with him when the program became more real to him than the room around him and he found himself swimming through a tide of ones and zeros. But it was a rip tide, torn by another stream surging through a jury-rigged gateway that shouldn't have been there.

Know your enemy—or at least, your opponent. Before Tony did anything to close that ramshackle gateway, he swam through it and upstream to find out where the alien signal was coming from.

In a bedroom on the other side of town, the cheering slackened and the short, pudgy African-American teenager clapped her hands over her keyboard. "I am so wicked!"

"You go, Randy!" The bass player slapped her shoulder. "You got us on the air!"

"Easy picking," Miranda assured him. "Seems they never stopped to think somebody might want to change their playlist."

The lead singer had his ear to the radio. "That really us? Sounds thin."

"Hey, they ain't got the kind of equipment I do," Randy protested. "'Course they're gonna sound coarse!"

"'Course they're gonna sound coarse!" the lead guitar player repeated, musing, and the drummer took it up. "'Course they're gonna sound coarse!" He hit the kick drum and added a lick on the snare topped by the tom-tom, then repeated it again and again.

"'Course they're gonna sound coarse!" the rest of the group chanted. "'Course they're gonna sound coarse!" They picked up their instruments.

Randy glanced at the CD light to make sure the recording was still spinning, then heard the music behind her and decided the nature of the problem had changed. Could she put this band on the air live?

Of course she could! She was almost tempted to tell those fat middle-aged listeners, "This is Randy, bringing you the music of today!" but there was no point in giving the cops her name and address, was there? After all, what they were doing was technically illegal.

"Tell the computer guy I want that racket stopped *now!*" Josh raged over the phone. "Then tell him to trace the hacker! I want that kid in jail for life!"

"Yeah, sure, Chief, but he's working as fast as he can." Gordon glanced at the engineer, who sat motionless, gazing at the automation computer's screen with a very thoughtful look on his face. It wasn't really a lie—hadn't Edison said brainwork was the toughest kind of all? And he should have known, he had hired enough brains to be an expert.

"Tell him to unplug the blasted thing!"

"He can't, it's hard-wired," Gordon explained. "So's the input from the music service."

"Tell him to cut the lines!"

"First off, he says that if we do that, it will take a day and a half to get the system back on-line," Gordon explained, "and the kid will just hack in again anyway. Says he has to find out how the hacker got in and unhack him. It'll be quicker and a lot more permanent."

Josh groaned.

A harried middle-aged woman called up the stairs, "Miranda! Time for dinner!" But she heard the music and started the climb, shaking her head with a sigh. Those kids would never hear her over that noise—and if it was that loud, they were practicing something new, not listening to a cut they'd recorded earlier. They wouldn't be happy about having to shut down—but they all knew what her cooking was like, and in teenagers, appetite just might win out over the need for self-expression. Good thing she'd cooked enough for a small army.

• • •

It was a tough problem for Tony—how to get the kids off the air, without leaving a trace for a security expert to follow. They seemed like good kids, and there was no point in getting them in trouble for a prank. A mighty big prank, mind you, and one that was costing the station a lot of money, but nonetheless a prank. He could scramble the code as a first step . . . He dived into the data stream and flailed about, making ones and zeros crash into each other, changing the music to static—and was shocked to see them being restored to their positions and the music clearing.

That was why—here came an unearthly-looking creature with more heads than Tony could count and at least a hundred tentacles, carefully setting the numbers back in order with a uniform distance between them. "Who the heck are *you?*" Tony cried.

"I am a Centimanes; I am the Hundred-Handed," the creature replied,

"A Centimanes?" Tony stared. "You can't be inside a circuit! You're a Titan! You're supposed to be the size of a mountain!"

"We are magical creatures." The monstrosity didn't miss a beat, or a digit. "I can take any size I deem necessary for the service of Order."

"Well, you're certainly performing a disservice to the radio station that's trying to broadcast oldies!"

"That is no concern of mine," the Centimanes answered. "I am the Servant of Order; I see to it that the data stream is kept neat and tidy."

Tony frowned. "And you don't worry about whose data you're ordering?"

"Neatness counts," the monster answered. "Tidiness is next to godliness."

With a shock, Tony realized he had met a supernatural obsessive-compulsive. "You're only dealing with the symptoms," he protested. "You have to attack the problem at its source."

"I care not whence the digits come," the Centimanes returned. "I only care that they stand neatly."

A wave toppled the numbers—a minor power surge. The Centimanes righted them.

Tony made another try. "The numbers keep scrambling because there are two information flows. Let's go find the junction."

But the Centimanes kept tapping numbers with its hundred hands. "I must be sure they stand in order."

With a flash of inspiration, Tony realized how he could lead the micro-monster to solve the radio station's problem without hurting Randy. "Let's go!" He shot away through the silicon, reaching out a hand to topple numbers like a child running a stick along a picket fence. The Centimanes gave a squawk of horror and dashed after him, righting numbers as it went.

Randy had an audio mixer for the band, of course—she had made it in electronics class, and the instructor had been so delighted he had given her an "A." She had designed it with an input for each instrument plus five singers' mikes, and they were all plugged in and showing green on her peak meter. With a devilish grin, she plugged the output into her computer, called up the audio card's mixer, made sure the levels were right, then routed the signal into the data stream. "You're on the air—live!"

Chapter 18

The drummer hit a triumphant lick topped with a cymbal crash and the lead singer began his chant:

> " 'Course it's coarse,
> Our music hoarse!
> Remember its source
> Is dirt and force!"

Nodding her head with the beat, Randy presided over the middle class of the city hearing from its angry youth—and about time, too.

Riding Randy's data stream, Tony shot through the gate she had opened into the automation computer. Ahead, he could see the other gate, the one she had closed to stop the flow from the music service. Now the problem was opening the one and closing the other, and he certainly couldn't do both at the same time; they were gates of digits, and he only had two hands.

But he knew someone who had more.

The gate that held back the music service was only a quadratic equation; Tony wrenched the factors apart and the digit-encoded music flowed. It collided with Randy's stream. Digits toppled one upon another, making for utter confusion.

Keening like an ambulance, the Centimanes dived into the maelstrom, its hundred hands sorting bunches of digits and righting others. It would take the creature only a second or two to straighten them both out. Tony had no more time than that to figure out how to shunt Randy's data stream away from the transmitter.

In Randy's room, the band froze, staring at the radio, which was emitting a blast of static that drowned out the band's music. "They're trying to jam us," she called over the roar. "I'll set up another gate!" Her fingers flew over the keys.

"Jam!" the drummer cried, and tore into a solo. The rest of the band cheered and added their throbbing notes to underscore his beat. The drummer topped his lick with a cymbal, and the bass took up a solo of his own.

Ahead, another gate materialized, but Tony shot through it before it could close and grabbed ones and zeros, assembling them into an algorithm that blocked it open. He swam on, searching for the output to the transmitter.

There it lay ahead, with Randy's data stream flowing through it! He rocketed on, formulating the equation that would divert hip-hop.

On the other side of the gate he circled back, fighting the current flow, and set his shoulder to the gate as he recited the code to shut it. Inch by inch, the gate began to close.

With a roar, the Centimanes slapped tentacles onto the gate, pushing against Tony. "The flow must not be impeded!'

"Why not?" Tony shouted. "It wasn't here in the first place! This gate is only shutting off the data stream that was intended to flow through this circuit!"

"I care not for was—I care for is!"

Tony gave a recursive curse and, while it was circulating between himself and the Centimanes, ran his hands over the gate, sensing its form, translating it into code in his head. When he had it, he worked out the countercode and recited it as he proceeded to take the gate apart bit by bit.

It took only nanoseconds and left him staring at the Centimanes through a snow-storm of ones and zeros that the Centimanes automatically righted and spaced as it demanded, "What have you done, mortal?"

"Eliminated the gateway," Tony said, "and the invading music with it. This circuit is as it was designed, creature. Keep it well!" With that, he withdrew his spirit-extension and found himself staring at the screen, fingers poised over the keyboard.

A hand slapped Tony's shoulder. "You did it!"

Tony frowned, looking up at a strange, middle-aged beefy face. "Sure. Kid stuff."

"I want the kid who did that stuff!"

"Uh, Tony Ricci," the announcer said hesitantly, "this is Josh Largan, our owner."

"It's not that easy to trace a hacker," Tony said, "especially after I've cut 'em off. Why would you want the kid, anyway? Didn't really do that much damage. There's no need to get her in trouble."

"Trouble?" Largan bellowed. "I want to hire her!

Any kid who can break into this computer, can figure out ways to keep other kids out—and at a quarter of the price I have to pay you!"

Tony was only too glad to pack up his laptop and head for the door—after all, he had a date that night.

The negative side—or maybe very positive side—of being back together was that Tony was much less inclined to resist temptation, if it meant hurting Sandy's feelings and maybe losing her. Sandy, on the other hand, was much less inclined to offer that temptation, or to push for anything more than petting. The result was mutual confusion and growing frustration.

Basically, Tony's approach was not to seek what wasn't offered, and Sandy wasn't about to offer anything that he would probably reject, no matter that he wanted it badly but was trying not to take advantage of her.

On a silvery Saturday, they went to roam the city, kicking through the snow, gossiping, stepping into coffee shops whenever the chill crept in, laughing over the newspapers at a bistro, strolling through three different museums, walking along a sidewalk lined with artists' pictures and pointing out several to remember, then going to another bistro to compare notes about the pictures they'd thought worth comment—but not exchanging those comments where the artists could hear. Museums, shopping for knick-knacks and paintings, talk and laughter and the occasional kiss made up a day Tony knew he would never forget.

When they arrived back at her apartment building, he said, "We're still on for the movies tonight, aren't we?"

"Of course," Sandy said with a smile.

"Okay, I'd better run home and change." Tony gave her a quick kiss. "Six-thirty?"

"Yeah . . . sure." Sandy sounded surprised, maybe disappointed, but gave him a kiss back—only this time, it lasted a bit longer, and when Tony backed away, she seemed more cheerful.

He went home, changed, picked her up, and had an evening that would have rivalled the day if Sandy hadn't kept glancing at him out of the corners of her eyes as though wondering if he were still there. Trying to reassure her, he held her hand whenever she wasn't eating popcorn, and it seemed to help a little.

They came out, happily dissecting the movie, but when Tony started to turn into their favorite club, Sandy held back, and said, "I don't think so. Not tonight."

"What?" Tony looked back surprised, then said, "Okay, then. Home?"

Sandy nodded, and he flagged down a cab. He kept asking her opinion of one aspect of the movie after another but received very short answers; Sandy seemed very nervous for some reason, and Tony started feeling as though he were in her way. When she turned the key in the lock of her outer door, Tony said, "Guess I'd better go, then. Thanks for a wonderful day."

"What?" Sandy turned, astounded. "Aren't you coming in?"

"If I'm invited," Tony said. "I'm not assuming that I'm welcome every night."

Sandy stood staring at him for a moment, then said very softly, "Thank you, darling. You were right; this is one of those rare evenings that should end here."

Tony forced a smile, making it as warm as he could, and kissed her on the cheek—only she moved her head, and his lips met hers instead. It was a long and lingering kiss, but when it ended, Sandy pressed a finger over his mouth, whispered, "Good night," and was gone through the door.

Tony stood staring at the doorbell for a few minutes, sorting out his confusions, then turned and went down the steps. He was surprized to find the taxi still there. He leaned down to the window and asked, "Are you free?"

"Sure am," the driver said. "I always stay to make sure my fares get in their doors. Pays off sometimes, too."

"This is one of those times, I guess." Tony slid into the back seat and gave her the address.

It was a cold, crisp December night. Outside the large building the snow sparkled on the ground, falling through the air like the pearl white seasonal sequins that would be heavily discounted in the next few weeks. Inside the building the white of fresh, sterile paint made the cold hallways even colder as Beth headed toward the studio once again.

As she opened the heavy metal door, one that always reminded her of a high-security bank vault, she was greeted with a blast of hot air. She took a deep breath and inhaled the heady scent of blue and pink gels baking over blazing lights, black cables freshly uncoiled, and the sweet aroma of canned coffee and melting duct tape.

Ah, there was nothing like the smell of Christmas, and to Beth the Christmas holidays always began with the WBEG Winter Pledge Drive. Yes, there was nothing like begging for money to get you into the true spirit of the holidays. That reminded her to make a mental note to call her mother when she got home.

She stepped into the studio and promptly sneezed as the searing heat of the lights for the set warmed her in

an instant. She'd been going back and forth all day—
and most of the week—between the warm control
room, the cold hallways, and the hot studio. Something
was clearly wrong with the heating controls in the
building. Add that to the long list of things that were not
working consistently, and it was amazing they were still
on the air.

Dodging phone volunteers and camera crew mean-
dering back to their positions from the break between
the breaks, and nimbly navigating around the dozens of
cables strewn across the floor, Beth finally arrived at
the cameras and began checking the tally lights for any
improvements.

"Seven minutes till the break," a tall man with a
bushy red mustache called out, then looked over at her.
"Any luck?"

"You tell me," Beth replied. "Did they work last
break?"

He shook his head, then readjusted his headset and
turned the volume up on the remote pack clipped to the
waistband on his jeans. She sighed and turned back to
the camera, slipping on the attached headset. "Mac?"
she asked, pressing down the TALK button.

"Yo," he replied, slightly out of breath as if he had
just run into position. He probably had. She could hear
the distinctive crunch of potato chips on the other end.
"Put up Camera Three."

She glanced at the monitor and saw the same image
as the one in her viewfinder, but the red tally light
wasn't lit. She looked over at the other cameras and noticed a red light on Camera One. Well, that tally light
worked, but by all explanations it shouldn't.

"Punch up Camera One," she insisted. A moment
later the image of a close-up on a telephone flashed
onto the monitor—but the tally light lit up on Camera

Three. She shook her head sadly. What was going on? The tally lights, like everything else, had been acting up for the last three days, and the engineers were working around the clock to fix the problems for tonight's breaks. The problem was, they couldn't find a problem. It defied explanation. The equipment only seemed to work when it wanted to. That was really nothing new in the TV industry, in this station in particular, but it was usually a little more reliable than this.

Suddenly the chatter in the room died down as a short man in a bad toupee entered the room, followed by an entourage of assistants. Beth took a deep breath, took off the headset, and marched over to him as Bill, the tall mustached man, helped him settle into the comfortable, Victorian-style armchair on the mock-library section of the set.

"Mr. Halloway, I'm Beth Grady, your director for the pledge breaks tonight."

The man smiled at her in a polite, distant manner as his assistants and Gerald Mann, the producer, began to fawn over him and get him ready.

Mr. Halloway was the newly-elected mayor and had built and won the election on his "Education for All" platform. He had openly touted the pedigree and excellence of the local PBS station, WBEG, and therefore had insisted on being the cohost for the Saturday conclusion of their Winter Pledge Drive. The other host, Stanwick Sage, a WBEG employee who oversaw production of a local show, was sitting on the round central podium surrounded by pledge gifts. He was a pro at keeping the pledge breaks quick-paced, entertaining, and on track. The mayor appeared to have none of those qualities. Beth doubted he could write a speech himself, let alone remember it.

That was why the little technical inconveniences

such as reversed tally lights and malfunctioning Tele-PrompTers, were a major problem now, and why Beth was sure her pet ulcer had developed a sister. The mayor was less than an amateur at live television and had been very hostile to the idea of looking foolish in any way.

Beth glanced at the phone volunteers and shuddered slightly, wishing there had not been a mistake with how the groups had been assigned. The local Bankers' Association was supposed to be here, but instead they had somehow gotten switched with a new group of some sort of sci-fi fan club. All the volunteers were wearing black cloaks with large green eyes painted on the backs.

Now, Beth had nothing against sci-fi fan clubs or dressing up to be on television. She liked to role-play herself and attended sci-fi/fantasy conventions whenever she could. WBEG welcomed their support as much as that of any group in the community—last night, the phone volunteers had been the *Doctor Who* fan club for WBEG's annual marathon, a very entertaining and nice bunch of people. Most of them had dressed up as characters from the show, several had tripped over very long scarfs either they or someone else was wearing, and one man had even tried to bring along his small schnauzer, dressed in tin foil and named K-9. Compared to them, green-eyed cloaks were tame, but there was something about the group that gave Beth a very uneasy feeling— as though they were watching her and waiting for something. Maybe it was the green eyes on their cloaks. That was what she told herself as she headed back to the control room. The volunteers could wait, and the producer could deal with the mayor—she had a break to run.

"Three minutes to air," Mac told her, as she dashed into the control room, realizing halfway down the hall how close they must be to air time. She threw on the headset and plopped down in the director's chair. It retaliated for the abuse by rolling backward into the wall. She grabbed the edge of the table and slid the chair back up to it, then flipped a bunch of switches, pressed a few buttons, and spoke into a small microphone.

"Ready in Master Control?" she asked.

Static answered; then a smooth voice, low and cool, spoke.

"Ready."

Beth frowned, trying to figure out who the engineer was, since it was obviously not Fred, the high-pitched computer nerd who'd been scheduled. Shrugging it off, she glanced at Mac, who sat behind the switcher, fingers poised above the buttons and twitching from too much coffee. "Ready?"

He nodded. She checked with the CG and Audio operators, then flipped on the permanent TALK button on her headset. "Ready in the studio?"

"Ready," Bill replied.

"One minute till air," she announced, looking at the red numbers on the countdown clock ticking away. "Whenever you're ready, go ahead and give it to us, Master Control."

There was an almost imperceptible flash in the image on the program monitor, one of ten monitors that were set up at the other end of the room across what the crew affectionately called "the Grand Canyon," empty space between the control desk and the monitors.

"We're hot and live with thirty seconds to go!" Beth declared. The nerves were killing her. She was so nauseous she was afraid she might throw up, and gripped the cool surface of the table for support.

"Fifteen seconds."

She closed her eyes and silently offered up a prayer

to St. Vidicon to keep the equipment working until they were off the air. Luckily it was only a six-minute break.

"Um, Tony—I could use a little help here . . ."

"Whassamatta?" Tony swam up from the depths of sleep, saw St. Vidicon's face, and tried to remember that he always felt refreshed after one of these errands. "Who's in trouble now?"

"Beth, that young television director you helped last June," St. Vidicon said. "Her equipment is rebelling again."

"Gotcha, boss." Tony stood up, looking around him at the maroon tunnel.

"Oh, and—you might need this." Father Vidicon pressed something into Tony's hand. A quick glance showed Tony it was a rosary. "Uh, thanks," he said, and stuffed it into his pocket, then spread his hands. "How do I get to the TV station?"

"Like this," Father Vidicon said, and Tony felt the floor drop out from under him.

"Ten seconds."

Under the table, Beth's leg was twitching anxiously.

"Ready open mike, ready cue talent, ready fade in one," she called. "Five . . . four . . . three . . . Open mike, cue talent, fade in one!"

They were live and on the air. Whether or not they stayed that way was up to the good Lord and St. Vidicon.

Flashes of light and miniature glowing squiggles flew past, the speed increasing. Finally there was an explosion of light and a pyjama-clad man tumbled to the floor of a pitch-black tunnel.

Hold on to your gigabytes and pass the Pepto—Tony had a new assignment.

He got to his feet and immediately fell down again as the floor moved beneath him. He looked down and saw, covering the floor of the tunnel (and taking up most of the corridor), four huge cables, each the width of a sidewalk and all moving around under his feet. They started to sway and jump more and he scurried to stand, bracing himself against the flexible rubber-coated wall. Then he realized that the tunnel was no longer completely dark and that each cable was a different color—red, green, yellow, and blue. He looked down the tunnel for the source of the light, but before he could pin it down, the cables began to shake violently, the red one in the middle shaking most of all. He gripped the walls for support and waited to see what new monster was savaging the world's technology this time.

He didn't have long to wait. A line of men and women, only as tall as his waist if that, appeared. They were dressed in brightly-colored long-sleeved shirts with coordinating trousers and vests. On their heads were pointed hats, the tips of which glowed as though they encased light bulbs. They looked like garden gnomes—like the tacky plastic kind you see in your neighbor's yard—only they had to be much smaller and were moving very quickly. In fact, they were running. Each one was carrying a giant letter, white and faintly glowing. The first one was capitalized and eventually Tony glimpsed a period running to catch up with the rest of the sentence. There seemed to be hundreds of them, racing through the tunnel and trying not to panic as a comma slipped and fell. Tony rushed to help him up. "Excuse me—what's going on?"

The gnome roughly shoved him out of the way,

grabbed the comma, and took off at lightning speed to jump back into the place he had deserted. The others brushed passed him, not even noticing him as he leaped aside to make way for a giant O. More than five hundred of them ran past, disappearing into the tunnel once more, the light going with them.

Since Tony didn't have anywhere else to go, he ran after the gnomes. He fell several times on the tricky, moving cables before he finally saw light ahead of him—red, this time, and coming fast. Two gnomes raced toward him, holding an enormous glowing red ball between them.

"Watch out! Tally light coming through!" one of them shouted.

Tony jumped back against the wall and the glowing ball shot past him at top gnome speed. He frowned after it, then turned to go on down the tunnel after the letter carriers.

Finally, he came to a glowing blue hole in the side of the tunnel. He took a deep breath and jumped through it, landing on a green cable on the other side. Looking around, he saw he was in another tunnel just like the first. He followed it, moving warily, since he really had no idea where he was going. At last the floor began to slope upward, the slope steepening until Tony was climbing more than walking, feeling as though he were three years old and trying to climb up a slippery steep slide.

Finally, he came to the top and crawled through a hole that was slightly larger then the biggest letter. He found himself in a glowing room with metal walls. Looking up, he saw that the light came from a hole in the ceiling that gave a glimpse of a more brightly-lit room above. Looking down again he saw, about a third of the way from the back wall, a huge blackboard with slim metal bands forming rows in equal widths across it. Half a hundred gnomes were standing on platforms beside the blackboard, holding their letters in front of them, while still more were climbing into place and even more were waiting to get on. In front of the blackboard ran three slightly taller gnomes, all dressed in yellow with gold stars on the tips of their hats. One held a scroll of what looked to be computer printout, shouting out words to the other two, who were arranging the letter-gnomes in order. The entire blackboard was moving upward into the even more brightly-glowing room above them.

Their speed seemed to vary, and as Tony stepped forward, hoping to get a better look, he noticed that there was another blackboard behind the first that was moving down, toward the room he was in. Letter-gnomes stood on the thin platforms and jumped down as soon as they were within three feet of the floor; then, still holding their letters, ran back to the larger group, waiting to get cycled back in.

They were making words and sentences. A speech. Suddenly he realized what he was seeing. He had been sent to help out with the often-malfunctioning PBS station WBEG once again. A few months before he had fought against a swarm of gremlkins who had attacked the character generator. The problems had escalated beyond that now, just when the station seemed to be doing better financially, and the equipment was either not working at all or working sporadically. He'd been sent inside the system to find out what was wrong and fix it, paying particular attention to the tally lights. He realized that what he was looking at was obviously the inner workings of the TelePrompTer. However, he had never in his life heard that TelePrompTers were operated by gnomes.

A voice boomed inside the room, echoing off the walls. "Ten seconds . . . Five . . . four . . . three . . ."

Tony realized the "room" was connected to the intercom system.

"Two," the voice said. "One . . . we're off the air."

Every gnome in the room, except the ones on the platforms, collapsed, taking deep gulping breaths as if they had just come up from an underwater battle. No more gnomes appeared on the blackboard in front and gnomes riding down on the back blackboard jumped off it, tossing their letters toward the outer edge of the room and falling to the floor in a crumpled heap. Eventually both blackboards slowed to a stop and the gnomes, having recovered somewhat, slowly stood up, holding on to each other for support.

"The next break is in twenty-one minutes," the echoing voice boomed.

There was a resounding cheer from the gnomes, and they all charged toward Tony.

Chapter 19

Once again, the gnomes barely noticed Tony as they ditched their letters and jumped into the hole that led back into the tunnel. He watched each one slide down the slope crying out in joy and running off into the tunnel—which, Tony realized, was the cable that connected the camera to the control room.

The room was emptying fast. In a few moments he would be alone and more confused than ever, and given some of his recent missions, that was really saying something. Before he could think about the consequences, he threw himself in front of the exit hole. Four or five gnomes promptly collided with each other, creating a gnome pile-up. Several of them cried out, and a younger one even squeaked in panic.

One of the yellow-clad gnomes—a sturdy-looking, middle-aged female with small spectacles—skidded to a stop near the pile and glared at Tony furiously. "What exactly did you think you were doing, young man?!?"

she demanded. "Do you realize how many gnomes you could have hurt?!? And every one of us is important if we're going to help the station survive the night!"

Tony stood up as soon as the gnomes had de-piled themselves, all glaring at him ferociously. He looked around apologetically, brushing off his clothes. "I'm sorry. I just need to know what's going on. Who are you?"

Several of the gnomes harrumphed and a few laughed. The yellow woman looked at him skeptically. "You don't look like an imp or a gremlin. Are you the one damaging the system?"

"Oh no," Tony said quickly, eyeing some of the more burly gnomes who were shaking their fists at him. "I've been sent to help."

"Sent?" another gnome, this one various shades of brown, demanded. "Sent by whom?!?"

"St. Vidicon." Tony figured he might as well be honest, since they probably didn't know who Father Vidicon was anyway—but a murmur of surprise and gasps of reverence echoed through the steel chamber. In a single smooth motion all the gnomes swept off their hats and bowed their heads. After a moment of silence they replaced their hats and looked at him with new respect.

All but the yellow lady. "Prove it," she snapped.

Prove it? How? Tony stared, at a loss, then remembered Father Vidicon's gift. He felt in his pocket and pulled out the rosary.

The yellow lady gasped, staring.

So did Tony. He had never before seen a rosary made from computer chips and strung on a strand of fiber-optic cable. The cross that dangled from it was made from four burned-out capacitors.

The gnomes murmured and took off their hats,

bowing their heads. The yellow one nodded, apparently satisfied.

Tony, however, was still confused. "How did you hear of Father Vidicon? He's scarcely been martyred yet."

"Silly boy," an older gray-haired gnome with a pocket protector and slight potbelly answered. "We operate clocks and watches and hourglasses and sundials!" He paused. "Well, okay, not sundials—but time doesn't matter to Technomes!"

"Technomes?" Tony asked. He had never heard of such a thing.

The gnomes were outraged. "Who do you think runs the stoplights and the telephone wires?!?" one demanded.

"And the TVs and VCRs and microwave ovens! Who runs those?!?"

Tony was confused. "Well, electricity, cables, sound waves . . ."

He was cut off by a rush of voices. "And what keeps clocks ticking in a power outage?!?"

"What if there's a short in the system? Who runs it then?"

"Who did Thomas Edison think he was, inventing that light bulb contraption? Have you ever been inside one? It's horribly hot in there!"

Tony was feeling overly overwhelmed. Luckily the woman in yellow seemed to notice and silenced her fellow Technomes with a wave, then turned back to Tony and held out her hand. "I'm Beatrice. Call me Bea."

"Tony."

They shook hands, and she led him back to the exit hole. "We'll explain it all to you back at the break room," she announced.

Tony tried to ask another question, but Bea reached

up and grabbed his shoulders, bending him down, then shoving him through the exit hole. He slid down the slide with a yelp and hit the bottom with a bouncing thud. He got to his feet as quickly as gravity allowed and stepped aside just in time to avoid being hit as Bea came sliding down behind him. She jumped up and took off running down the tunnel, the light on her hat showing the way.

"Follow me!" her voice cried, echoing down the tunnel behind her.

Tony took off after her, trying to keep up with her amazing speed and following the bouncing light in the tunnel ahead. He had been in TV studios before and knew there were yards and yards of cables. It would take forever to get out of the system.

He couldn't have been running for more than a minute or two when there was a flash of blue light and to his great surprise, he stepped out of the cable and into the back of the break room refrigerator. He stumbled forward and nearly landed facedown on a large plastic container of pudding, clearly intended for someone's lunch box—a normal-sized someone, not gnome-sized.

He looked around, amazed at the huge cartons of orange juice and half-and-half, the giant Tupperware containers full of salads and soups, and lots of other leftovers from lunches. Even a mammoth box of donuts peeked out around the mustard at the front. He'd never spent any time standing at the back shelf of a fridge before, but it was really quite fascinating. Bea looked at him and smiled.

"I told you time didn't matter to us," she declared with a hint of superiority. "We're sent wherever and whenever there's trouble." She looked around at the groups of gnomes who had already started to party down. Spaghetti streamers decorated the shelf ceiling and five gnomes were rolling two very large cans of soda over to another group. One gnome ran forward and stuck what had to be some sort of a tap into each can, and the gnomes promptly filed up in line, filling tiny mugs with cold, cool, carbonated goodness. Bea flashed him a smirk and a shrug. "And when the trouble's over, we like to relax."

Apparently gnomes had taken relaxation tips from college students. Some were chugging soda. There was a high-stakes poker game going, using colored sprinkles from several of the donuts and set up on a clementine with cherry tomatoes as stools. One group had even managed to get the lid off a container of red Jell-O and proceeded to swim in it. The bright light of the fridge bulb illuminated the whole rowdy scene, and Tony realized he had finally found the answer to whether or not the light stays on when the fridge door closes.

The brown-clothed gnome with the gray hair and pocket protector handed him a small ceramic mug and led him over to the soda keg as Bea followed.

"I'm Robert, call me Bob," he said, holding out a hand. Tony clasped it and shook. Bea led them into a quieter corner of the fridge, near the god-only-knows-how-long-it's-been-in-here lettuce. They sat down on a large, but mostly, empty bag of cheese cubes.

"We're Technomes," Bea repeated, once they were settled.

Tony shivered as the chill of the fridge began to creep into him, but focused on paying careful attention to what she was saying as she continued. "Our job is to make sure that things work. Obviously we can't fix everything—there's simply not enough of us—so we help out in emergencies."

"Most people don't even know we exist," Bob added, "but we've been around since the dawn of civilization. 'Course there wasn't as much to do back then, but we kept ourselves busy regluing tablets and making sure fires didn't go out too often."

"Mending socks," Bea added.

"Fixing quills and refilling ink. Then there was the Renaissance. Leonardo da Vinci kept us busy for a while."

"So did the Wright brothers, remember them?" Bea and Bob exchanged pained glances, and Bea turned back to Tony. "You know, we did stuff like that. But these days we're run off our feet. We've even had to divide into subgroups."

"Which are?" Tony prompted.

"I'm a school gnome," Bea declared proudly. "I help straighten up teachers' desk drawers, unjam the stapler, scrub the bad stains off the blackboard, and such. Then there are the computer gnomes who basically have their own sub branch of Net gnomes, who fix problems on the Internet, get Web sites back up and running, destroy spam, and try to head off viruses. Traffic gnomes control the stoplights and walk/don't walk signs. They also freelance in construction work. That's where we got the red tally lights—we borrowed them from the streetlight on the corner."

"But that means someone could get hurt," Tony exclaimed.

"No, no, no," Bea assured him. "We set the yellow lights on blink. Whenever you see that happen—stoplights stuck blinking on one color—it's because the traffic gnomes had to borrow the light for something else."

Suddenly Bea frowned and looked at a green-, yellow-, and red-clad gnome drying off from a swim through the Jell-O. "Edgar, when you pulled the red light, did you remember to set the yellows on blink?"

Edgar frowned, trying to remember.

They heard the muffled sound of a distant crash.

Edgar took off running.

"Apparently not," Bob muttered, then looked at Bea with a sad sigh. "Edgar's getting more and more forgetful these days. We'll have to do something about that. We could get him a nice job in the CD department."

Bea nodded, thinking, and sipped her soda. Bob turned back to Tony.

"Anyway, there are also two kinds of tele-gnomes," Bob continued. "I'm a telephone gnome—I run back and forth fixing telephone lines, phone jacks—cell phones are a royal pain, let me tell you. Then there're the television gnomes who take care of TV stations like this one and try to keep cable signals and reception clear. They also have to worry about cameras and lenses now, as well as DVD players, VCRs, satellite dishes, and digital programming."

"I'm glad I don't work in that office," Bea muttered. Bob agreed.

Tony looked around. "Which ones are the television gnomes?" he asked.

"Oh, they're still stuck in the control room fixing the problems there. The cooking gnomes send them catered snacks when we're not on the air. You know all the lights on the video switcher?"

Tony nodded.

"Right now, each one of those is a gnome."

Tony stared, struggling with the sheer magnitude of the idea. But something was puzzling him. He turned to Bea. "I was sent here to help fix the station's technical problems, but you seem to be doing fine—so why am I here?"

They shrugged, and Bob said, "Maybe you can find the root of the problem. We're just trying to keep it on the air."

"Haven't you looked for the source of it?" Tony asked.

They nodded, then looked away. "It was the first thing we did," Bea told him. "Nothing seemed to be wrong with the equipment, so we figured something was down in Master Control—the engineering headquarters."

"And what did you find?"

They shrugged. "The gnomes we sent there never returned. We sent two more parties, and they didn't come back, either. No one goes near that area who doesn't disappear without a trace."

"Could a gnome be behind it?" They looked offended, so Tony quickly added, "I mean, has any gnome ever gone bad?"

"Where do you think Imps come from?!?" Bob declared. "Those are serious offenders, and we don't take no responsibility for them! Oh sure, some gnomes get carried away and play a trick or two, like stealing a single sock out of the dryer, but what gnome hasn't wanted to do that?"

Gnomes were the reason for odd socks? Tony shook his head and turned his mind back to the problem at hand. What was going on inside Master Control? He sat back and mulled over the information as he sipped his soda. Clearly he needed to find a way in there.

And find a way back.

"Three minutes till air!" someone shouted from over by the soda kegs. "Get to your positions!"

One by one the gnomes got up and hurried over to the door back into the cables. Tony held Bob back as he moved to join them. "How do I get to Master Control?" he asked.

Bob looked at him as if he were crazy. "Why go there? You won't come back!"

"That's my problem. Can you tell me how to get there or not?"

Bob nodded and called out to a cooking gnome, dressed in white with a fluffy baker's hat. "John, can you show Tony here to Master Control? Take him to Roger." He turned back to Tony. "Roger can show you the way there."

"Thanks." Tony followed John to a side entrance. They jumped into a hole in the wall and disappeared into the darkness.

Well, the first break had gone pretty smoothly. Beth sighed with relief as she drained the soda can, crumpled it, and tossed it into the recycling bin, heading back to the control room. One down and six to go. *Please let the machines keep working*, she silently pleaded.

She slipped back into her seat and put on her headset. She'd a chance to talk with the mayor, who was pleased with how the last break had gone—though she'd had to assure him that in spite of their strange costumes, the volunteer phone operators were really very nice and were certainly not taking the spotlight off him. He was satisfied that the evening would be a success.

Unfortunately, the phones were not ringing off the hook as she had hoped. Well, maybe they would pick up later, although given how boring the last break had been, no matter how Stan tried to lighten it up, she doubted it.

Mac wandered back in and sat down at the switcher, brushing some potato chip crumbs off his shirt. He smiled sheepishly as Beth gave him a reproachful look. Cockroaches in the control room, that would be all they needed now.

"To you in ten," the sepulchral voice from Master Control said.

"Ready mikes, ready fade in three," Beth called. "Three . . . two . . . one . . . Open mikes, fade in three!"

The break was underway.

Unfortunately, it promised to be even more boring than the last, as the mayor launched into a speech on sewer service reforms. It wasn't boring for the crew, though—they were all praying silently for the equipment to keep working. *Come on, just a little longer. Just a few more minutes.*

Looking back on it, Beth would never be quite sure how it began, but someone on the set screamed. Beth, determined to keep the mayor on the air, kept the camera on him, but glanced at her preview monitors for the wide shot of the set. She couldn't believe what she was seeing.

The phone volunteers had abandoned their posts. Three of the dozen were standing on the set, pointing an odd assortment of guns at the crew and the remaining, non-cloaked, volunteers. The rest of the cloaked club were rounding up everyone who wasn't manning the equipment and forcing them over to the phone bank.

The mayor, realizing what was happening, stopped his speech and looked off screen. "What the hell is going on?" he demanded.

Beth still knew better than to change the camera angle, even with Mac asking her a dozen times when she wanted to switch. "Do we really want the folks at home to know about this?"

The leader of the cloaked club pointed a gun at Stan's head. "I want us on the screen! NOW!"

"Do it," she ordered, and Mac punched up Camera Two.

"Please, no one panic," Beth told her crew over their headsets, although she felt as if she were going against her own orders. "Please stay calm. Everyone will be okay. I'm calling the police."

"Don't call the police," the leader said into Camera Two. "If we hear one siren, if anyone enters this building from now until we get off the air, we will shoot everyone in this studio."

There was an audible gasp, and Beth waited breathlessly in the control room to hear their demands. What did they want? Money? Fame? Who would be stupid enough to hold a PBS station hostage? It's not like anyone was watching.

"We regret using the threat of violence," the leader went on, "but we feel it is necessary. We don't want to kill anyone, but we will if we have to. We are fighting a war, and we understand that there may be casualties."

War? *Oh my God, they're terrorists,* Beth thought wildly. What could she do to stop them? Were they going to die?

"As some of you know and many of you do not, aliens are among us," the "volunteer" declared.

Everyone froze, unsure if they had heard him correctly.

"That's right, aliens. We are not the Fly-By-Night Candy Foundation, who deliver to pregnant women and college dorms around the clock as our banner claims. We are, in fact, The Interglobal Confederation of Totally Outrageous Conspiracy Theories."

The what? Beth thought about the name for a moment and figured out their initials. TIC TOCT. They should have had clocks on their cloaks, not green eyes. Alien eyes, she realized with a start. Why hadn't she seen it before? Even if she had, she would never have expected this.

"We are a secret organization of civilians dedicated to destroying the threat of alien interference in our daily lives and of preventing the great Intergalactic War that will soon be upon us. Do any of you realize how many evil things in the history of our world have been the treacherous plans of beings from another world?"

He walked over to one of the mayor's staff, sitting by a telephone looking pale and worried. "You!" he demanded.

She squeaked with fear.

"Who was responsible for the assassination of JFK?"

"Um . . . Lee Harvey Oswald?" she mumbled.

"WRONG!" he yelled. "It was aliens! And who was responsible for the Black Plague?"

"Um . . . rats?"

"ALIENS!" he shouted. "Who started both world wars in an attempt to destroy our planet?"

"Um . . . aliens?" she suggested meekly.

"Exactly!" he cried, beaming with delight at her understanding.

Well, give them points for creativity. Beth had certainly never learned THAT in a history book.

He turned back to the camera and addressed the audience, all ten of them. "We do not like violence," he said again, "but we are very good at it. We appeal to the people of this country . . ."

Country? Didn't they realize this was a local PBS station? It couldn't even reach the whole state.

". . . to donate to our worthy cause! After all, we are fighting to save your lives as well as our own; we are fighting to save the world. But we need more money so that we can develop weapons powerful enough to defeat our enemies! Donate to us, here at this station, and save the lives of these brave volunteers while you help us save the world!"

There was a resounding cheer from all the black-cloaked volunteers.

Stan smiled, still sitting on the central, circular podium in the center of the set. "Hey, that's not a bad slogan—WBEG-TV—saving the world through public broadcasting."

"I'm in charge here!" the leader shouted. "I'll come up with the slogans!" He turned back to the camera once again. "Citizens of the world, unite!"

Oh, the country wasn't enough, he now assumed this broadcast was global. As if they had the money for THAT.

"We have long fought against the alien menace—join us now and fight for your world! Fight for your future! Send money to secure the safety of your home, of your children, from the alien scum! We must protect ourselves! Now is the time for action!"

"And for pledging at the hundred-dollar level we have a VHS copy of tonight's program," Stan declared, desperately trying to get back to the break's script. "At the seventy-five-dollar level . . ."

"I'm talking!" the leader yelled. "And when I'm talking, you shut up!"

"But we—we have lovely thank-you gifts," Stan offered.

"I have no interest in your pathetic gifts!" the leader glared at him, then looked at the VHS tape. "Ooh, *Lord of the Dance* . . ."

There was stunned silence in the control room.

"Well," Beth declared. "At least the equipment is working."

"Yippee," Mac declared without enthusiasm. "Those nutjobs get to stay on the air."

Beth knew the group was crazy, but they were holding the guns, and however far-fetched their theories, they were serious. Deadly serious.

Suddenly the phones in the studio began to ring.

Chapter 20

Every single phone rang, all at the same moment. Beth realized with a start that the phone number had been up the whole time. Reflexes took over, and she called, "One on the phones . . . Quick, quick! Pan right . . . Now! Take One."

The picture of the two rows of phones appeared on the screen, the mayor's frantic staff talking into them, and Beth could only watch helplessly. There were so many ringing that some of the cloaked conspirators even had to put down their guns and pick up pencils, taking down donation pledges.

Beth couldn't believe that people were actually calling in. She realized that the whole town was probably watching by now. Did they realize this was real? Or did everyone think it was some kind of *War of the Worlds* publicity stunt to get money pouring in? If it hadn't been for the fact that this was a real hostage situation, it might not have seemed like such a bad idea.

"Guess what?!?" a phone volunteer cried, jumping up and running to the hosts' table where the leader was standing. "Someone from Springfield will pledge one hundred thousand dollars if you can save the world by the end of the evening!"

"Yes!" the leader exclaimed. "I love a challenge!"

And just when things seemed to be getting better, and the TIC TOCTians were getting distracted, the worst possible thing happened.

Everything stopped working.

They were off the air. There was no light, no sound, nothing. It was as if every piece of technology in the building suddenly stopped. Beth could only imagine what the group would do, now that they were off the air.

"Please turn back on, please turn back on," she muttered.

Tony and John had just dived into the switcher when everything went dark. The room was a mass of confusion as all the tele-gnomes stopped what they were doing and froze, uncertain of what was going on outside, but all knowing that something was terribly wrong.

"What's happening?" Tony demanded, fighting his way through the darkness to the nearest gnome.

"No one knows," she replied, standing perfectly still.

Tony realized that whatever was happening on the outside, having the station go off the air could only make things worse. "Get back to work!" he commanded. "Whatever happens, we have to stay on the air!"

This seemed to jump-start everyone. The Technomes began moving again. In a few minutes the lights came back on, and Tony found himself in a huge rectangular room, full of moving platforms and thin, tiny cables. Hundreds of gnomes stood perched on platforms or ran between the narrow aisles and into a hole at one end of the room. Each gnome had a very bright light in his or her hat and Tony realized they were lighting up, and operating, the switcher buttons.

A tall gnome walked over to him briskly and held out his hand. He had a bristly beard and a mustache, both reminiscent of a college professor, and gripped an unlit pipe between his teeth. He removed the pipe and shook Tony's hand.

"Roger," he said, introducing himself.

"Tony," Tony replied.

"You're the one sent by the saint himself?"

Tony nodded, and Roger quickly moved him to the center.

"Look, I need to know what's going on." Tony tried to quell his mounting apprehension. Whatever made the gnomes stop came from outside the equipment, even outside the studio itself. "I have to get out of the equipment and into the Master Control room somehow," he said, almost pleadingly. "Whatever happens, you have to keep the gnomes working—make sure the equipment stays on!"

Roger nodded gravely and turned to several telegnomes, who had just run into the "room." He told them Tony's orders and sent them back into the cable tunnels to tell the others to get the station back on the air.

Tony looked around, trying to figure a way out of the switcher. He fumbled in his pocket and clenched St. Vidicon's rosary tightly, rubbing the computer chips and thinking as hard as he could. Then he saw it.

A shadow came over one of the gnomes and the gnome jumped up and down on the platform, making the outside button move. Tony realized that the shadow was a human finger. Maybe he could get inside a person on the outside and see what was going on? He had gotten into the inner workings of all kinds of things—why not a person? It could work. If only he knew how.

The shadow descended again and without thinking, he ran for the platform it was heading for, mumbled an apology as he shoved the gnome off, and jumped up, hitting his head against the orange plastic ceiling.

Suddenly he was flying and falling all at the same time, surrounded by darkness. Then he emerged, breathless, into a glowing red-and-pink tunnel—a vein, he realized, and dived in to swim through the red liquid. He found a section heading north and let the current carry him past fat cells lying around sipping piña colada, muscle cells flexing themselves and arguing about which of them was strongest, and several groups of white blood cells wearing martial-arts black belts and attacking nasty-looking leather-clad gangs of bacteria.

Tony lay back in the stream of blood that carried him along and settled in for an interesting ride.

It seemed forever, but could really have been only a few moments, before the switcher suddenly came back to life, lighting up the rest of the control panel. They were live and on the air again.

At first the studio had been pandemonium, with the TIC TOCTians' leader running around screaming at the crew, until Stan—good ol' professional Stan—turned to Camera Two, and said, "Please bear with us, viewers— we're having a few slight technical difficulties. We're sorry for the interruption—but it does show you why we need your donations: to keep on the air."

"Order! Order!" The leader shouted, brandishing his weapon, The mayor's staff fell silent, jumping back into their seats by the phones.

Satisfied that the studio was back under his control, the leader turned to Camera Two, and cried, "See! The aliens conspire to deprive you of our inspiring words! Send in your pledges now to keep them from conquering the world!"

He was, of course, standing in front of the brightly-painted flats with the WBEG logos. No one would ever forget which station was putting his little army on the air!

In the background every spare person was answering phones—all except the mayor, of course, whose face was a blotchy mixture of white and red, looking both frightened and furious at the same time and, not knowing what else to do, was sitting in his chair quietly.

"They will eradicate us all!" the leader screamed. "They will destroy your government and rule over your pathetic little lives! You will be mindless slaves, and they shall feast on the flesh of your children!" He paused in his frenzy and added with a gracious smile, "And that's why we'd like you to donate to the 'Save the Earth from Alien Attack' fund."

"The phones are ringing off the hook," Stan said, genuinely pleased with that fact at least. It meant people were watching. Which was a good thing, right?

"Yes, they are, Stan," the leader agreed. "And that's good, for if they were not, I would have to massacre the entire phone staff and force their families to watch!!" He paused again and smiled. "Now let's go over to my second-in-command—Major Paine—and see what lovely gifts we're offering tonight."

"Dissolve Three," Beth said, resigned, and the screen changed to an image of Paine standing in front of a tote board.

"Thank you, General, first—at the thousand-dollar level—we have your basic membership in the 'Inter-global Confederation of Totally Outrageous Conspiracy Theories,' including an all-expense-paid vacation to our training camp, as well as your very own gun. Now at the five-thousand-dollar level, you can start off with a commission as a lieutenant, guaranteeing at least five other 'Friends of the Federation' under your command. As an additional incentive, if enough people make a pledge at the ten-thousand-dollar level then we will NOT kill your mayor. However, if enough people pledge at the hundred-thousand-dollar level, then we *will* kill your mayor. Now back to you, General."

All the color had drained out of the mayor's face. He was looking both horrified and embarrassed.

After what seemed like hours, and many wrong turns into strangely fascinating organs, one actually shaped like a pipe organ (clearly, gnome travel laws did not apply to human blood vessels)—Tony finally reached what he had been looking for: the brain.

He had thought it would be impressive, but then of course, what did he know? He'd never been inside someone's brain before. He stood in a narrow hallway at the top of the spinal cord staircase in front of a plain wooden door. He reached out, turned the handle—and found it unlocked. His host must be a very trusting sort. Of course, it was his body. Tony only hoped he wasn't violating some unspoken law about not trespassing within thy neighbor's mind as he stepped inside.

What greeted him was a huge mess. Filing cabinets lined the walls, half-open, with papers falling out of them, dangling from the drawers, and littering the floor. He looked down at the papers near his feet and read them out of sheer curiosity. Some of them were chewed-up math problems, others were scribbled notes such as *do homework*, or *go to grocery store*, or *call home*. Still others were questions: *what is the meaning of the universe?* or *how does a toaster work?* The majority of papers, however, simply had one word written on them in block letters: RANDOM.

Tony wondered what his mind would look like if he were inside it. He looked around the room again and saw four or five dusty armchairs sitting in a circle around a bricked-up fireplace that had a rusty, tear-stained plaque hanging above it that read: THERE IS NO SANTA CLAUS.

At the other end of the room, there were two doors several feet apart. The one on the left was covered with finger paint, bright stickers, and crayon drawings. The one on the right was sparkling clean—the only thing in the room that was—and ornamented into neat, geometric designs. In between them stood a tall dresser, covered in dust and cobwebs. It contained three drawers that clearly had not been opened for quite some time.

Tony walked over and examined the dresser, looking at each neatly-labeled drawer in turn. From top to bottom they read: Childhood Fantasies, Brilliant Ideas, and Sex Drive. Figuring that this was more than he should know—certainly more than he wanted to know—he stepped back and nearly tripped over someone standing behind him. Stumbling backward, he caught himself before hitting the floor. He climbed to his feet and looked down to see what had tripped him.

Standing there was a small child, possibly as old as ten, though he would have had to be short for his age. He was dressed like a biker in black jeans and leather jacket. His hair was tousled and messy; he wore dark sunglasses and had a candy cigarette dangling from the corner of his mouth.

"Who are you?" Tony asked. He hadn't realized there was anyone in here. He hadn't seen anyone when he came in.

The kid shrugged and pretended to light his cigarette, chewing on the sugary end. "I'm the Rebel."

Tony stared at him. He'd heard someone say once that everyone had a little rebel in him, but he somehow doubted this was what the person had meant.

Before he could ask the child any more questions, both doors burst open and several people came charging into the room, arguing with each other. They yelled and cried and in some cases even swung punches at each other. Tony didn't know what was going on, but he noticed that the people—all men—looked vaguely alike. They all had dark brown hair, brown-green eyes, and some sort of facial hair, a beard or mustache or goatee. Only the boy beside him was clean-shaven. All the men were different sizes and dressed differently, except that each one wore a black T-shirt with something written on the front in white, bold letters. Tony looked down at the boy and noticed his T-shirt for the first time. The word REBEL was printed across the front, and Tony immediately turned back to the others, who were marching past him and carrying their arguments over to the messy filing cabinets. One by one he tried to read their shirts and was able to make out various words such as COURAGE—a muscleman type wearing a musketeer hat and a superhero's cape; SELF-PITY—a very large and strongly-built man; SELF-CONFIDENCE—a small, puny, straggly-looking guy with greasy hair; VANITY—a perfectly-groomed, very handsome man in an expensive Italian suit; and DEFENSE MECHANISMS—a large jumble of bulky bodyguards connected by a five-person vest.

The argument only stopped when a man appeared in the doorway to the right. He looked like a geeky nerd who wore glasses and a pristine striped shirt over his visible T-shirt, which read INTELLIGENCE across the front.

"Could you plebeians keep the shouting to a minimum?" he demanded. "There are a few people here who have jobs to do!" With that, he disappeared back inside the room and slammed the door shut.

The argument barely paused, then continued unabated until another man appeared, this time out of the left-hand door. He was dressed in an artist's smock that was spackled with paint of every color, a black beret perched on his head, and a Vandyke-style goatee. The word CREATIVITY glowed from beneath his smock.

"Excuse me!" he shouted angrily. "Some of us are trying to work here!!!" And he ducked back into the room and slammed the door.

The argument paused a little longer, but within minutes had started up again, even louder than before. Tony knew something had to be done, or he wouldn't find out anything—he might not even be able to get out. He glanced at the group, hurling insults and scrap paper at each other, then realized no amount of time he had was going to solve their problems. He turned back to the doors, looking from one to the other and trying to pick. Figuring INTELLIGENCE was bound to understand the urgency of the situation better than CREATIVITY, he opted for that door, knocked, then entered.

The room was neatly organized with rows of computers and blackboards. Harsh fluorescent lighting illuminated every nook and cranny. A table was set up in the center with a chart of the human body, clearly monitoring every movement.

"This is a restricted area," Intelligence snapped. "No unauthorized personnel allowed."

"The station's in trouble," Tony explained. "I've

been sent to help." He'd never had to explain his presence so many times on one mission.

"Sent by whom?"

"Saint Vidicon," he announced.

Intelligence looked thoughtful, as if trying to remember where he'd heard that name before. He turned to a man cowering under a nearby desk. "Fear, go check the files, see if you can find Memory—he's probably asleep in the cerebellum. Check for the name, 'Saint Vidicon.' I want all references on him immediately."

Fear, a medium-sized man in clothes two sizes too big, quickly nodded, shaking and trembling as he stood up and ran out of the room. Intelligence stared at Tony, looking him up and down and clearly trying to decide whether or not to trust him.

"Decisions!" he bellowed, and for a moment Tony wondered what he was talking about. Then two men appeared in the room from the back and walked up to him, past him, and over to Tony, walking around him in a circle and looking him up and down thoroughly as Intelligence had done. One of the men was dressed all in white with the words GOOD DECISION printed on his white T-shirt in black letters. The other was dressed all in red with the words BAD DECISION printed across the front of his red T-shirt in black letters. They reminded him of the angel and the devil that sit on the shoulders of cartoon characters.

"Well?" Intelligence demanded, addressing Good Decision. "Should we trust him?"

"Absolutely!" Bad Decision cried. "Trust everyone!"

"I wasn't talking to you." Intelligence gave him a scathing look, then turned back to Good Decision and looked at him questioningly.

"I think we can trust him," Good Decision said with finality.

Apparently he didn't have to give a reason why, his opinion was good enough. Intelligence nodded and looked at Tony.

"What's your name?"

"Tony."

"And what is the purpose of your visit to the land of Mac?"

Land of Mac? That was a new one. "I need to know what's going on in the TV studio and see if I can help."

Intelligence nodded again and looked almost relieved. He gestured for Tony to follow him and led him to the back of the room, where there was a white door. He opened the door and walked into another room. The only objects in it were three plain chairs, the door they'd come through, another door several feet away, and two gigantic television monitors, oval, like Mac's eyes. Huge, fringed curtains descended quickly, then rose again as Mac blinked. From this room, Tony could see everything that Mac could see. Loudspeakers set into the walls somewhere allowed him to hear everything that Mac could.

Mac looked up at the monitors across the room, and Tony saw the black-cloaked leader with his fellow TIC TOCTians holding the mayor's staff and the crew hostage. He turned to Intelligence, who motioned him to sit and quickly but thoroughly explained what had happened while Tony had been in the system.

"Well, Stan," the leader of the TIC TOCTians was saying, "the evening is going very well."

"Yes," Stan agreed, and turned to look at the camera, "I've often wondered what it would take to get the people of our lovely community and surrounding areas truly to appreciate the quality programming that WBEG brings them every year. Who knew it would come in the form of a group of Anti-Alien Activists holding us hostage?"

"Very true," the leader agreed. "I've been a fan of WBEG and the quality sci-fi shows that air on it for many years now."

"So what's your favorite show?"

"The local gardening program."

"Really?"

"Yes, I usually call in every other week. I raise petunias."

"I'm a spider plant man myself."

In the control room, Beth slammed her head on the desk repeatedly, trying to wake up. Not only was this the most dangerous, bizarre, and surreal pledge night ever in the history of public television, it was also by far the most successful. Who knew?

The current conversation between the cohosts—now involving the mayor, who was discussing his favorite rosebush and jade plant—segued into a discussion on lawn care.

The crew and the mayor's staff watched, feeling as though they were in a surreal dream.

Beth was watching a director's nightmare.

Stan, the mayor, and the TIC TOCTian leader had currently covered every topic of conversation from politics ("Well, yes, we think he's a good mayor, but what are his policies on Alien Control?") to religion ("Of course we believe in God! God created aliens!") and even comic books ("Superman is an Alien, doesn't anyone else realize that?!? They're all out to get us!")

The mayor was taking everything rather well. Apparently everyone but the producer and the crew now thought this was an elaborate joke. The mayor—who had only had people pledge to save him and had been shown great support by the community—was now acting like the hero of the hour, pledging some of his own assets to help save the world from the Alien Menace. The guns, on closer inspection, turned out to be spray-painted BB guns, modified into what the cloaked group called their Multi-Action, Double-Barreled Lasers.

So the threat of imminent bodily harm was gone— but why were they still on the air?

Two reasons. The first was that they were still generating dozens of phone calls. It had been close to an hour since the last break, and the crew and volunteers needed some downtime, not to mention the audience, who had to be at least beginning to get bored. A few calls had come in requesting they go back to the program, but so far they hadn't been able to.

That was the second reason. The TIC TOCTians simply refused to leave. There were enough of them that, guns or no, they could have overpowered the others.

At first, no one had bothered to call the police because of the leader's threat—then, after the situation settled down, because no one really thought there was still a danger. But when they'd realized the guns were harmless, Beth had given in and called them on her cell phone. The SWAT team was outside but had told Beth they'd decided not to interfere when it became clear the incident was staged. Beth tried to tell them it wasn't, but they chose to believe what they saw on the screen instead of the director.

There had to be a way to get the TIC TOCTians to back off without anyone getting hurt. Beth simply had no idea how to do it.

Chapter 21

⌨

Tony, however, did. After listening to the whole story from Intelligence, he stood up and paced the room, an idea forming inside his own mind—a perverse idea, but the whole situation they were in was perverse, and what was it that Father Vidicon had told him? Sometimes you had to fight perversity with perversity?

Well, the idea was far-fetched, but it just might work. All he needed was a few answers from the studio and a few directions from Intelligence.

"Can you tell me how to"—he paused, trying to find the right word—"operate Mac? I need to have him ask the director a few questions."

Intelligence nodded and led him to a control panel at the front of the room, complete with microphone and sound system.

"Hey." Mac leaned over to Beth and gently poked her shoulder.

"What?" she asked, irritated, but not with him.

"I have an idea. Have any of the cloaked group tried to operate the equipment yet? Like the cameras, anything like that?"

Beth frowned. "I don't think so." She turned to her headset. "Bill, have any of our crew been replaced by members of the organization?" She waited for his reply, then turned to Mac. "No, they haven't. Why?"

"That means they can't operate the equipment. They've probably never even been in a TV studio; otherwise, they would have come back to the control room and tried to run it from here. They could have run through the whole place, but they've stayed in the studio."

"What's your point?" Beth asked. "If you've got an idea, let's hear it."

By now Tony knew the power of saying you were sent by someone else—someone respected. His message would be even more powerful if they thought he was that person himself. Not Father Vidicon, of course— that would be unthinkable, and they probably didn't know who he was anyway. But something Intelligence had told him—some of the totally outrageous theories they had—gave him an idea.

"Have you got a phone book?" Mac asked, and Beth handed him one with a curious glance. She watched him flip through the book and find an address; then, before he could think twice, he leaned in front of her and punched up the studio intercom on the large control box in front of her, adjusting the microphone so that it pointed at him. Inisde Mac, Tony prayed that the TIC TOCTians were as superstitious as they were suspicious.

In as deep and booming a voice as he could manage, Mac spoke, his voice echoing through the studio. "This is the ghost of Abraham Lincoln."

The cultists all looked shocked; several of them

gasped. He had guessed right—none of them knew about the surround-sound intercom the architect had insisted on building into the studio.

"I, too, was assassinated by beings from another world," he announced, and had to fight seriously to stop himself from laughing.

Beth stared. This was a Mac she had never seen.

One of the cloaked men sitting behind a phone jumped up and cried out, "I knew it!"

"I have appeared to you today to give you this dire warning," Mac intoned. "The threat of Alien Attack is upon us. Save the Union as I fought to save it! You must stop them from destroying us all!"

The cloaked group gave a cheer, and the leader fell to his knees, awed and inspired. "Tell us what you know, great leader, and we will save our world!"

"Go to the place where their first ship has landed, cloaked and disguised as a tall building in the downtown area." He proceeded to give them the address, and they proceeded to write it down. Then Mac boomed, "Farewell!"

The leader stood up, addressing his fellow TIC TOC-Tians. "Our time has come! Let's save the world!!"

They cheered and followed him out of the room, out of the building, and into their cars.

The mayor's staff watched them go. The mayor simply smiled at the camera, and said, "Well, folks, it's not what I usually think of as educational, but hey—entertainment is also a necessary part of life."

"That's right, Your Honor," Stan chimed in, then turned to address the audience as well. "And now for the moment you've all been waiting for: part 2 of *Lord of the Dance*."

"And we're out in five ... four ... three ... two ...

one!" Beth cried joyfully. "We're off the air! Take the phone number off the screen, I never want to see it again!"

Tony was amazed that it had worked. By all accounts it shouldn't have. No one was that dumb—but perversity was perversity, and saints be praised, it was over.

At least, one particular saint be praised.

"Where did you send them?" Intelligence asked.

"The police station." Tony shrugged. "They'll barge in waving their guns, and the police can deal with them from there."

Intelligence smiled and watched the camera crew celebrate by running off to the break room.

"How did you ever think of anything like that?" an admiring Beth asked Mac.

"Like what?" Mac seemed genuinely puzzled.

Beth sighed and followed him out of the studio. Sometimes the man's modesty was infuriating.

Tony knew his job wasn't done yet. He still had to get inside the engineering room. Still being in Mac's body allowed him to check out Master Control from outside the equipment. If there was nothing wrong there, he could hop back into the cables and check it out from the other end. He turned back to Intelligence.

"Can I ask a favor?"

Ten minutes later they were at the door to Master Control. Tony—or rather Mac—knocked, but there was no reply. He tried the handle; it was unlocked, so he stepped in.

The room was a mess. Tapes lay scattered on the floor, extension cords were knotted and jumbled, and all seemed to be plugged into one socket—full to bursting—yet none of them were plugged into anything on the other end. Ripped and crumpled script pages were strewn across every surface, and stale pieces of potato chips, donuts, and other ant traps were littered everywhere.

But the most telling sign of who had been there was the can of dark, sticky, acidic cola that lay on its side on the control board, the liquid oozing out all over the keys and into the circuits.

Mac gave a cry of anguish, and Tony knew who had been there. It was obvious. No engineer would have ever left soda near equipment that expensive, or dumped tapes on the floor like that. It would have cost him his job. Cola could ruin electronic equipment.

This had to be the work of Finagle.

Of course, whoever he had sent this time was nowhere to be found, though Tony/Mac searched the room thoroughly. The culprit must have left as Mac was turning the door handle, and Tony now had no doubt as to who had arranged to have the TIC TOCT group volunteer to answer the phones tonight.

No matter the plot, it had been successfully foiled. And to Tony's great surprise, it had not even required fighting some sort of horrible monster. He had to admit it had been refreshing. Unusual, but nice.

Mac went back to the control room and unknowingly dropped Tony off in the audio booth, since the lights on the switcher were all gone and Tony assumed that the gnomes had gone back to the fridge to party. He said good-bye to Intelligence and the others, most of whom were still arguing in the outer room, slipped back into the bloodstream, rode out to Mac's fingertips, and sank into the CD player as the man reached out to check the theme music.

After apologizing to a gnome for landing on him, then getting caught up in running fast enough to keep the CD spinning until the gnome regained his feet, Tony headed back toward the fridge. A few wrong turns and a quick tour through the computer editing systems later, he was guided back to the fridge by a young female editing gnome, rather round around the middle, where he thanked Bea and Bob and the others, who thanked him in turn (some even asked for his autograph). After a few minutes of relaxing on a loaf of bread, drinking freshly tapped cola from the keg, and diving into the red Jell-O for a refreshing swim, he felt that strange and wonderful sensation that he was going home.

On the next date, Tony's reserve frightened Sandy. He was as courteous and cheerful as ever, but there was something a little forced about it, some strange holding back. Of course, it didn't help that they'd been watching a Wagner opera, but when they arrived at her building, and Sandy forced brightness, saying, "Come on in," and Tony hesitated, she took the bull by the horns. "What's the matter?"

"The clinches aren't my strong suit, are they?" Tony looked like a man waiting for a noose.

Sandy stared in surprize. Then she said, "You're fantastic. But a girl's got a right to say no when she isn't in the mood, doesn't she?"

"Of course." Tony leaned forward for a kiss.

Relieved, Sandy leaned forward, too—after all, she was a step higher than he was—but was amazed how cool his kiss was, and how brief. "Good night, then," he said, and turned away.

"Hey!" She stepped down to catch his arm. "I didn't say I wasn't in the mood tonight."

Tony turned back, surprised. "Are you?"

Sandy gazed at him a moment, then said, "Not a nice

question to ask. How about you do your best to persuade me?"

Tony smiled, and for the first time that night, it was a real smile. "All I ask is a notice telling me it's open season."

"Then don't forget your rifle," Sandy retorted. "Coffee?"

The next night, however, she definitely wasn't in the mood—or the next, or the next. They fell into an easy rhythm of going out to a movie or ballet or opera on weekends and sitting together talking at Nepenthe on the weekdays when neither of them had to work late— but after the first three nights when Sandy thanked him for a great evening at the door to her building, he started asking the cab to wait again. It was like their first few dates but without the suspense, and it went on and on. Sandy began to feel doom hovering once more.

Finally, one evening, she screwed up her courage while he was getting the coffee, and when he brought it back, she said, "Something's wrong."

"Yeah." Tony set her cup down in front of her and sat down. "We're being so virtuous a person would think we're married."

Sandy stared, then gave a laugh that made people at nearby tables look up. Tony grinned with relief. Sandy clapped a hand over her mouth, throttled the laugh down to giggles, and said, "That's why I'm not too sure about getting married."

"Maybe you're right," Tony said.

Sandy stared at him in shock and felt as though a lump of cold lead were growing inside her.

"It doesn't have to be like that." Tony reached forward to clasp her hand. "If we do marry, we'll have to work at keeping the romance in it. I've seen enough of my married friends to know that."

"Marriage isn't supposed to be work," Sandy said.

"Yeah." Tony's smile was rueful. " 'They got married and lived happily ever after,' right? Only they didn't. They had their ups and downs, same as everyone. A wise old man—well, older—told me your courtship lasts your whole life."

"Then what's the point in getting married?" Sandy demanded.

"It's a hunting license," Tony explained. "You don't have to feel guilty when the courtship succeeds."

Sandy sat still, thinking that over. Then she said, "So you felt guilty?"

"Only once," Tony said.

Sandy hadn't known she could feel smug and ashamed at the same time. Then she realized the silliness of it and leaned forward. "Should I feel guilty about making you feel guilty?"

Tony smiled. "Let's put it this way—I also felt proud."

"Oh, that you were such a real stud, huh?'

"No—that I'd made you happy."

Sandy stared into his eyes for a moment, then said, very seriously, "If you asked again, I might say yes."

Tony stared, feeling as though he were a conductor for a high-voltage current. When it ebbed a bit, he managed to say, "Will you marry me?"

"Yes," Sandy said.

Tony kept staring, stunned. Then she could see the energy building in him, knew he was about to give a yell that would have shamed a Rebel, and smiled again. "Drink your coffee."

He managed to hold in the yell and gulped the rest of his cappuccino. Then Sandy took him home to celebrate their engagement.

Epilogue

Father Vidicon strode onward down the throat of Hell, and he was resolved to confront whatsoever the Good Lord did oppose to him. Even as he went, the maroon of the walls did darken to purple and farther, till he did pace a corridor of indigo. Then the light itself began to dwindle and to darken until he groped within a lightless place. Terror did well up within him, turning all his joints to water and sapping strength from every limb, yet he did resolve upon the onward march, rebuked his heart most sternly, and held the fear within its place. He did reach out to brace himself against the wall—yet it was damp and soft and yielding, and did seem to move beneath his palm. He did pull his hand away right quickly and did shudder, and was nigh to losing heart then; yet he did haul his courage up from the depths to which it had plunged and did force his right foot forward, and his left foot then to follow; and thus he onward moved within that Hellish tunnel.

Then as he went, the floor beneath him did soften till he did walk upon a yielding surface, and he stumbled and did fall, and caught himself upon his hands. He did cry aloud and backward thrust himself with a broken prayer for strength, for that floor had felt as moist and yielding as tissue living. "In truth," he muttered, "I walk indeed within the throat of Hell."

He plucked himself up and pushed himself onward, bowed against the weight of his fear, yet going.

Sudden light did glare and did sear his eyes, so that he did clench them shut, then did slowly ope, allowing them to accustom themselves to such brightness, whereupon the glare was gone, and Father Vidicon did see a grinning death's-head that did glow there—yet not of its own light, for it was of a pale and sickly green that did shine too brightly for the light to be within it. Yet naught else could Father Vidicon see there about him. He did frown and held his hand before his face; yet he could see it not. "In sooth," he breathed, "what light is this, that is darkling in itself—what light is this, that doth not thus illuminate? How can light cast darkness?"

The answer came all at once within his mind, and he did pull his Roman collar from out its place within his shirt, and did hold it out before him, to behold it as a strip of glaring bluish white. "It doth fluoresce!" he cried in triumph, and he knew thereby that light did truly fill the hall but was of a color that human eyes see not. Yet his collar, in consequence of the detergent held within it, did transform that color, and did reflect it as a one that human eyes see as glowing.

Father Vidicon replaced his collar then within his shirt with hands that trembled only slightly; and he murmured, "I have, then, come within the land of the Spirit of Paradox." His heart did quail within him, for he knew that the perversities he'd faced ere now were naught indeed when set against the reversals and inverted convolutions of the spirit that he soon would face. Yet he bowed his head in prayer, and did feel his heart to lighten. With a silent thought of thanks, he lifted up his head and set forth again down that gigantic throat. The death's-head passed upon his left, and on his right he did behold a skeleton frozen at odd angles, as though it were running and was small with distance. And onward he did pace, past skulls and crossed bones on his left, and on his right, skeletons in postures that might have been provocative, had they worn flesh—and as they must have been to the Spirit of Paradox. Father Vidicon did pray that he would not behold a being fully fleshed, for he felt sure that it would lie as one who's dead.

The passage then did curve downward toward his left, past bones and left-hand helices inverted widdershins. A galaxy did reel upon his right, yet the spiral arms were on the rim and darkness dwelt within its heart, a disc of emptiness. Then did stars coalesce upon his left to form a globe elongate, and it did seem as though the universe entire did move backward and invert.

The throat he paced did upward curve, still bending leftward, and he did hear above him footsteps that did approach in front, then did recede behind. He frowned up at them, yet still did march ahead, past glowing signs of death in birth, on and on through hallways that did ever curve unto his left. Yet they did begin once again to curve downward also, down and down, a mile or more, till at last, he did behold, upon his left—

A grinning death's-head.

Father Vidicon stopped and stood stock-still. A chill enveloped him, beginning at the hollow of his back and spreading upward to embrace his scalp, for he was certain that this death's-head was the first he had beheld within this viewless tunnel. Then did he bethink him of the footsteps he had heard above his head, and knew with certainty (though he knew not how he knew) that those had been his own footsteps going past this place. They'd seemed inverted for, at the time, he had walked upon the outside of the throat he was now within; yea, now he walked within it once again. "In truth," he whispered, "I do wander a Klein flask." And so it was—a tube that did curve back upon itself, then curved within itself once again, so that he passed from inside to outside, then back to inside, all unawares. Aye, forever might he wander this dark hall and never win to any goal except his own point of origin. He might well press onward, aging more and more, till at last he would stumble through this hall, a weak, enfeebled, ancient spirit. Yet, "Nay," he cried, "for here's the place of paradox—so as time goes forward, I shall grow younger!" And hard upon the heels of that realization came another—that he might wander where he would, yet never find that spirit within whose throat he wandered—the spirit that did invest this place.

Or did the place invest the spirit? "Aye!" he cried in triumph. "'Tis not Hell's mouth that I did enter, but Finagle's!" And so it was, in truth, and the throat of Finagle was like unto a Klein flask. Therefore did Father Vidicon set forth again with heart renewed and fear held in abeyance, to pace onward and onward, downward to his left, then upward left again, until the wall did fall away beneath his hand and the floor curved down beneath him. Then he cried in triumph, "I have come without! Nay, Spirit, look upon me—for I have come from out to stand upon thy skin! Behold him who's sent to battle thee!"

A door thundered up scant feet away, nearly knocking him backward with its wind of passage. He did fall back, plunging downward, and cried out in fear, flailing about him, near to panic—and his hand caught upon a spike which did grow from that surface there below. More such spikes caught him, pressing most painfully against him, for their points were sharp; yet he heeded not the pain, but did gaze upward, and beheld a great and glowing baleful eye that did fill all his field of vision.

"Indeed, I see thee now," a great voice rumbled. "May there be praise in censure! I had begun to think I would never have thee out from my system!"

"Nor wilt thou," Father Vidicon did cry in triumph, "for the outside of thy system is the inside! Indeed, thine inside is thine outside, and thine outside's inside! They are all one, conjoined in endlessness!"

"Do not carol victory yet," the huge voice rumbled, "for thou dost address Finagle, author of all that doth twist back upon itself. I am the fearsome spirit that doth invest all paradox and doth make two aspects of any entity separate and opposed as thesis and antithesis, in Hegellian duality."

"Ah, is it Hegel's, then?" Father Vidicon did cry, but . . .

"Nay," Finagle rumbled, "for Hegel thus was mine."

"Thou dost affright me not," Father Vidicon did cry. "I know thee well at last! Thou art the bridge from Tomorrow to Yesterday, from Positive to Negative, from nucleus's strong force thus to weak! Thou art the bridge that doth conjoin all those that do appear opposed!"

"Thou hast said it." Finagle's voice did echo all about him. "And I am thus the Beginning and the End of all. Bow down and adore me, for I am Him Whom thou dost call thy Lord!"

"Thou art not!" the saint did cry, and righteous wrath

arose within him. "Nay, thou art a part of Him, as are we all—yet but a part! Thou must needs therefore be within His limit and control."

"Art thou so certain, then?" The great eye did narrow in anger. "For an I were the Beginning and the Ending joined, how could I lie?"

"Why, for that," Father Vidicon replied, "thou art the Spirit of all Paradox, and canst speak true words in such a way that they express mistruth! Thou dost lie by speaking sooth!"

"Thou hast too much of comprehension for my liking," Finagle then did rumble. "Ward thee, priest! For I must annihilate thy soul!"

Light seared, and did shock the darkness, turning all to fire, lancing the good saint's orbs sightless with light. He did clap his palms over them, and closed them tightly—yet the light remained. Recalling then that he was within the Realm of Paradox, he did ope his eyes to slits, and the little light admitted did darken dazzle till the saint could once again distinguish form and detail.

He beheld a gigantic, fiery bird that did drift up from ashes, its wings widespread and cupped for hovering, beak reaching out to slash at him. Then terror struck the priest's stout heart, and he grasped the spikes that held him kneeling on Finagle's flesh and, throwing back his head, did cry, "Oh Father! Hear me now, or I must perish! Behold Thy servant, kneeling here in helplessness, beset by that dread raptor called the Phoenix, in whom resides vast power, for in its end doth it begin! Give me now, I pray Thee, some shield, some weapon here for my defense, or I must perish quite! Even the last shreds of my soul must be transformed and subsumed into pure, unmodulated energy devoid of structure, an that fearsome predator doth smite me!'

He held up hands in supplication—and light did glare

within his palm, pulling back and pulling in, imploding, gathering together, coalescing—and the saint did hold an Egg of Light!

Then did the spirit's vasty laugh fill all the Universe, bellowing in triumphant joy, "Nay, foolish priest! For all thy pleas to thy Creator, nothing more than this hath He to give thee! An egg—and thou wouldst oppose it 'gainst the bird full-flown! Now yield thee up, for thou must perish!"

But, "Not so," the saint did cry, "for I do know thee well, and know that when thou most doth laugh, thou art most in dread—and when thou dost most gloat on victory, thou art most in terror of defeat. Thou must needs be, for to thy Phoenix grown out of an ending, I do bring a beginning that must needs bear its death!"

Then he did rise, that he might face the greatest peril of his existence upright and courageous; and he held the Egg out in his two hands cupped, as though it were an offering.

The Phoenix screamed, and fiery wings beat downward to surround him. The beak of flame seared toward him, like unto a laser; and he bore himself bravely, though he did feel his spirit quail within him. Fire did surround him on every side, closer then and closer— and the spirit of pure energy did envelop him and did sink in upon him . . .

And inward passed him. The heat of that passing did sear his flesh, and he closed his eyes against it. Cool breath then touched his face and, opening his eyes, he saw the bird, shrunken now unto a handsbreadth, shrinking still, diminishing and growing smaller. Its despairing cry did pierce his ears and heart; for as it shrank, it sank. The Egg absorbed all flame and every erg of energy, until the Phoenix's head did shrink at last within its shell. There it sat, glowing within Father Vidicon's cupped palms, brighter and more pure than e'er it had been.

The priest breathed a sigh, and cried, "All praise be to Thee, my Lord, who hath saved me from the mountain of the Light of Death."

Then the dazzle faded from his eyes, and again he saw that huge orb, still glinting balefully upon him. "How now, then, priest," Finagle's voice did rumble. "Thou hast defeated my most puissant servant. What shalt thou, therefore, do with me?" His voice did sneer. "Shalt thou now annihilate me? Nay, do so—for then thy race shall be free of this urge to self-defeat that doth invest it!"

Fathomless tranquillity enveloped the priest. "Nay," quoth he, "for I cannot make thee cease to exist, nor can any—for thou art part of God, as are we all, and thou art spirit—the Spirit of fell Paradox. Nay, tempt me not to *hubris*, arrogance—for I do know that, did I eliminate thee, thou wouldst turn that, even that, about, and make of it Creation. Thus wouldst though blaspheme—for none can create, save God. Thou wouldst not die but wouldst simply change thy form—and 'tis better to have thee as thou art, so that we know thine appearance. Go thy way—thou art a necessary part of existence."

"So, then." And the huge voice rang with disappointment quite profound—nay, almost with despair. "Thus thou wilt let me live."

But Father Vidicon knew that when the Spirit of Paradox did seem desperate, it was in truth triumphant. "Be not so proud," he did admonish it, "for thou art even now within the hand of God, and 'tis that which He hath proven through me—that even thou canst be comprehended, and accepted within a person's harmony of being. Thus thine urge to self-defeat can be transformed into growth. Thou wilt ever be with Eve's breed, fell Spirit, and with Adam's—but never again need any man or woman fear thee, for they will know thou art as much a part of the world about them as the rain and wind, and as much of the world within them as the urge to charity."

"So thou dost say," the spirit rumbled, "yet doth that not make a mockery of thy victory? Dost thou not see that I have triumphed finally? What shalt thou do with that Phoenix thou hast at long last slain by bringing within the scope of Birth? Wilt thou then destroy it, and with it, all beginnings?"

The priest then shook his head. "Nay; for 'tis not mine to do with anywise. I must surrender it unto its Source." Then he cried, "Oh, Father! I give Thee now Thine Egg of Rebirth, with all the thanks and praise that I do own—thanks that Thou hast preserved me, but more: that Thou hast deemed me worthy to become Thine instrument for this restarting!" He thrust the Egg up high, an offering there within his hands, and it rose above his palms and arced upward, and farther upward and farther, and Father Vidicon did cry out, "See! This is the Egg of All, the Cosmic Egg, the Monobloc!"

Then at its zenith did the Egg explode, filling all that emptiness with light, searing barrenness with its seeding of Energy and Matter, investing all the Void with the Cosmic Dust and with it, the structure of Time and Space, thus bringing Order out from Chaos.

And Father Vidicon did rise within it like to a flaring candle, for flame surrounded him transcendent and unburning; and thus did he ascend through Space and Time, unto the Mind of God.